The Chronicles of Lamis

Book One

Aliyyah and the Quest for the Lost Treasures

Ayesha A. Scott

Published in the UK by Beacon Books and Media Ltd, 60 Farringdon
Road, London EC1R 3GA

ISBN 978-0-9926335-5-4

www.beaconbooks.net

A CIP catalogue record for this book is available from the British
Library.

Printed in the UK

Aliyyah and the Quest for the Lost Treasures

Ayesha A. Scott

BEACON BOOKS

About the author

Ayesha A. Scott was born on April 5th 1960 in the small fishing village of Shoreham-by-Sea, Sussex.

The daughter of Alan and Carol-Ann Scott she was educated at Steyning Grammar School before going on to University. She won her first writing completion at the age of seven with her poem *'If I had to be an Animal.'* In 1981 she went to live and work in Malaysia with her husband and except for a period of six years (1987-1993) when they returned to England, has remained there.

In 1995 her first series of thirteen children's books for primary schools entitled 'Children's Supplication' series was published by Dewan Bahasa dan Pustaka. They have been republished several times as well as being translated in the Malay language. In 1996 she represented Great Britain at the International Istiqual poetry festival in Jakarta, Indonesia reading extracts from her poetry book *Search*. At the end of the festival she was awarded the title of Istiqual Honorary Fellow of Poetry. In 2003 Dewan Bahasa dan Pustaka began the publication of her Series of 200 books called 'The Glorious Prophet' series telling the stories of the prophets from Adam to Jesus fully illustrated with many historical and scientific facts for young adults.

She has also written for various newspaper and magazines within Malaysia. A mother of eleven children she is also active in social welfare work as well as being a cancer councillor. An active woman who is also a great bookworm she writes an average of 4-6 hours most days.

This trilogy that was partly inspired by Tolkien is the author's first novel, and first book for adults.

Dedication

I would like to dedicate this trilogy to my beloved husband who has been my constant companion, friend and support throughout the years.

Also to my children, especially Ruqqayah and Zainab, who could not wait for the next chapter to be written.

Finally, to my beloved parents Carol and Alan Scott, who I love dearly, always.

Contents

CONTENTS

Chapter One

The Dragon Chamber

Aliyyah made her way along the damp, dark, stone passageway slowly and cautiously. The only light there was came from the orbs of fire floating just above her head. Each orb gave out a green luminous light, which cast weird and frightening shadows all around.

Soon, Aliyyah knew, she would face her first and maybe final test, the dreaded Dragon Chamber. Every single 'seeker' had to enter this secret chamber and answer the riddles of the nine mystical dragons. Those who failed, and that was many, never left the chamber again. No one except maybe the elders knew what happened to them. There were rumours, dark and horrible rumours, but no one spoke these rumours out loud for fear of bringing the dragons, terrible curse down upon them.

Aliyyah, however, had a weapon, which no one else knew about, not even the elders. She knew the dragons' names - Golden Claw, Dark Wing, Silver Back, Fire Eye, Light Chaser, Wild Wind, Mercury Tongue, Sayning, and the oldest and wisest of all the dragons, Greenthor.

Only a true ruler, or the child of the true king of the nine magical Islands of Lamis, knew their names and they would become instantly obedient to whoever spoke those names. All that is except Greenthor, for he had another even more secret name that not even the kings knew.

The elders who sent her to be tested did not know who she truly was, for if they did her life would be in constant danger. She was in fact from a long line of ancient and noble kings who had ruled the islands wisely until her father had been murdered by the Dark One, an ancient who had been so corrupted by power and greed he had fallen from the light and embraced the darkness.

Had the Dark One known where she was she would have died a long time ago, but she had been well hidden shortly after her birth.

As was the custom, her father had looked into the Mirror of Dirtaq when she was born and had seen his death and her future. In order for her to succeed in her destiny, he had asked the only elder he could trust completely to look after her and keep her birth secret.

Mahin was old; he was so old that he was ancient when Aliyyah's father was just a child. He had known the elders of Atlantis before their greed and desire for more and more power had brought the curse of God down upon them, which destroyed their magnificent civilization.

He knew all the secrets of the old ways and the hiding places of the ancient treasures, the Book of Fazma, the Keys of Hanaj, the Mirror of Dirtaq, and the double-edged Sword of Ila.

Mahin, however, had no desire for wealth or power. He was a trusted guardian who stood between the dark and the light, trying to protect the light and defeat the dark. He could not fight himself, but only aid a seeker along the way. He had great powers, but he knew that if he misused them his fate would be far worse than even that of the Dark One.

Mahin hoped with all his heart that Aliyyah was the one foretold in the ancient Book of Fazma. The one who would reclaim the four ancient treasures and whose son would destroy the Dark One and his minions forever.

Aliyyah blinked as she saw a door suddenly appear in front of her, as if some old and strange magic was playing tricks on her. Written in glowing red letters that seemed to shout at her were the words,

*'For those who enter this chamber beware Nine dragons
await for those who dare To answer the questions each
one has to say If wrong this will be their final day'*

As Aliyyah apprehensively approached the door she heard a
deep booming voice demand, "Who dares to approach the Dragon
Chamber?"

In her bravest voice she replied, "A searcher for the way of
light."

"By which name do you go by, seeker?"

Knowing she could not lie she replied, "Aliyyah, daughter of
Dor, the son of Nuh."

Almost as if it was amused the voice replied, "Long have we
waited for you to begin your quest, but still my riddle you must
answer to start your test. Fail and with your life you will have to
pay.

> *"In a white dress to show the way
> I get thinner each and every day
> What am I?"*

Smiling, Aliyyah replied, "That one is easy, it is a candle!"

"You may pass, but beware the dragons' riddles are much
more difficult to answer."

Slowly, with a loud creaking noise, the great oak door swung
open on its rusty hinges. Cautiously Aliyyah walked into the
Dragon's Chamber. As her eyes adjusted to the gloom she caught a
glimpse of a silver scale and the glint of dragon eyes staring at her
from the dark shadows.

Suddenly, as if by magic, a fire leaped to life in the middle of
the chamber, spreading a greenish light that chased the darkness
back to the corners of this strange room.

As the fire danced, Aliyyah saw the nine dragons sitting on
elaborately carved stone platforms in a semi-circle around her.
Each of these platforms was inscribed with writing that was so
ancient that only the dragons themselves knew how to read it.

3

Looking at the dragons one by one she could recognize each one by his colour.

Golden Claw had beautiful golden talons almost like a work of art, but at the same time looking cruel and razor sharp. Dark Wing had huge black wings that seemed to melt into the blackness of the chamber. Silver Back was a slightly smaller dragon, green with a silver stripe down his back.

Fire Eye was red, as red as the burning fire, with eyes that danced like the flames making it appear both fierce and angry at the same time. Wild Wind was slimmer than all the other dragons, an athlete so to say. Aliyyah remembered that Mahin had told her that this dragon was so fast it could out fly the wild west wind. Hence his name. Light Chaser was pale silver in colour, with scales that appeared to change colour every few seconds, almost like a rainbow that could not make up its mind what it really wanted to be.

Mercury Tongue, as his name suggested, had a long silver-coloured tongue. It was said that among all the dragons he was the most eloquent of speech. Sayning wore a crafty, cunning look on his face and Aliyyah was quickly reminded of Mahin's warning.

"Beware Sayning, of all the dragons he is the most cunning and deceitful. No one, not even the other dragons, trusts him. However, if you can win his friendship he would give his life for you."

Finally, seated on the largest and grandest platform in the middle of the semi-circle, was Greenthor. Of all the dragons Greenthor was the largest, most dignified and truly the most magnificent. His emerald green skin glistened in the fire light like some bright, precious jewel.

As Aliyyah looked at Greenthor she saw that he was looking at her with benevolence. A mixture of pride, pity, compassion and sadness seemed to fill the dragon's eyes.

"Aliyyah," Greenthor's deep yet mellow voice echoed. "Approach us."

Moving closer, Aliyyah waited to see what her fate would be now she was at the mercy of the nine dragons.

"Aliyyah, daughter of King Dor, the rightful Queen of the Islands of Lamis, why did you come?"

Taken aback that they knew who she really was, she nevertheless replied without fear, "I come as a seeker."

Sadly, Greenthor asked her, "You know what the test involves?"

"Yes," Aliyyah replied. "I know and I am prepared."

"You know the penalty of failure? If you cannot answer even one of the questions then your life is forfeit. Do not think you can use the knowledge of our secret names for I have another secret name that even the other dragons do not know. Do you still accept our challenge?"

Shaken a little that Greenthor knew her father had revealed their secret names to her she bravely replied, "Yes, for there is no other choice for me."

Looking closely at her the dragon said nothing for a few minutes, then with a nod of his beautiful head he commented, "You are right, what has been written must be fulfilled. Turn around and face Golden Claw and your first riddle."

Aliyyah did as she was told and saw Golden Claw beaming at her from the end of the semi-circle.

> *"Answer my riddle if you please*
> *And try not to shake at your knees!*
> *What gives life to all, but does not live?"*

Aliyyah thought for a moment before answering, "The sun, which is as golden as your claws. Golden Claw."

"Well done, now come closer my princess." Unafraid, Aliyyah went nearer Golden Claw. "Take this," said the dragon, as he handed Aliyyah one of his old claws. "Keep this with you always. If you need my help at any time, rub the claw and I will appear. Proceed to the next dragon."

The dragon sitting next to Golden Claw was Dark Wing, who asked in a melancholy voice that echoed with hidden mysteries and deep sorrows,

> *"I hide all men's sins beneath my dark cloak.*
> *What am I?"*

Aliyyah looked puzzled as her mind raced for the answer. Dark cloak, dark cloak, what could that mean.

"I know," Aliyyah almost shouted, as she realized what the answer was. "The answer is night, Dark Wing, as black as you, great wings and just as mysterious."

"Well done, and as you have used my name I must obey you. However, I warn you, never misuse my help." Then holding out one of his claws he gave Aliyyah a black cloak. "This is my gift to you. This cloak will hide you from your enemies as the night hides the sins of men. Proceed."

Light Chaser was the next dragon to question Aliyyah.

"Princess, answer me if you please,

> *A promise I am, I do not tease*
> *For everyone to take as they please*
> *No more floods will come to drown the land*
> *I am the sign, a colourful band.*
> *What am I?"*

Aliyyah replied without any hesitation, "It is a rainbow, Light Chaser, a promise from the Creator that never again would He destroy the earth and all the creatures living on it by a mighty flood."

"Well done my fair princess, and for your reward please take this bracelet." So saying the dragon handed her a golden bracelet, which was embedded with many different coloured stones that seemed to change as the scales on the back of Light Chaser did.

"This bracelet will aid you whenever you have to cross a river or an ocean. Each stone will call a different river or sea creature who will come and obey you in any way you ask. Proceed."

6

Silver Back then asked his riddle. "Princess, answer if you can.

> *I am neither gold nor diamond, copper nor pearls*
> *But when a talisman is engraved on me,*
> *Try to harm me at your peril.*
> *What am I?"*

Aliyyah knew this one straight away as she had learnt about the use of talismans from the ancient books.

"Oh, Silver Back it is silver, like the stripe down your back. Whenever a protective verse is engraved upon it no harm can befall the one wearing it."

"Very good, now step forward and receive my gift." So saying he pulled out one of his silver scales and using his claw scratched some ancient verses upon it. Handing it to Aliyyah he told her, "Carry this with you at all times. As long as you are wearing it no harm can befall you. Continue."

Impatiently, Fire Eye stood and said, "Answer my riddle and I will give you a firestone to light your way.

> *I eat, but I have no mouth,*
> *I destroy and preserve at the same time.*
> *What am I?"*

Aliyyah looked at the ground, then at the other dragons, until she finally faced Fire Eye once again. As she stared at the striking red dragon she saw what looked like small flames dancing in his eyes. Suddenly she realized that the answer was fire.

"Oh, Fire Eye, the answer is fire."

"Yes, you are correct, and like my brothers, as you know my name I will aid you when you need me. Take my gift and proceed." So saying he handed her a red stone that flickered yellow and black as if a fire was burning inside it trying to get out. At the same time it let off a bright glare, lighting the darkness around her.

Gratefully taking the stone, she placed it in the deep inner pockets of her long, thick travelling cloak. Aliyyah then waited for Wild Wind to question her.

Wild Wind was a young dragon, only five thousand years old. Playfully he asked,

"No man can see me, but all men feel me when I pass.
What am I?"

Just as playfully, Aliyyah replied, "As your name is Wild Wind, I think it must be the wind. Am I right?"

"Correct. Take this whistle. If you need me just blow it and I will be with you faster than the wind."

Mercury Tongue was the next dragon to question Aliyyah.

"Do you know who I am, Aliyyah?"

"Yes," replied Aliyyah. "You are Mercury Tongue the most learned and eloquent of all the dragons."

"You flatter me, but Greenthor is the wisest and most eloquent, not I. Now if you please, answer my riddle,

In the ancient scrolls and the books of old
The answers to all are told.
It is written that in order to succeed in your quest
What is it you must look to, to pass the test?"

"This riddle is easy, for my teacher has always taught me to follow my heart."

"Very good, and I think we must have had the same teacher, for Mahin taught me as well many thousands of years ago. It seems you have learnt well, Aliyyah. Now to receive my gift you must come closer." Aliyyah stepped closer. "You must come even closer than that to receive my gift, Aliyyah."

Taking a few more steps Aliyyah found herself standing directly in front of Mercury Tongue. Without warning the dragon grabbed Aliyyah and held her tightly against his chest. As she struggled for breath she felt a great warmth and light enter both her

8

heart and her mind. Just as she thought she was going to pass out the dragon released her.

"Whatever Mahin poured into my heart I have now poured into yours. Use my gift well and remember me to Mahin."

The next dragon was Sayning, the most tricky and deceitful of all the dragons. Staring at Aliyyah with his unblinking eyes he asked, "What do you know about me, Princess?"

Smiling, Aliyyah replied, "You are Sayning, the most cunning of all the dragons, no one trusts you, not even your companions. However if anyone wins your friendship you would defend them with your life."

"You are correct, but just out of curiosity, what would you say a friend is?"

"A friend is someone who sticks by you through good and bad. Someone who helps without being asked, someone who would give their life for you and someone who is always there when you need them. That is a friend, and if you would allow it, I would like to be your friend."

Sayning remained silent for a while before replying, "We will see, Princess, we will see. I do not befriend anyone easily, but in your case there may be a chance. Now answer my riddle and be careful for it is not what it may seem.

I am pure, but can be polluted
I am eternal yet imprisoned in decay
I know all, but know nothing
Only death can set me free.
What am I?"

Sayning's riddle was indeed difficult and would have proved Aliyyah's undoing, however the knowledge that Mercury Tongue had poured into her heart showed her the answer.

"Oh, Sayning, truly you are most crafty, but I know the answer to your riddle!"

"Indeed, then tell us, Aliyyah, daughter of King Dor!"

"It is the soul. Created pure by our Creator, but can be polluted by the sins of the body. Before birth it knew everything, but at birth a veil falls so it knows nothing. Only when death of the body occurs is the soul returned to its pure eternal form."

"Most impressive, Princess, did you answer this riddle from your own knowledge or did my brother's gift aid you?"

Smiling at Sayning's question she answered, "Indeed your riddle has been the most difficult so far and I would have been unable to answer it but for your brother's gift."

"You are most honest Aliyyah, but beware of always being so open. Now as you have answered my question you have earned my gift, take this and wear it at all times." So saying he handed Aliyyah a gold amulet. The bright golden chain supported a dark stone that was encased in a golden circle shaped like a dragon chasing its own tail.

As she looked carefully she saw the stone seemed to be alive, flickering from one colour to another. As she placed the beautiful amulet around her neck Sayning told her, "This amulet belonged to an ancient sorceress. It is a truth stone and will change colours to let you know if a person is telling the truth or not. It will warn you of any danger and if you know its secret it will also protect you from that danger."

Puzzled, Aliyyah asked, "What secret, Sayning?"

"That, you find out for yourself. All I will say is that if you are true to the stone it will be true to you."

Straight away Aliyyah realized what that secret must be. "Oh, Sayning, I think that I know the key. Does it mean that if I am truthful and do not lie then the stone will protect me with the truth?"

If a dragon could smile then Sayning's expression would have been so. "Indeed you are as clever as you are beautiful. Your name suits you well. I hope that you will be as noble and truthful as the sorceress who this stone once belonged to. Her name too was Aliyyah, Aliyyah the Pure, Protector of the treasures of the nine mystical islands."

Sayning then indicated she should go to the last dragon, Greenthor, the oldest and the wisest of them all.

Looking kindly at Aliyyah, Greenthor asked, "Are you prepared? For my riddle is even more difficult than Sayning's. So far not one single seeker has been able to answer it."

"Oh, Greenthor, as I said before, I have no choice but to try. This is my destiny and I cannot run away from it."

"Very well, listen closely and think carefully before you answer. Unbeknown to you, more than your own life depends on your answer.

Older than the mountains am I
Changing everything yet remaining unchanged.
No man can see me, but all men can feel me pass
No man can outrun me, I outlast them all.
No force can contain me nor defeat me
I am more precious than any mine full of
Gold and diamonds,
What am I?"

The silence in the chamber grew ominous as Aliyyah strove to find the answer. What could it be? She felt the dragons' eyes staring at her even though she did not see them. Surely she was not going to fail at this last riddle? What she needed was more time, more time to think, more time to find the answer. Suddenly it hit her. Of course, how simple yet how difficult it was. The answer was time, time that no man can defeat or outrun. With a look of great relief on her face she said, "Greenthor, your answer is time. Time is something that no man can outrun or contain. It destroys everything except for the Creator himself and what He desires to be eternal, for time was created by the Creator himself."

No sooner had Aliyyah finished speaking than a bright white light sprung up illuminating every nook and cranny of the chamber. As her eyes grew accustomed to the light after the gloom she saw lined around the walls of the chamber cold, grey statues of young men and women. She had not noticed them before as they had been hidden by the dimness.

"Aliyyah," began Greenthor. "These statues were once flesh and blood; young men and women like yourself. They are the seekers who came before you and failed in their quest. This too would have been your fate if you had failed to answer my riddle. You have done well, but now you have an even more difficult decision to make. The first step of your quest has been successful, you now have the choice of two paths. You may leave this chamber now and continue on your quest without freeing these seekers, or you may free them first before going on."

Interrupting Greenthor, Aliyyah replied, "There is no difficulty there, of course I will free them first!"

"Wait," cautioned Greenthor. "Let me finish. If you continue your quest without freeing them and you fail, another seeker may try to answer the riddles, but you condemn these seekers to remain as stone forever. However, if you choose to free them you must not fail in your quest. Once they are released there can be no more seekers."

Aliyyah felt as if the weight of all the nine islands had been placed on her shoulders. What must she do? She could not leave the seekers to their stony fate, but what if she failed in her quest? If that happened then there would be no more seekers to defeat the Dark One and he would be able to claim the islands forever. As she struggled to find an answer she could almost hear Mahin's voice. "Remember, the quest is to save all those who have been enslaved by magic. If it is in your power to save even one soul you must do so, no matter what you fear the consequences may be."

"Greenthor," addressed Aliyyah firmly. "How can I continue my quest without releasing these poor souls from their enchantment? No matter what else happens, they must be set free!"

Quizzical, Greenthor looked at Aliyyah. "Are you sure my Princess?"

"Yes, I must follow my heart and what I have been taught."

"You have chosen wisely," Greenthor replied in a kindly voice. "For if you had abandoned them you would have failed in your quest and would have joined them in their stone prisons. We will release them, but first, accept my gift."

In his talons Greenthor held a ring containing a heart-shaped stone of the most incredible beauty and radiance. Its ever-changing colours melted into each other with perfect harmony.

"This is the Heart Ring," explained Greenthor. "It is a companion to the Truth Amulet you already wear. It will guide you when you are unsure of your path. Wear it at all times, for when it is combined with the amulet no black magic can harm you nor will anyone be able to deceive you."

Carefully taking the ring, Aliyyah placed it on her finger where it seemed to glow, if it was possible, with an even greater brilliance than before.

"Thank you Greenthor, I am indebted to you and your brothers for such great and priceless gifts."

"Gifts you have truly earned, Princess. Now step back and cover your eyes."

Then in a language that was so ancient only Greenthor knew how to use it, he began a strange incantation in his deep and mellow voice. As he droned on, the light in the chamber flashed from one colour to another, each light more brilliant and blinding than the last. Finally a magnificent white light filled the chamber.

As Aliyyah slowly lowered her hands from her face she saw the thick stone walls began to flicker and fade away to nothingness. As she stared, the statues that had lined the walls slowly turned from a stony grey to a healthy pink as life once more flowed back into the petrified bodies. As the seekers came back to life they looked around, dazed and confused, not knowing where they were or even who they were.

Concerned, Aliyyah asked Greenthor whether they would be all right.

"Do not worry, Princess, their memories of the quest have been wiped away to protect them from the Dark One. They will be transported back to the elders, who will take care of them until they can be safely returned to their families. Now you must bid farewell and continue the quest."

Even before Aliyyah could ask how they were going to be sent back, a white mist began to swirl up and entwined itself around each of the unsuccessful seekers. Then, before she could even blink her eyes, they vanished from sight.

Staring at the white twirls of disappearing mist, Aliyyah heard the slow but distinctive sound of flapping wings. As she turned around she saw, one by one, the dragons open their wings and majestically rise up into the evening skies above them, until only Greenthor was left in the chamber.

"Aliyyah," said Greenthor in his deep voice. "Although you did not know it, when you chose to set the seekers free you also set us free. A powerful magic, much stronger than our own, has kept us imprisoned here until the chosen seeker arrived. Thank you my Princess, for releasing us from our enchantment. Now we too can return to our homes, but if you ever need my help just recite *Hadsha Drogna Lamis Ni* and I will come to your aid. Farewell for now Princess, farewell." With these words he unfolded his magnificent wings.

"Wait, Greenthor," cried Aliyyah. "Where do I go from here?"

"Follow your heart," replied the dragon as he slowly rose up. "Follow your heart and remember to use our gifts well." With these final words he slowly disappeared into the darkening skies, leaving an apprehensive and somewhat puzzled Aliyyah standing where once the dragons had sat to question her.

Chapter Two

Which Path to Take?

As she looked around her, Aliyyah saw that she was in a small clearing surrounded by an ancient forest, so thick that not even a single ray of sunlight seemed able to pierce the darkness that gathered beneath the twisted and gnarled branches of the massive trees.

As she stared in front of her in the gathering gloom she could vaguely see three different paths leading into the forest. At first Aliyyah thought of using the firestone to explore the paths, but after a few minutes she decided that she would wait till daybreak to continue. She was tired and needed to rest. Lying down and wrapping her cloak tightly around her, she put her travelling bag under her head as a pillow. Then, before closing her eyes in an exhausted sleep, she looked at her ring and amulet to see if there was any danger nearby.

As she slept the trees seemed to whisper to each other, for unbeknown to Aliyyah, this forest was under an enchantment as powerful as the one that had kept the dragons imprisoned in their chamber. The forest, like the dragons, was waiting for the right seeker to break the black spell.

The ancient trees slowly moved towards her, closer and closer until they formed a protective ring around the sleeping girl. As the night grew colder and colder, some of the trees shook their boughs so that a thick blanket of leaves covered Aliyyah, keeping her warm and dry throughout the night.

Just as the first rays of sun appeared like fingers in the sky, the trees slowly retreated to their original places leaving Aliyyah still asleep, covered with leaves.

Shortly after this Aliyyah awoke refreshed, but startled to find herself covered with a thick blanket of leaves. Shaking them off, she got up and stretched wondering what had happened during the night.

Before exploring her surroundings, Aliyyah sat down and opened her bag, removing a small loaf of bread and a flask of water. Eating just enough to take the edge of her hunger, she washed down the bread with a few swigs of water. After replacing the remaining bread and water in her bag she looked carefully around her.

As the daylight flooded the clearing she could now clearly see that three separate paths lay in front of her. The path on the right was rough and overgrown, shaded by ancient gnarled trees. The branches made an impenetrable canopy like the old withered fingers of some forgotten giant, knotted together as if in prayer.

The middle road was clear and smooth as if it was used daily. However, the sides of the trees and the undergrowth were blackened, as if they had been scorched by fire. Aliyyah did not know, but this path was used by the fire-worms. Great creatures whose round segmented bodies reached almost to the tops of the trees. As they slithered through the forest, black-red flames shot out of their bodies, burning and blackening anything in their way.

These fire-worms were terrible, evil creatures, for they ted not on their victims' bodies, but on their immortal souls. Sucking the soul from the body, they devoured it, leaving behind them a walking corpse.

If anyone strayed upon their path, the fire-worms would pursue them, never giving up until they had destroyed that person or had perished in the attempt. The worms, however, never left their paths, following the same routes that all the fire-worms before them had followed. They never changed or made new paths so as long as you did not cross them they were no danger to you.

The third path was blocked with the massive trunks of fallen trees, it seemed as if a giant hand had picked them up and stacked them together in an untidy pile. However, unseen to Aliyyah, behind these trunks was a clear path that led out of the forest.

Confused as to which path to take, Aliyyah stood for some time pondering which way to go. Then carefully she started walking towards the middle path. As she got nearer both her ring and amulet changed colour to a black-red as if warning her against that path. Slowly she walked away a little and as she did so the ring and amulet returned to their normal colours. Once more she walked towards the middle path and once again the ring and amulet changed to a black-red colour.

"Well it seems that is the wrong path," commented Aliyyah.

Next she tried the other two paths, but the ring and the amulet colours did not change.

"Now what am I to do?" said Aliyyah to herself. "How am I going to choose the right one?"

Sitting down on a grassy knoll she looked from left to right and right to left, still she could not make up her mind. Just as she was going to call on one of the dragons for help a beautiful bird flew out of the forest and around her head. Although she had never seen this type of bird before, she knew what it was from the drawings in the books she had studied with her teacher Mahin. As she looked at the bird she remembered sitting in Mahin's private gardens under the strange Abut tree listening to her lessons. The bark of this tree was as soft as silk and its boughs were laden with juicy fruits. No two fruits were alike, each one was a different shape, size and colour, and every fruit tasted more delicious than the fruit before it. Whenever the wind blew, the leaves rubbed together making a gentle tinkling sounding like a child's lullaby. She could almost hear Mahin's voice as he told her about the bird.

"This bird is the fabled phoenix. See its beautiful feathers, all of which have magical powers. Every thousand years it builds itself a nest and then, sitting on the nest, it burst into flames. Then from the ashes it is reborn again to live another thousand years. Its tears have healing properties and it is wiser than any other living creature. It aids the ones who fight against evil and has its own powerful enchantments. If ever it appears to you, make sure you follow it for it will lead you on the right road."

As Aliyyah stood up, the phoenix started leading her towards the right-hand path. As she stepped onto the overgrown path she heard the beautiful singsong voice of the phoenix.

"The left-hand path is clear after the fallen trunks and will lead you out of the forest, but you must not take that way."

Puzzled, Aliyyah asked why. The phoenix replied, "In order to recover the Mirror of Dirtaq you must free the forest from its black spell."

"How do I do that?" shouted Aliyyah as the bird flew higher and higher.

"Free the unicorn from the glass castle, when you do that you will break the spell and find the mirror."

"How do I find the castle, Phoenix?"

"Follow the path, and remember not to eat or drink anything from the forest or you too will fall under its spell."

Wearily, Aliyyah walked along the narrow path. Sometimes it became so dark she was forced to use the firestone to light her way. Hour after hour, passed and still there was no sign of a castle or a unicorn. Eventually, hungry, tired and thirsty she stopped to rest. As she sat with her back against one of the trees, her eyelids drooped and she fell asleep. Shortly after she had fallen asleep the phoenix returned carrying a small bag in its beak. Inside the bag were juicy berries and nuts and a small flask of cool spring water. Placing the bag beside Aliyyah, the phoenix opened its beak and began singing the most beautiful song you could ever imagine. As it sang, rays of light started to crisscross around the sleeping girl forming a golden dome, as the phoenix wove its powerful spell of protection. Then, having finished its song, it stood guard until Aliyyah awoke the next morning.

As she opened her eyes, the golden dome quickly faded and disappeared and all that Aliyyah saw was the phoenix watching her from the branches it was seated on.

"Eat and drink from the food in the bag. I took it from a forest far away from here. I am sorry it is not much, but it will give you strength and quench your thirst."

Thanking the phoenix, Aliyyah gratefully ate and drank before asking, "Wise phoenix, how do I free the unicorn from the castle of mirrors?"

"Aliyyah, among the mirrors is hidden the Mirror of Dartiq, once you hold it, all the mirrors will break and the unicorn will be freed."

"Phoenix, one more question, how will I know which mirror is the Mirror of Dartiq?"

"Use your amulet, use your amulet! Remember the mirror is small, but it may appear to be large. Only when it is in your hand will it reveal its true form. Now goodbye until we meet again, goodbye seeker and good luck."

These words echoed in Aliyyah's ears as she watched the phoenix slowly and gracefully disappear from sight. Stepping firmly, Aliyyah continued on her way. As she walked she noticed that the path was opening up and the ground was no longer overgrown. It was as if someone had been looking after the grass. As she followed the widening path she caught her first glance of the enchanted glass castle. She gasped as she had not realized that something so evil could be so beautiful, it was like an enormous cut diamond sparkling in the bright sunlight. There must be thousands of mirrors, how was she ever going to find the right one?

As she approached the doorway she could hear a multitude of shrill voices all screaming at her.

"Aliyyah, I am the one you seek, look no further!"

Their screams were enough to drive a person mad and Aliyyah already felt as if her head was about to break. What could she do?

Suddenly inspiration flooded her mind as she remembered Mahin telling her the story of Jason and the Argonauts, who outwitted the sirens by placing wax in their ears so they could not near the alluring songs of these evil sea creatures. Quickly, Aliyyah broke the small candle she carried in her bag and carefully placed some of the wax in each ear, blocking out the shrill voices.

As she entered the castle she saw herself reflected a thousand limes over and at the same lime she also saw the reflection of the most beautiful white unicorn, which although not tied, was imprisoned in a courtyard of mirrors. No matter which way he ran, the unicorn saw only its reflection and veered this way and that in fear.

"Hold on," Aliyyah cried out in compassion and pity for the frightened but noble beast. "I am coming, I will free you, don't despair!"

Even as she said these words she wondered how she was going to reach the magical creature. Each room she entered was the same, filled with reflections and leading to another identical room. You could spend your whole life searching for and never finding either the unicorn or the Mirror of Dirtaq. Aliyyah gradually realised that she was also trapped, as there was no way she could find her way back to the entrance. She must succeed or remain a prisoner in the castle forever.

As this realization hit her, Aliyyah remembered the phoenix's words, 'use your amulet to find the mirror'. Taking the amulet out from underneath her dress she allowed it to lay across her breast. No sooner had it been taken from within the folds of her clothing than it started to glow. At first it was a dull light, but as she walked the light increased in intensity until she was standing in front of the largest and most beautiful of all the mirrors. It was here that her amulet glowed with the brilliance of an exploding star.

This must be the right mirror, but it is so big! How am I going to take it? she thought. Surely there must be a way. As she pondered she remembered what the phoenix had told her, 'the mirror may appear to be large, but when in your hand it will take its true form'.

"Well, let's try and see what happens." Aliyyah slowly stretched out her hands and grabbed both edges of the mirror. As soon as she touched it there was a deafening breaking sound as all the other mirrors cracked and fell to the floor in a shower of broken glass. As the shattering sound faded, Aliyyah opened her eyes to see the Mirror of Dartiq in her hands. Looking at the mirror in its true form Aliyyah admired the workmanship that had gone into its creation. The mirror was slightly smaller than her hand, a perfect circle. The surface of the mirror was cloudy, only revealing the future when the time was right and the proper words sung. It was encased in a gold frame that had two handles, one on either side. One handle was shaped like a dragon chasing its own tail, with ruby red eyes, while the other was in the form of a lion standing on two paws, with emerald green eyes. On the case, inscribed in the sacred language of the elders, was line after line of protective verse. Aliyyah knew how to read some of these verses having being taught them by Mahin, but others were much more difficult to unravel.

Carefully she wrapped the mirror in a purple velvet bag that she had been given by Mahin, then placed it into one of the deep pockets of her thick travelling cloak.

Looking around she saw to her surprise that all the sharp shards of mirror seemed to be dissolving into pure white sand. As she watched, a strong breeze started blowing the sand away until, within a short while, nothing was left except a sward of green grass and a beautiful white unicorn standing free at last.

As she walked over to the gentle creature, she heard it speaking to her, not physically but mentally. Aliyyah had never realized that unicorns were telepathic, but it pleased her that they were able to communicate.

"Princess Aliyyah, thank you for freeing me from the evil spells of the Dark One."

"How do you know who I am?" asked Aliyyah with some surprise. "Who told you?"

"The phoenix told me to have hope as you were coming. This castle has robbed me of my magic and was slowly draining my life force as well. If you had not saved me I would have surely died."

"I know the Dark One is evil, but why would he want to kill you?"

"A unicorn has very powerful magic, more powerful than you humans know, and with it the Dark One would become invincible. Our magic has been drained from us, but it takes many years and the person who robs us can only use this magic if we die. Now that you have freed me the Dark One cannot use my magic," replied the unicorn with a graceful nod of his head.

"Can you regain your magic again?" asked Aliyyah.

"Yes, but it will take time and I will have to travel to the hidden island of the unicorns, far, far away."

"Then you must leave at once," said Aliyyah. "Before you are captured again."

Shaking its head from side to side it told Aliyyah, "No, I cannot abandon the one who saved me. According to our laws I must accompany you and help you until I succeed in paying back my debt. Then and only then will I be permitted to return to my island."

"I will be glad of your company, but you have no need to follow me. I release you from all obligations to me. My quest will be long and dangerous and I would not like for you to get hurt," replied Aliyyah with a smile.

Shaking its head and pawing the ground with its snowy white foot it once more spoke telepathically to Aliyyah. "Even if that is so, I would still come with you for I too want to see the Dark One defeated.

I think I will be able to help you, even without my magical powers."

Aliyyah felt very glad to have a companion and asked the unicorn his name.

"I am called Najputih, the white star, among my kind I am well known for my wisdom and beauty." Then looking around him the unicorn enquired where they were going next.

Aliyyah had no idea where she was supposed to go next. She looked at both her amulet and ring, but this time they gave her no indication of where she was meant to travel.

"I do not know, Najputih. All I know is that after I had retrieved the Mirror of Dartiq I must next find the Keys of Hanaj."

"Well we cannot stay here," thought the unicorn. "Let us continue the quest, I am sure before long we will find our next test, or it will find us."

"Yes," agreed Aliyyah. "Let us see how far we can walk before nightfall."

So saying, they started walking out of the forest. As they walked Aliyyah could hear the trees whispering their thanks to her for releasing them from their enchantment. The darkness of the forest had been lifted and the songs of birds and the noises of the wild animals broke the silence.

"Thank you," the trees whispered. "Thank you, come back again our Princess, come back."

Just as they were about to leave the forest a strange shape appeared before them, it was not a tree yet it was not a man, rather something in between.

"I am a Dryad, one of the tree spirits, we are the guardians of all living trees and plants. I have been sent to thank you and to give you this gift." Holding out his twig-like hand he gave Aliyyah a flower of the most incredible beauty and scent.

"This is the Day Bloom. It comes from the hidden gardens of the wood elves. It can heal any wound or slop poison. All you have to do is place it in water and use this water for healing. This flower will not die as long as your heart remains pure. Now listen carefully, for I have also been told to teach you how to call for the aid of the forest if ever you need us."

So saying, the Dryad taught her part of the language of the trees, a strange creaking kind of speech, as old as the speech of the dragons and just as mysterious.

"Now Princess, as it is near nightfall the trees have asked if you wish to sleep here tonight. They will protect you and in the morning you can continue."

Aliyyah, not wishing to offend the Dryad or the trees, agreed and she and the unicorn lay down on the grassy knoll the Dryad showed them. As Aliyyah's eyes began to close she saw the trees slowly moving to form a protective circle around them. At the same time she felt a gentle layer of leaves falling down and covering her and the unicorn, providing a warm blanket against the cold of the night.

Sleepily Aliyyah said, "It was you who covered me before, thank you, my friends, thank you." Before long both Aliyyah and the unicorn were fast asleep under the protection of the forest she had freed.

Chapter Three

The Fortress of Illusions

From far away Aliyyah could hear the noise of raucous laughter and coarse song coming from the dilapidated old fortress, sitting bleak and forlorn on the top of the black basalt rocks, which jutted out over the sea of despair and misery.

The sound of merrymaking contrasted deeply with the mourning sighs of the black waves. Sighs that spoke of unimaginable grief and endless despair. It was easy to believe that these waters could drive a person to madness.

The fortress of dreams and deceptions, the old man had called it.

"Beware," he had warned her. "The fortress is not what it appears to be. It is pure evil and will trap you with the things you desire the most."

Puzzled, Aliyyah had asked him who he was.

"I am a stranger from an even stranger land. My job is to guide those who truly wish to be guided," he replied, staring at her with eyes of fire that seemed to burn deep down into her very soul. "And you, Princess Aliyyah, are a seeker trying to free your lands from the black enchantments of the Dark One."

Speechless, Aliyyah just looked at his amused face, half smiling, yet not unkindly. As soon as she had recovered her wits she asked him who he was and how he knew who she was.

"Did I not tell you?" he replied. "I am a stranger from an even stranger land. I am known by many different names, the green one, the one who speaks in riddles, the guide and many others. I know who you are, who your father was and why you came here, I even know your teacher Mahin very well."

Thoughtfully, Aliyyah questioned the confusing old man. "If what you say is true, then I think my next task must be to set them free and destroy the evil of the fortress forever. Can you help me?"

Shaking his head the old man replied, "I can only guide you, no more than that. You must not listen to the whispers you will hear the moment you enter the castle. This time your candle wax will not help you. These whispers you will hear inside your head, not with your ears. You must remember, whatever you hear is lies, illusions and deceit. Do not look at or speak to anyone inside the castle or you will lose your soul as they have. Find the black stone that beats at the very heart of the old fortress and remove it. Beware, however, for it is well guarded and you will need all your wits to outsmart the guardians of this evil place."

"But how am I going to take the black stone?" questioned the bewildered Aliyyah.

Smiling, the old man told her, "A game to win a stone, oh daughter of King Dor. A game you have already played and won." With this he slowly began to fade away. "Goodbye Aliyyah, till we meet again goodbye and good luck."

Standing near the drawbridge that led into the gloomy fortress, Aliyyah wondered who the old man really was. She had heard stories of an old man who was able to take any form he desired. It was said that he had drunk from the waters of eternity and since then he wandered among all the lands, hidden and open, aiding all those who fought against evil.

By her side Aliyyah felt the unicorn begin to tremble and shake. Stroking Najputih's mane gently she asked the unicorn what was wrong. In her mind she heard the unicorn replied, "I am a creature of purity and goodness who has been weakened by my long imprisonment in the Castle of Mirrors, I dare not enter into such a place of evil in my present condition, please forgive me!"

Smiling gently, Aliyyah replied while still stroking the unicorn's magnificent white mane. "I too have no desire to enter such darkness, but I have no choice. In order to fulfil the quest I must not only recover the treasures that have been hidden, but also release all those who have been bewitched by evil. Will you wait for me or do you wish to return to your hidden islands?"

Once again Aliyyah heard the unicorn's melodious voice inside her head.

"I have not yet repaid my debt to you for releasing me from my glass prison. I will wait for you for three days, if you have not returned I will know you have failed and I will return to my islands before it is too late."

Nodding her head, Aliyyah slowly walked towards the looming walls of the fortress. As she crossed the drawbridge and neared the huge wooden doors she tried to empty her mind of all emotions and desires. She did not want to give the evil powers inside this place any weapons with which to trick her.

As she neared the old, heavy wooden doors she began to hear whispers, distant and incoherent at first but becoming stronger and clearer as she approached the doors. As fear began to grip her heart she almost turned and fled, but she heard another stronger voice inside her head, 'a stone to conquer a stone'. Quickly she looked at the heart stone she was wearing. Its colours were changing rapidly as if it too were fighting a battle with some unknown force. Suddenly it flared and started to shine with a brilliant white light, which seemed to push nil the other voices and whispers out of Aliyyah's head leaving her with clear unfettered thoughts.

"That's it, I must concentrate on the heart stone if I am to be safe from the evil whispers."

As the doors swung open of their own accord, Aliyyah cautiously entered. The stench of filth and decay was so strong she felt that she would vomit. Keeping her eyes on the heart stone she was still able to see what was going on around her. Men and women, dressed in rags and covered in dirt and sores, were sitting on piles of rotting food and eating it as if it was the most delicious banquet ever prepared.

Disgusted, Aliyyah recited some of the verses of the ancient books, which contained in them all the knowledge, guidance and wisdom any person could ever need.

"Teltel em ese hwat yeht ese." Aliyyah then asked with her heart, show me what they see.

Instantly the scene in front of her changed. Now all the people were dressed in expensive clothes made of fine silks and satins trimmed with fur and lace. The women were bedecked with precious jewels and golden rings while the men wore hats with bright plumes mid heavy gold chains hung around their necks. The courtyard itself was gaily decorated with bright banners and flags flying from the ramparts. Where the piles of rotting food were stood tables laden with
mouth-watering dishes of every kind of food you could imagine, all on plates of the finest gold and silver. The goblets were of crystal and were overflowing with rich red wine. The piles of dung to these people appeared to be chairs of richly carved wood with velvet cushions.

As Aliyyah blinked her eyes the vision disappeared and once more she was facing the reality of the fortress. No wonder this fortress is called the fortress of lies, illusions and deception! She thought. Those people really believe they are fine ladies and gentlemen. They have already lost their minds and maybe their souls to this evil place.

Slowly and carefully, so as to avoid treading in the piles of dung and rotting food, Aliyyah made her way across the courtyard to the main entrance of the fortress keep.

As she walked as swiftly as she could, one after another of the poor victims of the fortress came to her trying to talk to her and offering her rotten food, which seemed to change to her favourite food before her very eyes. Each time she shook her head and quickly turned her gaze back to the heart stone around her neck, which caused the illusions to disappear straight away. Nearing the main castle building she could hear a terrible screeching noise like nails being scraped across a piece of sandpaper mixed with a methodically thumping noise, which seemed to pound deep into her head, threatening to break her eardrums.

"Lokani lokani vel nee knai lokanu ti," she quickly recited and with these words the sounds in her head disappeared, even though the horrible music continued playing within the castle walls.

"What on earth is making those terrible sounds?" she said to herself.

Cautiously she approached the huge oak doors, which were black with age and evil. The massive doors slowly creaked open at her approach, inviting her in like a spider to a fly.

Telling herself to be brave she stepped into the main castle building. As she did so the huge doors slammed shut behind her, barring her way out Aliyyah looking around and reeled with horror at the scene in front of her. The hall was long and dimly light with tall black candles that hid whatever was lurking in the shadows. Large rats with red eyes ran across the giant beams that crisscrossed the ceiling. Ragged banners of previous families hung limp and dissolute from the walls, reminders of a day before the evil came.

At the far end was a raised platform on which sat an orchestra, which must have come from the fires of hell itself. The musicians were not humans, but skeletons, dressed in ragged uniforms and playing upon instruments made from human skin and bones.

The people that were slowly dancing to this cacophony of sound were even more horrific. Although some of them were human, others were living dead and what was more horrific was as they were dancing with those who were still alive, they were biting and eating their flesh. As they turned and twisted Aliyyah could see the dead with their decaying bodies feasting off the flesh of their living dance partners. As their blood leaked down their bodies, the ones who were not yet dead laughed and continued this morbid dance as if nothing was happening to them.

Shrinking backwards Aliyyah watched for a few minutes trying to decide what she should do next. Suddenly the music stopped and the dancers, both living and dead, turned round to Aliyyah and began to move towards her.

Panicking, Aliyyah searched for a way to escape these hellish forms and their clear intention to add her to their banquet. Looking around furtively she spied a small archway at the far end of the hall that seemed to lead down into the dungeons. Aware that it could lead even more horrors, but seeing no other way out, she decided to risk going down there. Taking the firestone out of her cloak she held it high, blinding the hellish forms surrounding her. Without a second thought she quickly ran across the long hall, dodging and weaving around the gruesome forms that tried to catch her in their bony and bloody fingers. Panting, she managed to reach the archway, which did indeed have a flight of very steep stairs leading down into the foreboding darkness below.

Lifting the firestone up, Aliyyah carefully started to descend the winding stone stairs. As she went lower the air became colder until she was shivering uncontrollably. Faintly at first, but becoming stronger with every step, Aliyyah could hear what sounded like a heartbeat. As she reached the bottom of the stairs she saw several dark passageways leading in different directions. Each passage had a dank smell of decay and age and in each passage strange and frightening sounds could be heard. Above all these sounds, the heartbeat could be heard even stronger and louder now she had reached the bottom of the stairs. Taking the cloak that Dark Wing had given her, she quickly put it on, disappearing at once from the sight of whatever was waiting for her down here. Using the heart amulet and ring, Aliyyah went to the entrance of each tunnel and looked to see what colours they changed to. Finally, at the entrance of the largest tunnel, the ring, bracelet and amulet all flared up in a brilliant red flash followed by a blinding white light.

Well, thought Aliyyah to herself, it seems that the ring is not just showing me the right path, but also giving me a warning.

Walking into the tunnel, Aliyyah could hear the heartbeat getting louder and louder, but now there was another sound. A strange sound, like someone snoring, but it was not a human sound. Soon she could smell a strong smell of sulphur and fire and she noticed that the walls of the tunnel were blackened as if someone or something had thrown fire at them.

At the end of the tunnel there was a large chamber filled with the greatest treasure you could ever imagine. There was enough treasure there to make the person who owned it the richest king that had ever lived.

Aliyyah, however, was not interested in the treasure, for she had seen what was causing the snoring sound as well as what the heartbeat was.

On the top of one of the piles of gold and silver lay an enormous black dragon curled around a solitary black stone. It was from the dragon guarding the egg that the snoring sound was coming, while the heartbeat was coming from the stone.

Aliyyah realised that the black stone was not a stone at all, but a dragon's egg. Now what was she going to do? Careful so as not to disturb the sleeping dragon she tried to remember everything she had ever learnt about dragons.

She knew that although most of them were wise and just, there were those that were totally evil.

Racking her brain Aliyyah slowly recalled the story of Ne'alder. She was one of the oldest and wisest of all the dragons till her pride and vanity became her undoing. She was chased out of the Council of Dragons and banished from their court. Swearing revenge, she left the land of the dragons and began wreaking havoc in whichever land she stayed. Century after century she killed, burnt villages and stole all the treasure she could steal.

Terrified delegation after delegation pleaded with the Council of Dragons to help them and stop Ne'alder's reign of terror. The dragons agreed and they sent out their wisest and strongest dragons to capture and imprison the rebellious and proud dragon.

The eldest dragon had forbidden them to kill her, for no matter what, she was still a dragon. The dragons chased her for many months until finally they cornered her and using powerful magic, bound her. They took her back to their lands and locked her up in a deep cave for all time. However, she was a clever dragon and using her magic she managed to persuade the young dragon that had been appointed to look after her to not only let her free, but to return to her the egg she had laid and had left behind when she was banished.

Dragons only mate once every five thousand years and there is never more than one egg from each mating. The egg will take many, many years to hatch, sometimes as long as 500 hundred years. The Council of Dragons had taken the egg away from her as they were afraid that if she was permitted to keep the egg, when it hatched it would become another dark and evil dragon.

All dragon eggs were kept in special nurseries surrounded by light and goodness so that when they hatched they hatched, into good dragons who did not follow the dark ways. However, if a dragon egg hatched into darkness and evil it would become black-hearted and evil as well. A danger to all living creatures.

Aliyyah knew that this dragon must be Ne'alder for she had sworn that she would have revenge on the dragons and she would use her egg to create the most powerful and evil dragon imaginable. She had no mercy in her stone heart, as the young dragon had found out, for once she had her egg she had attacked him and left him dying from his wounds before fleeing. The other dragons had found the young dragon before he breathed his last and had found out what had happened.

They had searched for Ne'alder, but had been unable to find her ns she had hidden here in this ancient fortress. No wonder it had become so evil over the years, acting as an incubation room for a dragon that its mother was planning to train in the ways of evil.

However, this did not solve her problem. She knew that even though Ne'alder could not see her, if she got any closer she would definitely sense or smell her. Not only that, how could she destroy the dragon's egg? It was also under a kind of enchantment as well.

If only she could rescue the egg it might still be able to grow into a good dragon.

Thinking to herself, she tried to remember if the dragon had any weaknesses she could exploit. She knew dragons loved riddles and treasures and she also knew that all dragons were bound by their word in the riddle game, no matter how evil they were. If a dragon lost the riddle game it would have to do whatever it had promised before the start of the game. However, if the dragon won, the loser would become its next dinner.

How could she use this to defeat this dragon? Thinking furiously she decided that she had no choice but to goad the dragon into playing the riddle game, but what bait did she have? It would be foolish to use any of the gifts the dragons gave her, but what else did she have to offer? Suddenly an idea entered her head - the Mirror of Dirtaq.

Ne'alder would never be able to resist the chance to see the future of her egg. Creeping as close as she dared without disturbing the dragon, Aliyyah stared at her sleeping opponent. She really was a beautiful dragon, covered in black-golden scales that seemed to make a mockery of the darkness that was in her heart. Her great wings were folded by her side and she lay in what Aliyyah thought was deep slumber. Without any warning, one blood-red eye opened and gazed around the chamber stacked high with treasure. A pair of nostrils started sniffing the air before the dragon slowly and deliberately stretched her magnificent body. A soft alluring voice addressed the invisible Aliyyah where she hid in the shadow.

"It has been many years since anyone entered my chamber, it was the last thing they did. Who are you and what do you want here, stranger in an invisibility cloak?"

"My name is unimportant Ne'alder. I know your name and your history."

"Well, well, in that case I am supposed to do as you say, but you know I no longer follow the rules of the Dragon Council, having been thrown out by those cowards and idiots centuries ago.

Shall I just roast you where you are, or maybe you have something to offer me? You are no thief, for if you were you would have fallen under the fortress's black spell."

"I have come to break the black spell on this place and save your egg from the darkness. I mean to return it to the Dragon Council so it can hatch in light and goodness."

With a snort and a sudden breath of flaming fire, Ne'alder exclaimed, "Who are you to try and steal my egg?"

"One who would set right the evils you have done and intend to do," replied Aliyyah.

"Hmph, how are you going to do that? You cannot defeat me, I am much too powerful for you. Maybe I will just swat you now like the annoying little fly you are!"

"Maybe, if you can see me!"

"I don't need to see you, I can smell you," retorted the dragon.

Taunting, Aliyyah replied, "If you do that you will never get your hands on the Mirror of Dirtaq."

Curiously, Ne'alder, in her gentlest and most seductive voice, said, "The Mirror of Dirtaq now I know you are mad, no one can get the mirror."

Smiling to herself, Aliyyah replied, "Not only do I know where it was, but I am now its keeper."

"Impossible," exclaimed the dragon. "No one knew where it was hidden."

"That is where you are wrong, Ne'alder, for I was the one who entered the Castle of Mirrors found the mirror and freed the white unicorn and the Forbidden Forest. So you see, I am more than a match for you!"

Sneering, the dragon replied, 'I am much more dangerous and cunning than you can possible imagine. Still, I would like to own that mirror. How do I know you tell the truth? Show me the mirror."

"Do you think I am that foolish, oh wise and wicked Ne'alder. However, I am willing to make a deal with you."

"That's more like it. What do you want? Silver, gold, power? I can give you all of them."

"No, I challenge you to the riddle game. If I win, you release this fortress and all in it from your dark spell, I will take the egg back to the Dragon Council to be hatched in light and goodness and you will leave these lands and go into the dark forever."

Ne'alder asked in a threatening voice, "And if you lose?"

"Then not only do I forfeit my life, but you get the Mirror of Dirtaq and all the other treasures I carry."

To Ne'alder the offer was almost irresistible. Never in all of her very long life had she lost the riddle game. It was too easy. However, to risk her egg? Ne'alder knew, powerful as she was, she was still bound by the ancient magic and if she lost, she would have no choice but to honour her pledge.

"I agree on one condition. Show yourself, for I wish to see who is going to be my supper tonight."

"You accept my terms and my challenge by the power of the ancient magic?"

"Yes, yes, whatever your name is! What was it again, for I have forgotten it?"

Laughing, Aliyyah said, "You will not trick me that way, Ne'alder, for I have no intention of telling you my name. You think I do not know the power of knowing the true name of a person. All I will tell you is I am a daughter of a man."

"Hmph, we will see if you are so clever when we start the game. Three riddles each. The winner is the one who gets the most riddles correct. Agreed?"

"Agreed," replied Aliyyah, removing her cloak of invisibility. "You go first."

Looking rather disgusted at the sight of Aliyyah, the dragon answered, "You are just a girl, but still, you should be nice and tender for my supper. Are you ready? Here is your first riddle.

Kings and Queens upon me walk
Bishops to the peasants preach
Knights they ride to certain doom

Only one can win this war.
What am I?"

Smiling, Aliyyah replied, "Ne'alder, I thought that your riddles were supposed to be hard and that is so simple."

In an angry voice Ne'alder snorted, "Really, you insolent girl! What is the answer then?"

"It is a chess board, with a king, a queen, pawns, knights and bishops. Am I correct?"

"Hmph, a lucky guess, no more. What is your riddle?"

> *"Of many colours is the scarf I wear,*
> *Gossamer silk of the finest thread,*
> *No human hands can fashion me*
> *I am born of rain and sun.*
> *What am I?"*

Ne'alder seemed surprised and puzzled at this riddle. Thinking furiously she began to realise that Aliyyah could be more than a match for her. After a few tense moments however, the dragon realised the answer and scornfully replied, "You will have to do better than that. I think I am right in saying it is a rainbow."

Aliyyah nodded her head and asked the dragon for the next riddle.

> *"From the earth I came*
> *To the earth I go*
> *Up and down*
> *Around and around.*
> *What am I?"*

Aliyyah sat thinking for a while as Ne'alder looked at her hungrily. "What's the answer then?"

Unfortunately for Aliyyah, Mahin had trained her well. It was quite simple once she remembered her nature lessons.

"Oh Ne'alder, it seems you are not the great riddle master you thought you were for the answer is rain."

Furiously Ne'alder let out a snort of fire.

"Temper, temper," said Aliyyah. "It seems you are not as good as you thought. Now listen carefully;

> *Two hands have I, but no arms*
> *I can speak, but have no tongue*
> *Day and night I work non-stop*
> *My job is never done.*
> *What am I?"*

Ne'alder seemed puzzled, then worried, finally fearful. Racking her long memory she tried to recall if she had ever heard this riddle. She had never, however, listened to children's riddles and this was one of them.

"Do you know the answer?" asked Aliyyah.

"Don't rush me, young lady, I am thinking."

"Well I don't have all day, Ne'alder, hurry up."

Eventually a furious frustrated dragon had to admit defeat.

"Well what is?" she snapped. "Something clever I suppose."

"Not really," replied Aliyyah. "It is, in fact, a children's riddle. The answer is a clock. Now give me your final riddle. Remember, if I guess this riddle you lose and by the ancient magic you have to honour your promise."

Smiling evilly, Ne'alder searched her mind for the most difficult riddle she could find.

> *"Older than the mountains am I,*
> *Changing everything yet remaining unchanged*
> *No man can see me, but all men feel me pass*
> *No man can out run me, I outlast them all*
> *No force can contain me or defeat me,*
> *I am more precious than any mine filled with*
> *Gold and diamonds.*
> *What am I?"*

When Aliyyah heard this she burst out laughing. "Oh Ne'alder," she finally managed to say. "Your riddle would have been difficult, but I have already answered it once. It is time."

In a towering rage, Ne'alder demanded to know where she had heard this riddle before. As far as she knew there was only one other dragon who knew it.

"You are right, Ne'alder, it was from another dragon I heard this riddle, a great and wise dragon called Greenthor."

When Ne'alder heard this name she went into a terrible fury and would have killed Aliyyah, but she was bound by the ancient magic and could not harm her.

Calming down, she changed her voice to the sweetest and gentlest tone one could imagine. "Now that you have won the riddle game I suppose I have to free the castle from its evil, but surely you would not separate a mother from her egg?"

Firmly, Aliyyah replied, "To leave it with you would be an even greater crime. I will return it to the Dragon Council so it may hatch into a good dragon and not dark and evil as you have become. As for you, you must release your spell and go into the dark forever."

"Hmph, how are you going to return it? It is too heavy for you to carry and no man knows where the island of dragons is."

Without answering Ne'alder, Aliyyah recited in a loud voice, "Hadsha drogna lamis ni, hadsha drogna lamis ni."

Shocked, Ne'alder asked, "Who has been teaching you the tongue of the dragons?"

Before Aliyyah could reply there was a loud flapping of wings as the wall of the treasure room was smashed open. There in all his magnificence stood Greenthor himself.

"My Lady, you called me?" he said.

"No," screamed Ne'alder. "It cannot be."

Turning to face the shaking dragon, Greenthor replied, "Indeed it is, Ne'alder. I told you we would meet again and thanks to the princess here, we have. Princess, how can I help you?"

"Greenthor, Ne'alder has just lost the riddle game, so she now has to free the fortress of its evil spell and go into the darkness. Not only that, but she has to leave behind this egg. I was going to destroy it, but the heart stone reminded me that a dragon's egg, if

38

hatched in light, will become a good dragon. Therefore, I called you to take it back to the Council of Dragons and ask them to put it once more in the dragon's hatchery."

In a harsh voice Greenthor told Ne'alder, "By the ancient magic, release your spell and leave this land forever. I will stay here until you do and make sure you do not try to trick or harm this girl."

"Very well," the dragon replied sulkily. "But can I at least take my gold with me?"

"No, nothing, it does not belong to you anyway. As always, you stole it from other people. Now break your spell or face the wrath of the ancient magic!"

Ne'alder now had no choice but to live up to her end of the bargain. In an angry and discontented voice she muttered the words dial would release the fortress from her dark spells. "Rakda sesae takda sesai rakda sesau rakda ontsesai ree ree fufi."

No sooner had she finished than a loud crack like thunder was beard and the walls of this ancient fortress seemed to quiver and tremble, as if some giant was shaking the whole building. Dark and frightening lights flashed one after another until they were eventually it placed by a soft and warm white light, as the dark spell was finally lifted.

Without a backwards glance, Ne'alder spread her wings and began to rise up through the hole in the chamber walls.

"We will meet again, young one, and when we do, beware. I will destroy you one way or another. Our battle is not yet finished!"

Ne'alder spat at Aliyyah before disappearing into the dawning light.

"Beware, beware," Ne'alder's final words came drifting down from the skies.

Turning to Greenthor, Aliyyah smiled and thanked him for his help.

"No, Princess I am the one who should thank you, for once more I am in your debt."

Puzzled, Aliyyah asked him what he meant.

"Many years ago, before she rebelled against the Council of Dragons and left the path of light, Ne'alder was my partner. The egg you chose to spare was from our mating. Without knowing it you have saved my child. For this I can never repay you, no matter what service you ask of me I will always be in your debt."

"Oh Greenthor, I am happy I have helped you. Take your egg back quickly so that it may hatch in light and goodness."

Lifting the egg tenderly in his talons, Greenthor flapped his magnificent wings and rose up out of the chamber, carrying his un-hatched egg back to the island of the dragons and safety.

Cautiously making her way back up the cold stone stairs, Aliyyah emerged into the ballroom. No longer did the skeleton band play nor the un-dead feast, for both had been vanquished when the spell had been broken.

Instead, the room was full of confused and bleeding people walking around dazed, as if they had just woken up from a terrible nightmare. Full of pity and compassion for them, Aliyyah looked around to see if she could find some water. Searching the room she saw a small fountain that she had not noticed before. Sparkling clean water, where once there had been a dark evil-smelling fluid, now trickled from it into a stone pool at its base.

Taking a bowl from one of the tables she rinsed it before filling it with clean water. Then, taking the day bloom from inside her cloak, she put it into the water. As she watched, the water turned a light blue colour, letting off the most wondrous aroma. Approaching the nearest person she gently poured some of the water over the man's wounds. No sooner did the water touch them than miraculously they began to heal and within a few minutes there was no sign of his injuries. At the same time, the man seemed to snap out of his trance. Shocked at what he saw it took him a few minutes to realise what had happened. Turning to Aliyyah, tears filling his eyes, he thanked her again and again for breaking the evil spell and healing his injuries.

Then without a word, he began to pull the other victims who were nil wandering around in a daze, over to Aliyyah.

"Pease help them as you have helped me," he pleaded.

Smiling softly, Aliyyah replied, "Of course, I will not leave here until all of your companions are healed."

One after another she poured the water over the bleeding wounds of Ne'alder's black enchantment and each time the wounds, both physical and emotional, were healed. Time after time Aliyyah was ha red to refill the bowl with clean water into which she placed the day bloom flower. Finally, after many hours, the last person had been treated.

Aliyyah was overwhelmed by their gratitude as their eyes filled with tears and they thanked her for saving them from their nightmare.

"It is nothing," she replied humbly. "Now I must leave you and continue on my quest."

The inhabitants of the fort begged her to stay for a while, but Aliyyah sadly shook her head. "I cannot, for as long as the Dark One null rules these lands I must continue on my journey. Farewell and take care."

Chapter Four

The Sea of Sorrow

After healing the last inhabitant of the fortress, Aliyyah made her way to the massive oak doors that led to the outside. As she crossed the courtyard that was now free of the filth, rubbish and decaying food, she saw the bright banners of the original owners flying proudly once more from the stone battlements. At last the fortress was free and Aliyyah could continue her quest. As she approached the ancient doors she heard a man calling her. Turning she saw the lord of the fortress running towards her.

"Wait, please wait, I must talk to you," he cried as he rushed towards her.

Aliyyah stood still, wondering what the man wanted.

"Oh brave and noble one," the man stammered as he tried to catch his breath. "Thank you, thank you, for freeing us from the dragon's evil spell. May I ask, are you a seeker?"

Glancing at her heart stone, which remained unchanged, she cautiously replied. "Yes, I am."

With a look of relief on his face the man continued, "I thought you must be. Do you know why the dragon chose this fortress rather than any other?" Shaking her head Aliyyah replied that she did not know. "Well, the story goes like this, many years ago when the Dark One murdered our true king, one of the elders came here with one of the four treasures and gave it to me to hide until a seeker came to reclaim it. He told me that the seeker would know who he was and J was only to give it to the one who could tell me his name. Many people came claiming to be seekers, but not one of them was able to give me the elder's name. Later, the dragon Ne'alder came, also demanding we give up our treasure. When we refused, she searched the whole fortress, but was unable to find it. In her anger she placed a dark spell upon as all and for many years we have been living a terrible nightmare. Now you have freed us and if you know the elder's name I will return the treasure to its owner."

Smiling, Aliyyah replied, "That is easy for it can be no other than my own teacher, Mahin."

"Thank God," exclaimed the man. "At last I can discharge my duty." Reaching into his pocket he removed a bunch of golden keys. "These are the Keys of Hanaj, you will need them to recover the Book of Fazma."

Taking the keys, she thanked the man then asked, "Where did you hide these keys? Surely Ne'alder must have searched all of you?"

Chuckling, the man replied, "When you want to hide something the best way is to put it in plain view."

"What do you mean by that?" said Aliyyah.

"The fortress's keys were lost a long time ago and the doors were never locked because of that. When we got the keys, we hung them on a hook next to the door and anyone who saw them assumed they were the keys for the doors. No one, not even Ne'alder realised that they were the treasure we were hiding."

"You are very wise," said Aliyyah. "Thank you, but now I must continue on my quest, wherever it leads me."

"I think I can help you a little there, Mahin told me that to find the Book of Fazma you must speak to the wise green turtle."

"How do I find him?" asked Aliyyah.

"I do not know," replied the man. "The only ones who know are the Screeching Owls who live on an island in the Sea of Sorrow. You must travel there to find the answer to your question."

Then, handing her a flask of fresh water and a small bag of provisions, he bade her farewell.

Leaving the Fortress of Illusions, Aliyyah was happy to see the unicorn still waiting for her. Smiling, she greeted Najputih. "I am glad to see you are still waiting, my friend."

"Of course," came the reply in her head. "I am still in your debt and by our laws I must do as much as I can to help you. Not only that, but I too wished to see the power of the Dark One destroyed forever. So where do we go now?"

Aliyyah slowly turned and pointed to the dark, sinister sea that lapped against the blackened rocks. The unicorn shuddered as it looked at the grim sea.

"Aliyyah, that is the Sea of Sorrow. Whosoever sets sail on that sea, it will draw all the happiness and joy from them leaving only increasing despair, sorrow and anguish in their hearts. If you stay too long on this sea you can die of despair."

Aliyyah nodded her head, still looking at the jagged waves of the dark sea.

In the distance she could just see a series of small islands illuminated by the constant flashes of lighting that seemed to rent the air.

"I know," commented Aliyyah. "But the Screeching Owls that live on those islands are the only ones who know where to find the wise green turtle. He is the only one that knows the hidden whereabouts of the Book of Fazma."

"I understand," thought the unicorn. "But how are we going to cross the sea? We have no boat."

Smiling to herself, Aliyyah told the unicorn, "I hope that you are not afraid of dragons." Then blowing the whistle Wild Wind had given her, she called, "Wild Wind, my friend, come, we need your help." Aliyyah had not even finished talking when the air was filled with the sound of flapping wings. As they looked up they could see a small black spot fast approaching them. As the spot got nearer they could see clearly that it was none other than Wild Wind, who true to his name seemed to be moving faster than the wind. Slowly he descended in front of Aliyyah and the unicorn, folding his enormous green wings to his side as his feet touched the ground.

'My Princess," he began. "I have come as I promised I would. How can I aid you?"

"Wild Wind, I am very happy to see you. We need to go the islands of the Screeching Owls, but we have no boat, can you help us?"

Thoughtfully the dragon looked at Aliyyah before replying, "I can of course, but this is a sea of despair. How are you going to protect yourself from its evil?"

Aliyyah shook her head, "To be honest, I do not know, Wild Wind. I can only pray that both myself and Najputih will be strong enough to withstand its effects. We have no choice if we want to know how to find the wise turtle."

Wild Wind said nothing at first, then he told Aliyyah, "Wait here and do not move, I will not be long."

Without any warning he unfolded his great wings and swiftly soared up into the stormy skies. Puzzled, Aliyyah and the unicorn waited, wondering where Wild Wind had disappeared to and why he had flown away so quickly.

However, after only a few minutes they saw the dragon once again, approaching faster than before. As he landed they saw that he carried in his talons some branches, which were laden with strange- looking berries. Each berry was an oblong shape and glowed with a bright golden light.

"These are berries of joy and contentment. Whosoever eats them will feel that their hearts are filled with peace and contentment. Eat one of them now and as soon as you feel your heart becoming heavy or upset you must quickly eat another one."

Thanking Wild Wind, both Aliyyah and the unicorn ate one of the berries. They tasted sweet, but unlike anything Aliyyah had ever tasted before. As she swallowed the berry she felt a warmth seep through her body, while a happiness that she had not felt since her childhood filled her heart.

"Where did you get these berries from Wild Wind?" asked Aliyyah.

"My Princess, these berries are only found on the Isles of Contentment in the Sea of Light. On these isles there are no wars, illness, envy, jealously or any bad things. The people are always joyous and contented. They live simple lives praising their Creator and helping one another. These berries are the fruit of their constant praise and are their main food as they do not eat any form of flesh. Now, Princess, if you are ready, climb on my back and I will carry you to the islands."

"Thank you Wild Wind, but what about my companion Najputih?"

"Do not worry, Princess, I will carry Najputih gently in my talons. He need have no fear as I will not harm him. Dragons do not like to eat unicorns."

So saying, Wild Wind lowered his neck to make it easier for Aliyyah to scramble up onto his back. Carefully, so as not to hurt the dragon, Aliyyah climbed onto his back and tried to sit as comfortably and as safely as she could. This was not easy as his scales were hard and slippery and Aliyyah prayed quietly that she would not slip down and fall off.

Wild Wind rose up, as a very nervous and frightened unicorn stood waiting below. As gently as a mother holding a new-born baby, Wild Wind clasped the beautiful unicorn in his sharp cruel-looking talons and carried him up into the darkening skies.

Within a few minutes they were flying over the dark and evil Sea of Sorrow. At first Aliyyah felt elated and exhilarated as they flew high over the black waves, but before long she began to feel an icy cold feeling creeping over her. Remembering the dragon's words she quickly ate another one of the strange berries. As she swallowed the berry she once again felt warmth and happiness flow through her veins. Aliyyah wondered how the unicorn was faring below her. She knew that he must be feeling very scared dangling like that in Wild Wind's talons. She hoped that he was all right!

Very soon they were approaching the largest of the ten islands of the Screeching Owls. As they neared the island, Aliyyah could hear the terrible noise made by the owls. The sharpness of their calls seemed to fill the air, while piercing Aliyyah's ears at the same time.

Gently, Wild Wind released the shaking unicorn before landing gracefully on the black soil. Quickly climbing down, Aliyyah ran to where the unicorn stood shaking with fear and the effects of the Sea of Sorrow. Stroking the white mane of Najputih she forced some of the berries into his mouth and gently encouraged him to eat them.

As the unicorn ate the berries he gradually stopped shaking, as warmth and happiness once more flowed through his veins, vanquishing the terror and darkness that had overcome him.

"Thank you, Aliyyah, thank you," thought the unicorn. "Never, not even in the Castle of Mirrors, have I felt such terror or darkness."

As Aliyyah smiled at Najputih she heard the voice of Wild Wind behind her. Turning, she saw the young dragon preparing to fly away.

"This is where I must leave you for now, my Princess. I cannot stay here for long as it will drain even my magic. However, as soon as you need me again, call and I will come to you faster than the wind."

With these words the dragon rose up into the air and was soon lost to sight.

Looking around her, all Aliyyah could see was black soil, stunted trees and giant boulders. Nowhere was there any colour, no green grass, no bright flowers, no light of any kind. It was as if the whole island had been drained of all goodness and burnt black by the touch of evil.

As her eyes adjusted to the gloomy light, Aliyyah noticed that towards the centre of the island was a thick clump of trees. As she looked closer she could see the red-yellow eyes of the screeching owls. Cautiously, Aliyyah and the unicorn approached the owls, trying not to scare them. As they got closer the owls began to screech even louder, deafening both Aliyyah and Najputih.

Eventually, when they were only a few feet away from the trees, the oldest and the largest of the owls flew out of the trees and landed at their feet. This owl was bigger than any owl Aliyyah had ever seen in her whole life. It was nearly three feet in height with massive round eyes and plumage of an astonishing pure white making a stark contrast with its grey surroundings.

After blinking its mournful eyes a few times the owl started to address Aliyyah and as it did so all the other owls fell silent.

"Too woo, who are you and what are you doing in this forlorn place?"

"I am Aliyyah, a seeker, and I have come to ask you where I can find the wise turtle."

"Why do you want to find the green turtle?" asked the owl.

Before answering Aliyyah looked at both her ring and her amulet to see if they had changed colour at all. She wanted to be certain that there was no danger in answering the owl's question. When she saw that both the ring and the amulet remained unchanged, she replied, "I am seeking the Book of Fazma and only the wise turtle knows where it is hidden."

"And why," continued the owl, "do you need the Book of Fazma?"

"As I said, I am a seeker and I must recover all the lost treasures of the nine islands of Lamis before the Dark One can be defeated and his evil spells and darkness removed from this land."

The owl remained silent for a while before replying, "We know where you can find the wise turtle, however, before we tell you, there is a task you must perform first."

Tentatively Aliyyah asked, "What is it you want me to do?"

Solemnly the owl began, "My name is Toowooni and I am the king of all the owls of these islands. A long time ago we were called the Singing Owls not the Screeching Owls. Our songs were so beautiful that they filled the hearts of all who heard us with peace and happiness. Our islands were green and fertile, filled with verdant grass dotted abundantly with bright, fragrant flowers. The trees bore succulent fruits and nuts while the sea that lapped our shores was a crystal blue. Sea creatures abounded in the azure waters and we all lived together in peace and harmony. Then one day the Dark One came to our shores demanding to know where the wise turtle lived. When we refused to tell him he stole the Luminous Pearl that guarded these islands and threw it into the Forbidden Volcano. He then placed an evil spell upon our islands leaving them dark and dissolute. Our beautiful voices were changed so that the only sounds we can now make is a horrible screech. The sea creatures all fled as the seas darkened and turned evil with the Dark One's magic. We now need your help to destroy the black magic so that our islands may be restored to their former beauty and our voices returned to the way they were before the Dark One came."

Realising she was honour bound to help them, Aliyyah asked, "How can I break the spell?"

Toowooni replied, "You must recover the Luminous Pearl from the Forbidden Volcano and return it to its shell in the Cove of Joy." "How can I recover the pearl?" questioned Aliyyah.

"Only a person pure of spirit and protected by the magic of the dragons can enter the volcano. You must use your firestone to show you the way in the darkness. To retrieve the pearl you must use both your ring and your amulet. You may also be able to release the lost souls," added the owl.

"Who are these lost souls?" asked Aliyyah.

"They are the souls of drowned sailors who are unable to rest or pass on to the next world. They roam the Forbidden Volcano making it a place of terror and horror for us."

"How can I set them free?" asked Aliyyah.

"To set them free you must find out the cause of their despair. If you succeed in restoring the pearl to its proper home, thus breaking the Dark One's spell, we will not only tell you where the wise turtle lives, we will take you there. Do you agree?"

With a half smile Aliyyah answered, "I don't really have much choice do I? If I do not help you I will fail in the quest and the Dark One will rule these islands forever."

"Yes," agreed Toowooni. "You have no choice. The volcano is on the last island and you will need a guide to lead you there." Toowooni then let out an ear-splitting screech and a smaller, much younger owl flew down and landed next to Toowooni. "This owl is called Tootooni and he will guide you to the Forbidden Volcano. There are hidden pathways that lead to the farthest island, which are known only to us owls. Now before you go you must pluck one of my feathers. This will show all the other owls that you are under my protection and are acting on my behalf. Otherwise, even though you are guided by Tootooni, they will attack you trying to protect our secrets."

As gently as she could Aliyyah plucked one of the great owl's brilliant white feathers and tucked it into the belt of her travelling cloak for all to see.

"Go now and be careful, may you succeed and return with the pearl." Tootooni flapped his wings and started flying towards the end of the island.

"Keep up, keep up, we must hurry before night falls, keep up, keep up!"

As they reached the end of the main island Aliyyah wondered how they were going to cross over. As far as she could see there was no way across.

Tootooni, landing beside her, began an incantation in the strange language of the owls, "Tootoo ni whoo tootoo ni woo woon ni woonno tootoowhoo whhoo nini."

As he recited, to Aliyyah's astonishment a series of stepping stones rose up out of the sea, leading across to the other islands.

"Quickly, the stones will only stay above the water for a short while. You must cross now while you still can."

Needing no second warning, Aliyyah and the unicorn began jumping from one stone to another. Neither one of them wished to fall into the dark evil waters of the Sea of Sorrow. Just as they reached the second island the rocks slowly began slipping back into the sea to be covered once more by the dark, sinister waters.

"The Dark One did not know about these paths, so when he cast his spell they were unaffected. You are the only person besides the owls who know of their existence. We ask therefore that you do not tell anyone about them."

"Of course, your secrets are safe with us, aren't they? said Aliyyah, looking towards Najputih who nodded his snowy white head in agreement.

"Thank you, now come quickly we have another eight islands to cross before we reach the Forbidden Volcano."

On and on they went until finally they came to the last island before the forbidden island.

"I can go no further," exclaimed Tootooni. "I will call the rocks for you to cross to the other side. I will wait for you here. If you do not return in three days I will return to my home. Please do not fail us Aliyyah."

So saying, Tootooni called the rocks once more and Aliyyah and the unicorn quickly crossed over to the island of the Forbidden Volcano. As soon as they reached the other side they became aware of an eerie silence, an unnatural silence that seemed to seep inside them like some unseen frozen hand, numbing them to the bones.

No sooner did they feel the icy silence then they quickly ate one of the berries Wild Wind had given them, before walking towards the looming volcano. As they neared the volcano it seemed that all the light was being swallowed up, leaving just a dim, half-light, a twilight zone of unknown dangers.

"Well," thought Aliyyah. "How are we going to climb that? The sides are sheer like polished marble and the pearl is inside."

"Remember what Toowooni said," thought the unicorn. "Use the firestone, maybe there is another way into the volcano."

Nodding her head in agreement, Aliyyah took the firestone out of the folds of her cloak. As she lifted it out it glowed with a bright red light that chased the darkness into the shadows. As they searched around the base of the volcano they found what they were looking for hidden behind a clump of bushes. It was a small cave into which someone had cut a series of uneven steps leading upwards towards the stomach of the volcano.

"It seems to lead inside the volcano, but the steps are very steep. Do you want to come with me or wait here?" thought Aliyyah.

The unicorn shuddered before replying, "I have no wish to remain here on my own, I will follow you even though even though it terrifies me to enter."

"Then keep close to me and be careful as the steps are very slippery."

Aliyyah and the unicorn began to climb the steps that led up into the belly of the Forbidden Volcano. As they climbed they saw strange shapes that seemed to flit before their eyes then just as quickly disappear. Before long, as they climbed higher, a soft low moaning sound was heard, it was not quite human but at the same time it was not animal. Looking at the unicorn, Aliyyah felt her skin shiver even though it was getting very hot in the long dark tunnel. Picking another two berries from the branch she gave one to the unicorn before eating the other one herself.

"Do not be afraid," she thought. "I think that it is only the lost souls that are trapped here. If we can, we must find a way to release them from their torment, we must."

Slowly and carefully they continued to follow the uneven slippery steps up. Now the moaning sounds were becoming louder, more human and heart rending. At the same time in the red-black light they began to see figures that seemed to melt out of the walls and stare at them hungrily, as if it was some kind of sin to be alive.

Najputih began to shake as he sent a mental plea to Aliyyah "What do they want? They seem so..."

"Lost," thought Aliyyah. "Do not fear them, the dead cannot harm the living, but we may be able to help them."

Quickly she made Najputih eat another two of their precious berries. By now they were surrounded by ghostly figures. As they neither moved nor tried to harm them, Aliyyah and the unicorn carried on only to be trailed by more and more of these lost souls.

Finally the stairs led into the caldera of the volcano and there, in the centre, was the pearl. It was suspended by fragile chains that held it across a pit of spitting lava. The red-black heat could be felt from where they stood, even though it would take at least half an hour to walk there. As Aliyyah stared she could see no way of releasing the pearl without sending it straight to its destruction in the hellish pit of fire beneath it.

As she stood in thought, the ghostly figures started to crowd in on them getting nearer and nearer while the moaning became almost unbearable. Fear began to enter Aliyyah's heart until she remembered Toowooni's words, 'find the cause of their sorrows'.

In a firm voice Aliyyah addressed the ghostly figures. "What do you want of us? We seek only to return the pearl to its proper place and break the Dark One's spell over the islands. Maybe we can free you as well."

The ghostly figures seemed to blur and merge only to separate once more then merge again. Each time the ghosts merged into one, the figure seemed to become more solid. Finally the figure solidified and the figure of a ship's captain appeared before them. The face was weathered, not unhandsome, but full of such despair and sadness the Aliyyah felt a great wave of compassion fill her heart for these souls trapped between this world and the next.

"Who are you?" asked Aliyyah. "What do you want from me?"

In an eerie, echoing voice, the spectre replied, "We are the men who came from the Isles of Radiance - a beautiful land full of peace and joy. We had one sacred treasure, which we guarded all the time from evil forces. This treasure was the Book of Peace, which contains all the magical spells to destroy the forces of evil and keep goodness and contentment safe in this world. However, when our queen heard that the Dark One was coming to our lands determined to seize the book and destroy it, the queen told us to take the book to another land and hand it over to the Sand Wizard, the only person she knew of that could stand up to the powers of the Dark One. In haste we set sail on our ship the Isle of Light, but before we could escape the Dark One sent a mighty tempest upon us. For three days and nights we were tossed on the violent seas until we knew that we were doomed. Our only thought now was to save the book from falling into the Dark One's hands. Using the strongest spells we knew we encased the book in a bubble of light, which can only be broken by one who has the magic of the dragons in their hands or the one who holds the Sword of Ila. When the Dark One boarded our ship he tried every spell he could think of to break the bubble, but without success. Every time he tried to touch the book he was burnt terribly. Finally, in his anger he sent the ship with us and the book to the bottom of the sea, drowning every single soul aboard. He then spread a lie that we had fled with the book and abandoned our duty. We were under a debt of honour to fulfil our task and until that debt is paid and our names are cleared, we are trapped here forever."

Shaking her head Aliyyah asked, "Why did you not use the book to defeat the Dark One?"

"Not everyone can open the book and use it. Even our queen was unable to use its great powers. It answers only to three people, the true ruler of Lamis, the one who possesses the amulet of Aliyyah the Pure or the one who holds the Sword of Ila."

Smiling, Aliyyah replied, "I do not yet hold the Sword of Ila, but I am Aliyyah, the daughter of King Dor, the true king of the sacred islands of Lamis and wearer of the amulet of Aliyyah the Pure, the ancient protector of the islands. Tell me where the book lies and where to send it and I will fulfil your task for you, as soon as I have returned the luminous pearl to the Cove of Joy."

The figure once again seemed to fade and then thicken before it replied, "If what you say is true, you must also possess the dragon's ring. Show us both of them."

Without any hesitation Aliyyah showed the figure the heart-shaped ring on her finger and the golden amulet around her neck, with their beautiful ever-changing coloured stones.

"We never thought that you would come and our souls were filled with despair. Now we have hope once more. Our ship lies close to the home of the owls under the waters of the seventh island. To retrieve the Book of Peace you must recite these words three times, 'Out of darkness there is light, out of light there is peace, out of peace there is joy, lacarda lacarda ni lacardi'. After you have recited these words the bubble will take the book to the Mountain of Light and restore it to its place on the Pedestal of Knowledge, where once more it will protect our lands."

"Will not the Dark One try to return and destroy the book once more?" questioned Aliyyah.

"He will be unable to. We could not recite the spell, for the book will not listen to us, but it will listen to you and the dragons' gifts to you. Once the book has been opened not even the Dark One can stop its power."

"Very well, I will find your ship and release the Book of Peace," replied Aliyyah.

"Thank you, Princess," they replied, separating into many different forms once more. "If we can help you in return, we will."

Aliyyah looked at the different forms now drifting around her and said, "Yes, I think you can. How can I retrieve the pearl without it falling into the molten lava?"

"My Princess, you cannot retrieve the pearl from above the lava pit for it is not there," replied the spectre. "It is only an illusion and if you try you will be either destroyed or trapped."

"Then where is the pearl?" asked Aliyyah. "How can I find it?"

'It is hidden near the bottom of the stairs that lead into the volcano. Use your ring and amulet to find it. They will both show you by their colours where it is, but beware, only a pure heart can remove it."

Thanking the lost souls, Aliyyah and Najputih began the slow and slippery descent back down the steps. As they neared the bottom Aliyyah asked Najputih to hold the firestone in his mouth so that she could use both her ring and amulet to find the pearl's hiding place. As she turned round slowly she looked at both at the ring and amulet, hoping that they would they would show the hiding place of the pearl.

As she looked carefully she suddenly saw a glimmer of light glowing just below her. As she cautiously approached the glimmer she realised it was coming from behind a jutting-out ledge that she, in the darkness, had not seen before. Calling Najputih, she took the firestone from him and held it high up so that she could see what was behind the ledge.

Letting out an exclamation of joy, Aliyyah told Najputih, "It's here, the pearl is here, it is so beautiful. I don't know how we missed it on the way up."

Amused, Najputih replied, "Maybe because we were not looking properly." Then more seriously he thought, "But be careful how you take it. We do not know what will happen once it is removed."

"That is true," replied Aliyyah. "I think as it is difficult for you to descend these steps you had better go down first and wait near the edge of the island. If I have to flee it would be better if you are not in the way. Let me know when you have reached the shore."

Najputih pawed the ground showing his dislike of this suggestion, but nevertheless he reluctantly replied, "I don't like leaving you here alone even for a few minutes, but you are right, the steps are difficult for me. I will do as you say, but if you are not out within a short time I will come back to search for you."

Smiling, Aliyyah thought, "Thank you, my friend, now go. I wish to leave this accursed place as quickly as I can."

Nodding his beautiful white head, Najputih made his way down the steps as quickly and as gracefully as he could. As the seconds passed, Aliyyah strained her mind listening for Najputih's mental message to tell her that he was outside by the sea. After what seemed to be an eternity Aliyyah heard his voice inside her head, "Take the pearl and be careful, I am waiting for you."

Grasping the pearl as firmly as she could, she began to pull it out of its hiding place. Although the pearl was slippery, Aliyyah was surprised to find it was quite warm to her touch, not cold as she expected. As the pearl began to move, so did the ground beneath Aliyyah's feet, at first very softly, but getting stronger as Aliyyah lifted the pearl. No sooner had she pulled it out from behind the ledge than there was an almighty cracking sound, as if the volcano itself was splitting into two. An unearthly scream filled the dark air, chilling her to her bones even as the temperature began to rise rapidly. Clutching the pearl closely to her chest Aliyyah bolted, tumbling over her own feet and nearly falling down the rest of the steps, scratching her face and bruising her arms and legs as she fled. All around her the rocks were crashing down, threatening to bury her alive beneath them. With a final spurt Aliyyah shot out of the cave as the volcano rapidly plummeted to pieces. Glancing behind her she saw the lava slowly licking its way towards her, gathering speed as it started to flow downhill towards the sea.

Panting for breath in the burning air, Aliyyah blew her whistle calling Wild Wind to help her and Najputih. As she continued to run for her life towards the shore and Najputih, she felt a strong wind behind her as the dragon swept down and snatched her in one of his strong talons. Without stopping, Wild Wind flew to where the shaking unicorn was and snatched him up in the other talon.

"Hold tight, Princess," shouted the dragon. "Do not let go." Flapping his wings as fast as he could, the dragon flew towards the first island they had landed on, where all the owls were huddled together in great fear.

Behind them they heard the lava as it hit the water, and as Aliyyah strained to see behind her, she was shocked to see a mighty wall of water begin to rise up as if an angry hand was trying to smash a small insect.

"Fly faster, Wild Wind, faster."

Wild Wind needed no encouragement to fly faster as he had already seen what was coming. "We must reach the owls, they know where the cove is," he replied.

It took less than a minute before they saw the owls trembling in fear, not knowing what to do or where to hide. Swooping down, Wild Wind dropped both Aliyyah and the unicorn so that they landed on the ground unhurt, but in a rather undignified way. Wild Wind landed heavily next to them and waited as Aliyyah called out to Tootooni.

"Tootooni, where is the cove? Where do I put the pearl? Quickly, before all the islands are destroyed!"

Flying towards them, Tootooni told them to follow him. Lifting

Aliyyah onto his back this time, Wild Wind followed the owl, who led them to the far end of the island. Before long they saw a crescent-shaped cove filled with the evil black water. At the far end of the cove there was a cave with a ledge jutting out. It was on this ledge that the shell the pearl belonged to sat. There was no way to reach the ledge by land, the only way was through the foul dark waters.

As the neared the waters Tootooni cried out, "The waters are not deep, but they will sap the energy and maybe the life force of anyone who enters them. Be careful, be quick!"

Wild Wind flew as near to the ledge as he dared. "Aliyyah, I cannot get any closer and I dare not touch the water. You must jump and try to reach the shelf before the waters harm you."

Nodding her head, Aliyyah quickly ate the rest of the berries before jumping off Wild Wind's back, holding the pearl firmly to her chest. As she hit the waters she felt as if a black hand had reached out and grabbed her heart and was now trying to squeeze her soul out of her body. Grasping for breath she felt that her lungs were on fire and her body felt like lead as she struggled towards her goal. Every step was torture to her and even though the water only reached up to her knees it was like trying to force her way through an avalanche of snow.

With her energy totally drained she saw the ledge only a few feet in front of her. With a supreme effort she managed to half fall onto the ledge a few inches from the empty shell. As her sight began to fade she dropped the pearl in its shell before falling back into the water, with only her head and shoulders resting on part of the ledge. Aliyyah, just before slipping into unconsciousness, saw a bright light fill her vision.

As Aliyyah lay motionless the pearl began to shine with a light so bright and pure that no evil was able to withstand it. The black waters seemed to shudder before they started to slowly turn back to their original crystal blue colour. At the same time the tidal wave that was threatening to destroy the islands froze in mid-air before crashing down to the sea, without causing any destruction to the islands. As the waters changed colours, the islands began to change as well. The trees, as if by magic, became coated with fresh green leaves, while buds, flowers and fruits appeared all at the same time. Meanwhile, the barren ground sprouted verdant grass that was dotted by beautiful flowers and bushes and crisscrossed by sparkling streams and springs.

As the islands returned to their former beauty and peace, so the owls' beautiful voices were returned to them, and once more they could sing like the famed nightingale.

Once the waters had changed, the fish and the other sea creatures swam back to their ancient homes. As they did so they saw the unconscious young girl laying half in and half out of the water. One of the sea creatures quickly swam to the shore where Wild Wind and the owls were waiting for Aliyyah to return.

In a language known to all dragons he told the young dragon that a young girl was lying unconscious in the cove, half in the water and half out with one hand stretched out towards the pearl.

Without a word, Wild Wind flew off towards the cove and reached it within a few minutes. Swooping down, he lifted the inert Aliyyah as gently as he could and carried her to where the anxious owls were waiting restlessly. Laying the young girl as gently as he could on a grassy, knoll Wild Wind then landed next to her and tried to revive her as best as he could. However, no matter what Wild Wind, Najputih and the owls tried, they could not revive Aliyyah who seemed to be hanging at the edge of death's door.

Lamenting, the owls cried out, "What to do, what to do. Who can save her, who can help?"

Wild Wind, in desperation, let out a mighty roar before reciting in the ancient language of the dragons, "Hadsha hadsha ne leda lageda hadsha."

Within a few minutes, a strong rush of wind was felt as the sound of flapping wings filled the air. Before the round blinking eyes of the owls, Greenthor, the most magnificent of all the dragons, slowly and majestically landed next to Aliyyah and Wild Wind.

In their own tongue Wild Wind explained to Greenthor all that had happened before asking how they could help her.

Shaking his noble head, Greenthor replied in a voice that all could understand, "Aliyyah has been struck with the black sleeping illness. Even as we speak her soul is slowly slipping away. The only thing that can save her is the seed of the Black Nummic, which can cure all illnesses except for death itself. Wild Wind you must fly with all your speed to the island of the ancient healers and beg them for some of their precious seeds. Tell them that Greenthor, who they are beholden to, asks this favour, but do not tell them why as that knowledge will place them in great danger. Go quickly, for Aliyyah only has until sunset before this evil sickness claims her life. Once the sun has set, no medicine in the world can save her. Fly now as fast as you can to save the life of Aliyyah, fly."

Without any further urging, Wild Wind lifted his wings and was soon lost to sight. Sitting next to Aliyyah, Greenthor kept watch as the owls and Najputih did all they could to make sure Aliyyah was as comfortable as possible. The dragon had already blown her clothes dry with his warm breath and had removed all the pieces of black weeds that had attached themselves to her clothing. All they could do now was wait and pray that Wild Wind would return in time.

Chapter 5

Shadow of Death

In the azure skies, the young dragon was flying the fastest he had ever flown. Even though he had only known Aliyyah for a short time, he already had a deep love and respect for the courageous young girl and he was willing to do anything he could to save her life. Hour after hour he flew until finally he reached the hidden island of the healers.

Flying low over the island that was dotted with numerous types of herbs, plants and medical trees and flowers, Wild Wind soon found the healers' simple village. Small houses with wooden walls beautifully carved were crowned with golden roofs of carefully thatched rushes. Surrounding each house were racks of drying herbs, roots and seeds, while in the centre of the village was a large green with an ancient well in the middle. This well provided crystal clear water for the healers, which was essential not just for them, but for their work in preparing medicines needed to cure the sick and wounded. Landing as carefully as he could, Wild Wind called out loudly for the oldest healer to come quickly.

Although they were used to visitors, a dragon was a rather unusual, guest so not just the oldest healer left his house, but nearly all the other healers as well. Stepping forward, an old man with a shock of long white hair asked the young dragon what his errand was.

Quickly Wild Wind delivered Greenthor's message and waited for the ancient healer to speak. Nodding his head, the healer replied, "Young dragon, for I do not think that you are very old, I am Kathir. I will not ask your name for I am well versed in dragon lore and I have no wish to offend you. Indeed, we are beholden many times over for Greenthor's help and protection, but still I must ask you for what reason does Greenthor need these most precious seeds?"

"Greenthor told me not to reveal to you the reason why he needs the seeds as it may put you in great danger if you know, but he adjures you by your debts to him to give me the seeds. All I can add is that if you wish the rule of the Dark One to end, you will help without asking any questions."

The ancient healer remained silent for a few minutes before replying, "I will give you the seeds, but I asked you why as we have very few seeds left and to gather more we would have to leave our hidden island and travel to the dry lands of the golden sands far away. A journey that, at my age, I fear I would not survive."

"Do not worry about that," answered Wild Wind. "For as soon as my errand is complete I can take you or one of your healers on my back and fly faster than the wind to collect as many seeds as you require."

Smiling, Kalhir replied, "Thank you, young dragon. A dragon's word can never be broken so I will happily give you all the seeds we have left, but be careful you do not lose them."

So saying, Kathir entered his dwelling and after a few minutes returned with a small bag containing the precious seeds.

"Soak them in warm water for a few minutes then give the water and the seeds to whoever needs them. Only a few seeds are necessary, however, if the victim is suffering from the black sleeping sickness as we suspect from what you have not said, you must administer all the seeds and water. You must also make sure that you give them before the sun sets as their power is diminished in the dark of the night."

Nodding his understanding, Wild Wind asked Kathir to place the seeds in the pouch he had tied under his right wing, where they would be protected if anything unexpected occurred. As soon as Wild Wind had lifted his wing, Kathir carefully placed the seeds into the pouch and closed it tightly, making sure that there was no way the seeds could fall out or be lost in any way.

"Fly fast, young dragon, faster than the wind, and all our payers and blessings go with you."

Without a word, Wild Wind took to the air and flew faster than he had ever flown in his life. On and on he went, desperate to reach the islands of the owls before the sun started to set. The Dark

One however, had other ideas and halfway back the skies suddenly darkened as if some malevolent evil had just appeared.

Not slowing for even a second, Wild Wind felt rather than saw his pursuer. Within a few minutes this evil force had overtaken him and Wild Wind saw what, to his dismay, was hunting him. A dragon has few natural enemies, but a chill seemed to seep into his scales as he saw it was no other than a Nogard that was about to swoop down upon him. This evil creature resembled a dragon in appearance, but it was not made of flesh and blood, rather it was made of shadows and mist from the darkest pits of damnation themselves.

With an unearthly scream that seemed to split the clouds in two, it dived, snatching wildly at the young dragon, attempting to injure him with its poisonous talons, sharp and cruel. Quickly turning aside Wild Wind managed to avoid injury. Again and again the Nogard attacked until Wild Wind was forced back, turning this way and that to protect himself. Minutes passed as the battle continued until Wild Wind realised that this creature was not out to kill him, but merely trying to delay him until it was too late to save Aliyyah. Twisting and turning Wild Wind used all his skills to out manoeuvre this evil creature, but as he began to tire the Nogard managed again and again to rip his talons into Wild Wind's side, not enough to kill him, but enough to weaken him if he did not escape soon.

The Dark One must have guessed what has happened, he thought to himself. I need help to escape or Aliyyah is doomed. Desperately, Wild Wind using the ancient language of the dragons, once more cried out, "Hadsha lacade hasdha laden."

Trying again to pass the Nogard, Wild Wind could only hope his fellow dragons had heard his cry. Wild Wind had no need to worry, for no sooner had his cry gone out than all eight dragons flew to his rescue as fast as they could. Within a short while they were in sight of the young dragon as he was attacked again and again.

"Brothers," declared Greenthor. "You cannot kill this creature for it is not of this world, but you can distract it and drive it off. Remember the ancient songs, the stories of lights triumphant over the dark. Recite them in the ancient tongue, the Nogard cannot bear this. Drive it away from Wild Wind, drive it back to the pits where it came from. I will fly with Wild Wind to save Aliyyah."

In unison the eight dragons swooped down, voices raised in the ancient tongue. As they dived and baited the Nogard the creature writhed and screamed in fear, agony, fury and frustration.

In the ensuing chaos, Wild Wind and Greenthor slipped through and headed straight for the island where Aliyyah lay.

The long afternoon slowly passed as seconds slipped into minutes and minutes into hours. Despite the newly restored beauty of the islands and sea, Najputih and the owls were saddened and worried about the stricken girl who seemed to be slipping away from them. Helpless, Najputih kept looking up to the skies, hoping to see a small black dot that would herald the return of Wild Wind.

It had been several hours since Greenthor had left and now they all feared the worst. What disaster could have possibly called away the great dragon? Had the Dark One captured, or even worse, killed the young dragon?

The leader of the owls had sent many of the younger and faster owls out to see if there was any sign of the dragons and the precious seeds that could save Aliyyah's life, but all had returned without sighting anything at all.

"Tuoo woo too woo, this is unhappy news, what could be keeping the dragons," lamented Toowooni.

Najputih did not even try to communicate with the owls. He knew that even if he still had his unicorn magic he would be unable to heal the black sickness that was threatening to snatch Aliyyah's life. Gently he lay down beside the young girl, trying to give as much comfort and strength to the unconscious Aliyyah as he could.

As the rosy glow of the late afternoon sun appeared, a golden light began to surround Aliyyah as a crisscross mesh of beams made a kind of net around her body.

Despair began to fill Najputih's heart for he knew that this was a sign that Aliyyah's soul was preparing to leave. Silent tears dripped down his snowy cheeks and he felt that his heart would break into a thousand pieces. If Wild Wind did not arrive soon, it would be too late.

As the sun began to sink, a loud flapping of wings was heard and the two dragons appeared on the horizon. Both dragons were wounded and bloody as if they had been in a great battle. Even before landing, Greenthor cried out to the owls, "Quickly, bring water, for we have very little time."

A young owl by the name of Norworol quickly flew down from one of the trees, carefully carrying a large shell filled with clear, clean spring water. Landing next to Aliyyah he laid the shell down on the ground between two rocks so that the water would not spill.

As the dragons landed, Norworol told them, "Mighty dragons, I have waited many hours for your return. I knew that you would need water for the seeds so I flew to the fourth island where there is a spring of water clear and pure that is known for its healing properties."

"Thank you, young yet wise owl," replied Greenthor as he removed the pouch containing the seeds from Wild Wind. Carefully tearing a hole in the bag, Greenthor tipped all the seeds into the shell and heated the water with his fiery breath.

"Quickly," the telepathic plea came to Greenthor. "Look at Aliyyah."

As Greenthor gazed he saw a shimmering light shaped like Aliyyah hovering slightly above her body, like a golden shadow held by the most fragile thread.

Sharply Greenthor ordered, "Wild Wind, lift Aliyyah's head up so that I may pour this medicine into her mouth."

As tenderly as a dragon could, Wild Wind lifted Aliyyah's head while Greenthor coaxed the black Nummic seeds and water into her mouth. Slowly but surely he managed to feed all the medicine to Aliyyah and as he did so the crisscross of golden beams faded, while the shimmering light seemed to slowly sink back into Aliyyah's body.

"Now we will have to wait and see. We will know by the morning if we were in time or not."

As soon as he had treated Aliyyah, Greenthor looked closely at Wild Wind and realised how badly injured the young dragon was. Long deep gashes ran along each side of his body, while one wing was bleeding profusely. Somehow he must stop the bleeding and treat the wounds as quickly as he could, but it would only be temporary. When the other dragons arrived they would have to help Wild Wind fly back to the island of the healers to be treated properly. Greenthor knew that there were only a few herbs that could treat the poison of the Nogard, among them the Day Bloom, which only grew in the ancient forests guarded by the Dryad.

Turning to the owls Greenthor asked, "Do any of you know the herb called Heal-all?"

Once more Norworol spoke, "Before the Dark One came here and placed his evil spell upon our land, it used to grow in abundance in the foothills of the sixth island. Maybe as the islands have been restored it is once more growing there. I will fly there and search for you."

"Thank you, but you had better bring some of your companions with you as we need as much as you can carry."

Norworol quickly flew off in a westerly direction, followed closely by four other young owls. Flying directly to the foothills of the sixth island they found that once more they were covered with the purple flowered Heal-all. Landing heavily, they plucked as much of the herb as they could carry. Then laden, with their burden, they spread their powerful wings and flew swiftly back to the wailing dragon.

"Good," exclaimed Greenthor when he saw how much of the precious herb they had brought. "This is more than enough to stop the bleeding and remove some of the poison. However, Wild Wind must go as soon as possible to the island of the healers."

Weakly, Wild Wind interrupted, "I will not go anywhere until I know for sure that Aliyyah is going to be alright."

Shaking his magnificent head, Greenthor replied, "You must go to the healers to remove all the poison. This herb will only remove the poison in your skin. It cannot remove the poison that has already entered your blood. You will be no use to Aliyyah if you die."

Giving in, Wild Wind pleaded, "At least let me wait until the morning, it is only a few hours away."

Very reluctantly Greenthor agreed. He knew how stubborn Wild Wind could be and he had realised how much the young girl had come to mean to Wild Wind.

Greenthor took the Heal-all little by little and after chewing it into a pulp he placed it on all of Wild Wind's injuries. Before the astonished eyes of the owls the bleeding stopped immediately, leaving the wounds red and angry as the poison slowly began to seep out and drop onto the ground. Wherever the poison dropped, the grass beneath it withered, turned black and died.

By now the sun had finally set and darkness lay upon the islands like a cloak. As the owls dozed restlessly a loud flapping sound was heard as the other seven dragons descended one after another and landed near Greenthor, Wild Wind and the still unconscious Aliyyah. "Greetings brother, how is Aliyyah?" asked Mercury Tongue.

"We still do not know, but I believe we were in time. Her colour is improving and her breathing is steady. We will know in the morning. If she awakes when the sunlight falls upon her she will be alright. However, if she does not I fear she will sleep forever. Wild Wind is badly injured by the Nogard's poison and you must help him fly to the island of the healers. He is so concerned about Aliyyah he refuses to go before the morning."

Nodding his head, Mercury Tongue tried to persuade Wild Wind to go straight away, but to no avail Wild Wind would not.

"Let me rest for a few hours, I am too weak to attempt the flight now. Especially in the cold of the dark night. A few hours is all I need."

So saying, Wild Wind tucked his head beneath his wing and refused to say anything more. Greenthor was very worried, for even a few hours could be fatal. If the Nogard's poison reached Wild Wind's heart, nothing would be able to save him.

Restlessly Greenthor and the other dragons waited for the dawn and the fate of those they loved. In his heart Greenthor knew that if Aliyyah survived then so would Wild Wind. If she did not make it, he dreaded to think what would become of Wild Wind. The young dragon had made the fatal mistake of allowing himself to love the young girl and this had created such a bond with her that he too would die if she did. Many years ago there had been dragon riders, but when the riders died so too did the dragons. The only way a dragon could outlive its rider was if the rider had a child that bonded with the dragon and took over from its parent. However, as most dragon riders never married, this relationship had proved disastrous for the dragons. Finally the Council of Dragons and the Council of Men had a long meeting and it was decided that there would be no more dragon riders, although the dragons promised to aid all those who travelled the path of light and protect the sacred Islands of Lamis whenever they were called to be the rightful rulers.

As the long night passed, Wild Wind seemed to slip into the same sleep that afflicted Aliyyah. His fate now depended totally on Aliyyah's.

Finally the dawn came and with it the first feeble rays of the new day. As the sun began to rise the dragons, owls and Najputih looked anxiously at Aliyyah. Slowly the rays of the sun spread across the islands and as they stroked Aliyyah's face she began to stir. After a few minutes she opened her eyes and looked around her in some confusion.

"Where am I, what happened?" were the first words she spoke.

"You are on the islands of the owls. You almost died after replacing the Luminous Pearl in its shell. The black waters would have claimed your life but Wild Wind flew to the hidden island of the healers for the medicine that saved your life," replied Greenthor.

Smiling, Aliyyah asked, "Where is Wild Wind, I wish to thank him."

Shaking his head, Greenthor moved aside so that Aliyyah could see Wild Wind lying motionless on the ground.

Shocked, Aliyyah demanded to know what had happened.

"Aliyyah, the Dark One must have known what happened for on his way back Wild Wind was attacked by an evil Nogard. Even though we all flew to his aid, he was badly injured. However, he refused our help to take him to the island of the healers and refused to leave your side. His love for you may be the cause of his death, for now the only thing that can save him in time is the water of the Day Bloom, which can only be found in the ancient forests that are protected by the Dryads."

No sooner had Aliyyah heard this than she began to smile, to the amazement of the dragons.

"Do not worry, Greenthor, but get me some water as quickly as you can. For freeing the forest around the Castle of Mirrors the Dryads gave me one of their precious Day Blooms and taught me how to use it. I will use it now to heal Wild Wind of his injuries."

Greenthor had not even moved when Norworol flew down with another seashell of water.

"Take this, I collected it for you to drink when you recovered, but use it now for the dragon."

Placing the shell next to Aliyyah, he stepped back to allow the girl to sit up. Aliyyah however was still weak and needed the gentle help of Fire Eye to sit up. Opening her bag that was still slung around her shoulders, she took out the precious Day Bloom and put it in the water. As the water changed colour, the fragrance lifted the hearts of all those who smelled it. After reciting the words she had been taught by the Dryad, she asked Greenthor to give the water to Wild Wind.

"I am still too weak to stand so will you please give the water to Wild Wind, I have used this before and it should cure him straight away."

Greenthor and the other dragons tried to wake Wild Wind and after what seemed like an age he finally opened his eyes.

"Take this medicine now," commanded Greenthor.

"How is Aliyyah?" demanded Wild Wind.

"She is well and it is she who has prepared this medicine for you. Now drink." Slowly, Wild Wind drank and as he did, all the poison of the Nogard flowed out from his skin and dropped onto the ground before seeping into the earth. At the same time all the wounds on his body healed themselves as if by magic. Within a few minutes not a mark remained of the injuries he had sustained. As the injuries healed and the poison left his body, Wild Wind felt his strength flowing back into his veins.

Getting up, he went over to Aliyyah and doing an awkward dragon bow he thanked her for helping him.

"No, Wild Wind, I should thank you, for if you had not tried to help me you would not have been hurt. Thank you.

With this she put her arms around Wild Wind's neck and hugged him. As she did so she heard a voice in her head. "Well then, what about me? I have not left your side and I too would have given my life for you if I had to."

Turning, she saw Najputih by her side looking slightly put out. Hugging him too she told him, "My dearest friend, you are my constant companion and I love you dearly. The dragons are our friends and I love them too, but you are by my side always and should never feel left out."

Greenthor, who alone of the dragons could understand the telepathic language of the unicorns' replied in the same. "We are all sworn to help Aliyyah in her quest, but you have the greater honour by being her travelling companion. Please extend your trust to us as we extend our trust to you."

Looking first at Aliyyah then at Greenthor, Najputih finally replied, "I am honoured by your trust and in return I give you mine. Although I do not want to ride or be carried by a dragon again."

Making a noise that sounded like laughter, Greenthor then spoke aloud for all to hear.

"Once more I am in your debt, my Princess."

"What do you mean, Greenthor? Surely it is I who is in your debt."

"No Princess, it is I. I am the oldest and the wisest of all the dragons. I am so old that no one remembers when I was hatched or whom my parents were. I have mated many times and have had many sons, all have passed away except for the egg you rescued, and Wild Wind."

Silenced filled the air, for not even the other dragons knew that Wild Wind was Greenthor's son.

"I kept this secret even from Wild Wind himself, for I wanted him to prove himself worthy before I revealed the truth. He has now more them proved himself to me and if the other members of the council agree I will now train him to become my successor on the Dragon Council when the time comes."

Shocked beyond belief, Wild Wind did not know who to thank first, Aliyyah or Greenthor. For many years he had wondered who his father was and now, thanks to Aliyyah, he knew. At the same time he realised that if his father was Greenthor, his mother must have been Ne'alder.

"But that means my mother is Ne'alder!" he said.

"Yes," replied Greenthor. "But that was long before she took the path of evil. At that time she still worked for the light and was wise and beautiful. But somehow her heart became corrupted and she turned against the light. It was for that reason I never told you who you were. I wanted you to prove yourself, not just to me but to the other dragons, so that they would not condemn you for who your mother is. Now no dragon can say you follow her, but they can all see that you follow your father and the way of the righteous. I am proud to call you my son, Wild Wind. I will never mate again, so you and the egg that is in the dragons' nursery are all the children I will ever have. By the way, the keepers of the egg tell me it is a female, so one day you will have a little sister to look after."

Overwhelmed at the events, Wild Wind bowed and bent his head, first before Aliyyah and then before his father.

"My father, I swear by the ancient magic always to honour and obey you in all things. I will fight to defeat the dark, even if it claims my life and I will strive always to make you proud of me."

"Good," replied Greenthor. "Now you and Dark Wing go and find food and water for Aliyyah and Najputih, for as soon as they have eaten and rested they must continue on their quest."

Chapter Six

King Poseidon's Palace

Within a short time Wild Wind and Fire Eye returned, laden with a variety of fresh fruits and nuts. Wild Wind had even managed to get hold of three loaves of fresh bread as well as two water skins full of cooling spring water. Landing next to Aliyyah, the two dragons urged her to eat and drink.

Smiling, Aliyyah took one of the strange yellow fruits that looked like an apple, but tasted like honey. As she ate she felt the strength returning to her body and all the effects of the sleeping sickness seemed to disappear completely.

"Where did you get these fruits?" enquired Aliyyah. "I have never tasted anything so delicious!"

"They are from the same island that I took the berries from," replied Wild Wind. "All the fruits we have brought are from there. It is where we got the bread as well. When we were collecting the fruit the head of the village came to us and asked if this was for a seeker, as he knew we dragons do not eat fruit. When we replied that it was he gave us the bread as well as this." Handing Aliyyah a small bag, Wild Wind continued, "The elder said to give this to the seeker only if she had already obtained the Keys of Hanaj."

Curious, Aliyyah opened the bag to find a strange dried weed, rubbery to the touch. It had been cut into three-inch pieces and there were exactly thirty pieces in the bag.

Wild Wind continued, "The elder said that when you reach the end of the world it will be difficult for you to breathe. When that happens you must eat one piece of this weed. It will allow you to breathe easily for one hour, but no more. He told you to use it wisely."

"Thank you Wild Wind and Fire Eye. Please, when you go back to the island thank him for me."

"Oh no, Princess," exclaimed Fire Eye. "The village elder insists that when your quest permits, you must visit him personally as he has a gift that was entrusted to him by your father."

"How does he know who I am or who my father is? I thought that only Mahin and Greenthor knew."

"I do not know, Princess, but the people of these islands know many things that are hidden to others. If you really want to know, you must ask him yourself."

Petulantly Aliyyah replied, "True, but I have no idea where this island is hidden."

"Do not worry, Princess, when the lime is right I will send you there, and Najputih, if he trusts me to carry him again!"

Shaking his snowy mane, Najputih retorted to Aliyyah, "I would rather grow wings first."

Laughing, Aliyyah quickly finished her light meal. Surrounded by the dragons and owls with Najputih by her side she felt safer and more loved than she had in a long time. Even though Mahin had loved her as if she was his own daughter, he was a very stem teacher who was very strict with her. He had made sure that she learnt all the skills she would need to survive and be successful in the quest. Although he had a great love for her, he dare not show it for he knew the future of the islands lay in her hands.

A few minutes after Najputih and Aliyyah had finished eating, Toowooni, with the greatest respect, approached them.

"Oh, pure-hearted one, thank you for saving us and restoring our islands to their former beauty and glory, never will we be able to repay you. Now as we promised we will show you the way to the green turtle, although the path is not easy."

" I thank you Toowooni, but first I must fulfil a promise I have made to the lost souls. They told me that their ship went down not far from your home. Do any of you know exactly where the ship went down?"

A small brown owl who had been listening said, "Just before the Dark One stole the pearl, I saw the ship floundering off our island in a terrible tempest. The sailors had no chance and in desperation they began to cast their most powerful spells around a book that shone with light. Terrified, I watched as the Dark One flew down on the back of a Nogard and tried to take the book.

However, each and every time he tried, something drove him back. In anger he sank the ship and killed all the sailors on her. Not one survived. I can still hear their screams as one by one they drowned and sank down to the seabed. It was soon after that the Dark One put his black spell upon our islands. I can show you where the ship lies, follow me, follow me."

With Aliyyah following, the owl led the way to the golden shore. A short distance away was a rugged outcrop of black rocks against which the waves shattered and smashed as if they were bent on destroying this obstacle in their way.

"It was here where the rocks are that I saw the ship sink."

Thanking the owl she asked him to wait, before turning to Wild Wind who along with the other dragons had also followed.

"Could you carry me again, Wild Wind over to those rocks?"

"Of course, Princess, but why?"

"I have a debt of honour to repay. The lost souls helped me so I must help them. By returning the Book of Peace their names will be cleared and their souls can then sleep in peace."

"Very well, Princess, climb on my back, it is so near it won't take long."

Carefully climbing once more onto Wild Wind's back, Aliyyah felt him lift up into the skies and almost straight away descend again to the rocky outcrop.

"Thank you Wild Wind, please wait for me as this should not take long."

Nodding his head, Wild Wind half stood, half hovered at the edge of the rocks so that Aliyyah would have plenty of room.

In a loud voice Aliyyah slowly and clearly recited three times, "Lacarda lacarda ni lacardi."

No sooner had she finished than a strange light could be seen rising up from under the deep, blue waters. With each passing second it became brighter until at last they could see a large bubble breaking free of the waves. Inside was a great book with an embossed leather cover. It was from this book and not the bubble that the light was coming from. As the bubble hovered over the surface of the sea they could see the book slowly opening. As it did, a bright golden light spread from east to west filling the hearts of whomever saw it with great joy and happiness. At the same time a melodious-singing haunting tune was heard of longing and mysterious secrets. As they stared, another light, still bright but slightly darker, began to form from the open pages of the Book of Peace. Slowly it took the form of a beautiful young woman dressed in the robes of one of the ancient and wise sorceresses.

"Thank you, Aliyyah," the figure of light began. "Thank you for opening once more the Book of Peace. I am Mimah, the sorceress whose job it is to guard the book. I am indebted to you for not just opening the book, but also for setting me free from my imprisonment within its pages. No one knew what had happened to me, some said I had died while others said I had fled, but the truth was I was tricked by an evil dragon called Ne'alder who wanted this book to destroy the other dragons. However, the book can only be used for good, as she found out, and in her anger she trapped me in the book as it was closing. Now I am free I will return the book to its rightful place and guard it properly so it may never be closed again."

With these words she faded away along with the book until there was nothing left to see at all. Aliyyah turned towards Wild Wind ready to climb on his back once more, when she heard a loud noise behind her. Turning, she saw the lost souls of drowned sailors soaring out of the sea. As they left their watery graves they became bright with light so they looked like a meteorite shower going up into the air instead of down. At the same time they heard a multitude of voices all repeating the same words, "Free, free at last, thank you, thank you."

Finally, one figure detached itself from the others and approached Aliyyah and the dragon. It was the young captain of the ship whose handsome face was now radiant and serene.

"Thank you, Aliyyah, for keeping your promise. Now at last we can rest. The sorceress has returned our bodies to our homeland and with the return of the Book of Peace we can now sleep until the time comes for us to live again. Goodbye, Princess, and may you succeed in your quest."

Then he too disappeared into the skies. Looking rather downcast Wild Wind said, "Well, Aliyyah, at last they can rest. Please forgive us dragons for what my mother did."

"Wild Wind you are not responsible for your mother's actions. No person will be judged by another's act. Do not worry, my dear friend,

I know nothing but good about you."

Embarrassed, Wild Wind said nothing, but feeling a lot happier he carried Aliyyah back to the island where the owls were waiting.

As they landed they were quickly surrounded by the owls who were singing a beautiful song of praise and thankfulness for their deliverance from the spell of the Dark One. Aliyyah's face turned red as they sang and she was relieved when they finally stopped.

"Thank you, kind owls," she said. "But without your help and the help of the dragons and the lost souls I would never have been able to succeed. I should be the one praising you!"

Hopping forward, Toowooni replied, "Your coming to our islands was truly a blessed event. Now we will fulfil our part of the bargain and show you the way to the home of the green turtle. However, I can only take you part of the way as his home is under the deep sea beyond the palace of the Merpeople, past the Whirlpool of Infinity and through the seaweed forest. You will have to pass the questioning of the guardian, only then will you be allowed to see the green turtle. The journey is long and difficult and you must find a way of breathing under the water. Do you still wish to see the green turtle or will you stay here in safety. We would be honoured to look after you."

Shaking her head, Aliyyah replied, "I have no choice I must continue, but thank you anyway. Shall we start while it is still light?" Before either Aliyyah or Toowooni could move, Greenthor spoke. "Aliyyah, what the owls did not tell you is that you must also pass the palace of the dragon king of the eastern seas who is my cousin. He is both wise and powerful and no friend of the Dark One. Seek his help in my name for his magic, is the strongest of any dragon."

Before continuing Greenthor handed Aliyyah a small piece of bark covered with strange marking, unlike any writing she had seen before.

"Show this to him and he will recognise it and know you truly are my friend. He will then ask you if you know his name. When he does, you are to tell him." With this he bent his magnificent head and whispered into Aliyyah's ear the dragon king's secret name. "He will know that you can be trusted, for only a dragon friend will know the secret name each dragon uses."

Turning to the other dragons he told Dark Wing, "Go with Aliyyah and the owls as far as you can and then return to the council." Interrupting, Wild Wind pleaded, "There is no need to send Dark Wing I can go with Aliyyah."

"No," stated Greenthor firmly. "You must go to the island of the healers and fulfil your promise to Kathir. A dragon can never break his word. When you have finished only then you may once again aid Aliyyah, but only if she calls you for you have much to learn if you are to take my place on the Dragon Council one day. Now go."

Not daring to disobey, Wild Wind, without any more words, slowly rose up in the air. "Look after her well, my brother," he cried before flapping his wings and disappearing over the horizon.

In a firm voice Greenthor told the other dragons, "The rest of you are to return to our island for there is still much work to be done. Dark Wing, I wish to talk to Aliyyah alone, please wait for her. Aliyyah, come."

Following Greenthor, Aliyyah wondered what it was that the dragon wanted. As soon as they were out of earshot of the owls and Dark Wing, Greenthor stopped and for a few minutes he just looked at her before saying, "Oh my Princess, I am already in your debt so much, but now I have to ask yet another favour from you. Wild Wind has already become very fond of you. For a dragon that can be a fatal mistake. If he gives his heart to you he will die when you die, unless he gains a greater love towards your child. Therefore, to save him from offering his heart to you, unless you have no other choice, please call on one of the older and wiser dragons for help. Any one of us will come at any time and willingly aid you. I myself would give my life to protect you. Wild Wind is my last son, I will have no others to carry on my bloodline. Even though we are blessed with a lifetime greater than any others we, like all creations, will die eventually."

Aliyyah felt tears filling her eyes as she replied, "Of course I do not want any harm to come to Wild Wind, for he too has become very dear to me. I will do as you say and I pray that Wild Wind is not too hurt if I ignore him."

"Thank you, Aliyyah, I know that this is hard for you, but a human will not die when a dragon does. I will keep Wild Wind occupied for he has much to learn if one day he is to replace me. Now you must continue on your quest. Take this," continued Greenthor, handing Aliyyah a silver flask covered with delicate engravings and protective verses. "The elder of the Dragon

Council made the liquid that is contained inside this flask. It is called Feillife and just a few drops it will provide you with energy to carry on even if you have used your last ounce of strength, it will also heal any wounds you have. Use it wisely for this is a gift beyond price!"

Taking the flask, Aliyyah asked Greenthor to thank the elder. "Please convey my thanks to the elder, he must be a great and generous dragon."

Looking at her strangely Greenthor replied, "The elder may be many things, but one thing he is not and has never been, a dragon!" Shocked, Aliyyah asked Greenthor who or what he was.

"My dear Princess, I'm afraid that I cannot tell you that. If you finish your quest, then and only then will you find out who the elder is. Until then you must be patient and concentrate on your mission. Now go with Dark Wing and with our blessings, go." Without another word Greenthor rose up into the air and flew away.

Aliyyah slowly returned to where Najputih and the others waited. Putting the remaining food that Wild Wind and Fire Eye had brought into her bag and slinging the water flask over her shoulder, Aliyyah prepared to continue the quest. With a frenzy of excited hoots the owls crowded around Aliyyah to say goodbye to her and the unicorn.

"Toowoo, Toowoo, take care and thank you, thank you. May you succeed where all others have tailed. Toowoo, toowoo, come again soon. Farewell."

After the last owl had bid Aliyyah farewell, Toowooni approached her. "Are you ready, Princess?"

Smiling, Aliyyah replied, "As ready as I will ever be."

"Good, but we have far to travel, do you wish to ride on the dragon or walk on the ground?"

Looking at Najputih, who was shaking his head violently while pawing the ground with his hoof, she said, "I think that Najputih has had enough of flying for the time being, so I will walk for now."

Turning to Dark Wing, she added, "Please do not be offended, Dark Wing, if I do not fly with you for now. When the time is right I will be greatly honoured if you will carry me."

Looking directly at Aliyyah, Dark Wing, in his deep and melancholy voice, told her, "Aliyyah, no offence is taken. We dragons know the fear the unicorn has of us. If he had been an ordinary horse we may have eaten him for our dinner, but we do not harm any creatures of light or white magic. He is more than safe with us."

Najputih seemed to doubt the dragon's word, but nevertheless asked Aliyyah to tell Dark Wing, "Thank you, as you spoke in the ancient tongue I feel I must believe you, but please never mistake me for an ordinary stallion."

Dark Wing made a sound something like short burst of laughter. "No chance of that, now let us proceed. I will fly overhead and check for any dangers. I will rejoin you when you stop to rest."

So saying, Dark Wing opened his jet black wings and majestically rose up into the azure skies. Aliyyah and Najputih followed Toowooni, who half hopped and half flew in front of them, leading the way.

As they walked across the island Aliyyah was able to appreciate its great beauty. Colourful butterflies flitted from one bright flower to another while the songs of the owls, now harmonious voices seemed to fill the air. Before long they had reached the shore and Toowooni called the stones once more so Aliyyah and the unicorn could cross to the next island.

After several hours they had reached the shores of the seventh island, just as dusk was tailing. Stopping, Toowooni looked around for a while before saying, "It is late and the night is falling and we cannot safely continue in the dark. Let us rest here and continue in the morning."

Nodding her head in agreement Aliyyah look around her to find a suitable place to rest. As she looked around, Dark Wing landed softly on the pristine sand near her.

"You are resting for the night?" he enquired.

"Yes Dark Wing," replied Aliyyah. "The owl told us it was not safe to continue in the dark."

"A wise decision," Dark Wing commented. Then noticing Aliyyah shiver as the air started to cool, he told her to move away from the clump of rocks she had been standing near.

Opening his jaws he let out a mighty jet of fire, which heated the rocks until they turned red hot.

"Ouch, be careful!" cried Toowooni as he flew up to the branches of a nearby tree. "You almost scorched my tail feathers."

77

"I am sorry little one, I did not see you there." Then, turning to Aliyyah he told her, "You and the unicorn lie down on the sands near the rocks where the heat will keep you warm. It will be many hours before the rocks are cool again. I will lie down in front of you to protect you from the cool sea breezes as well as keeping watch for any danger."

Gratefully Aliyyah lay down as close to the rocks as she could. They were so hot that even the surrounding sands were warm. Lying her head on Najputih's flank, she looked at both her necklace and pendant before pulling her cloak over both of them. As soon as she had settled down, Dark Wing elegantly laid down in front of them making a barrier against the wind. Enclosed on one side by the hot rocks and other by Dark Wing, Aliyyah felt warm, comfortable and safe.

Just before she drifted off to sleep she said, "Goodnight Dark Wing, thank you."

"Goodnight Princess, rest well," answered Dark Wing. Then as an afterthought he added, "Goodnight Najputih I will make sure no bad dragons get you in the night," then, chuckling to himself in his deep voice, he half closed his eyes to rest, but not to sleep.

Early next morning Aliyyah woke to find that Dark Wing had disappeared. Puzzled, she looked around to see where he had gone.

"Toowoo, toowoo," cried Toowooni. "The dragon has gone to look for food for you. He will not be long."

Smiling, Aliyyah found a small stream and washed her hands and face in the cool, crystal waters. She sensed rather than heard Najputih come up behind her. "Good morning," she thought. "How are you today? Ready to continue with our quest?"

Shaking his snowy mane, Najputih replied, "Yes, as long as it does not involve flying in a dragon's claws again."

Laughing, Aliyyah heard the sound of flapping wings as Dark Wing returned. In one claw he carried a dead deer and in the other a rough brown bag. Landing, he called Aliyyah.

"Princess, there is fruit, fresh bread and some milk as well as water in the bag. The deer is my breakfast, but I can roast a piece for you if you wish."

Sensing the distress the dead deer was causing Najputih, Aliyyah replied, "Another time, Dark Wing, please enjoy your food." Looking meaningfully at Najputih she said, "We must all eat, that is the way of things," as she took the heavy bag from Dark Wing.

Chuckling, Dark Wing carried his deer a little way off so the unicorn could not see him as he devoured the skin, meat and even the bones, until not one scrap of the animal remained.

Opening the bag she saw it contained five fresh loaves of bread, apples, plums, oranges and several fruits she did not recognise as well as wild berries. There was a large skin fall of water and a small gourd of fresh, creamy milk that was still warm. Faking one of the loaves she broke it in half and gave one half to the unicorn while eating the other herself.

"Toowooni, would you like some bread?" asked Aliyyah.

"No thank you," replied the owl. "I will go and hunt for my breakfast for like the dragon, I need to eat meat, but thank you." Flapping his wings he set off to catch his breakfast. Before long Toowooni returned refreshed and singing happily. "Aliyyah, my Princess, are you ready? For now the difficult part of the journey begins."

Nodding her head, Aliyyah slung the bag of provisions over her right shoulder and the water skin over her left.

"Yes Towooni, but where do we go from here?"

"Well, Princess, we must cross the ocean until we reach the Island of Mists, for only there will you find the way down to the home of the green turtle."

Before Aliyyah could say anything Najputih sent her an urgent plea. "Please Aliyyah, I do not want to be carried by a dragon again! Is there no other way?"

Najputih, unaware that Dark Wing who was the only other dragon apart from Greenthor could understand his telepathic thought, was shocked when he heard him say, "You have no need to fear me, I am bound by the ancient magic to protect you. However, if your fear of flying is so great, ask Aliyyah to use her bracelet Fire Eye gave, to call the sea creatures, one of which I am sure will be able to carry you on their back through the waters."

Ashamed, Najputih said, "Dark Wing, forgive me, I do not mistrust you, but unicorns were not meant to fly and an uncontrollable fear overcomes me when I am dangling in the air."

"It does not matter, but if it is unavoidable to lift you out of danger, I promise I will be as gentle as a mother with her newborn baby."

Aliyyah was unable to control her laughter as she listened to the unicorn and dragon.

"I think," she said, when she had finally stopped laughing, "that before this quest is over you two will become inseparable friends." Then going to the shore she looked at her bracelet before reciting over it the words Fire Eye had taught her when he gave it to her. "Hadsha kani hadsha awelth hadsha dangu hadsha mulase."

No sooner had the words left her lips than the stones of the bracelet lit up one by one, each with a different colour. As she watched the lights grew in intensity until one by one they seemed to shoot up into the air before falling back into the sea.

For a few moments nothing happened, then slowly they saw a variety of different sea creatures approaching the golden shores where they were standing.

The first to arrive was the great blue whale who stayed some distance away from the beach, where the water was deep enough to support him.

Following the whale were giant squid as well as manta's of all shapes and sizes. Dolphins, sharks and all sorts of unusual and strange sea creatures swam together, with fishes of every description. All of them drawn by the lights from Aliyyah's bracelet.

As the creatures swam around off the shores of the seventh island, one of the smaller dolphins swam towards Aliyyah and in its strange clicking language asked her how they could help. By the power of the bracelet, not only could Aliyyah understand their language, but they could also understand hers.

"We need to reach the Island of Mists. Could one of you carry myself and the unicorn. The dragon and the owl will fly ahead."

Clicking his understanding he swam back out to where the larger sea creatures were waiting. A few minutes later the dolphin returned followed by a giant manta ray. Never in all her life had Aliyyah seen such a creature, which seemed to glide just below the surface of the crystal clear waters. Its wingspan must have been at least twenty metres and its tail seemed to stretch on forever.

"This is Mantrayrini," clicked the dolphin. "He is the king of all the manta rays. There is no ray bigger or stronger than he is. Even though he is the king of all the rays, he has agreed to ferry you to the Island of Mists. However, he apologises, for even though he will try to swim as close to the surface of the water as he can, you will still have to get your feet wet."

Smiling, Aliyyah replied, "Thank him for us. Tell him we are greatly honoured by his offer and we do not mind getting a little wet to reach the Island of Mists."

Turning to Najputih she asked him, "Do you agree or do you want to fly?"

Unhappily Najputih replied, "I am neither a fish nor a bird although it seems it would be easier if I was. However, out of the two options I will choose the manta, though I do not relish the journey."

Once more laughing, Aliyyah told the glum unicorn, "My dearest companion, do you think that I would let any harm come to you? For your sake I have called the sea creatures, for I am quite happy to fly with Dark Wing."

Flittering about nervously Toowooni exclaimed, "Are we ready, are we ready? We must reach the island before midday the day after next, we have no time to lose."

"Yes Toowooni, we are ready, but why must we reach the island before midday the day after next?" questioned Aliyyah.

"On the island near the shore there is a pillar of stone. It is part of the ancient city of Atlantis that was destroyed many, many years ago. When the sun is directly above it at midday the day after next, its shadow will point to the hidden door that will lead you down to the home of the green turtle. However, we have to pass many dangers before that, so be prepared."

Nodding her head in understanding, Aliyyah started wading through the waters towards Mantrayrini, followed by a hesitant and reluctant unicorn.

The giant ray made an odd movement, which looked something like a bow, when he saw Aliyyah and then remained perfectly still as she climbed up onto his giant wings. For Najputih it was quite difficult to mount the giant manta and it was only with Aliyyah pulling him and several dolphins pushing him that he was finally able to get onto the manta.

"I think flying is beginning to look not so fearful after all," he thought. "At least I would not get wet!"

A deep, humorous voice replied, "Do you want me to carry you after all?"

Quickly Najputih replied, "No, there is no need. I am already on the manta, let's just get this journey over and done with."

"Very well," chuckled Dark Wing. "But do not worry, I will be watching, ready to rescue you if you fall in the sea."

Smoothly the manta glided away from the shore with the dolphin who had spoken with Aliyyah swimming next to him. As they reached the open sea, Aliyyah saw all the other sea creatures who had followed behind them disappearing one by one, each returning to their respective homes, until there was only the manta, dolphin and Aliyyah and her companions.

As they travelled the dolphin talked, telling her all about the sea and those creatures that live in it.

At first as they glided along Aliyyah fell refreshed as the wind blew the fresh sea breezes into their faces, leaving a salty taste on their lips. However, after a while both Aliyyah and the unicorn began to feel the strain of standing up on the back of the giant manta, Aliyyah more than Najputih.

The dolphin, noticing Aliyyah's discomfort, said, "Aliyyah, you look tired from standing so long, as well as cold. I can do nothing about the cold, but if you don't mind getting wetter you can ride on my back for a while, at least you won't be standing."

Gratefully Aliyyah accepted. "That would be welcome, if Najputih does not mind?"

"Go ahead, Aliyyah," responded Najputih. "Just don't ask me to ride a dolphin, a manta is enough!"

The dolphin, whose name was Aquas, swam as close as he could to Mantrayrini, and Aliyyah, as gracefully as possible slid onto the back of the dolphin. It felt good to sit once more after several hours of standing on the back of a moving manta with no support at all.

"Are you comfortable, Aliyyah?" came the clicking speech of Aquas. "Not too wet or cold?"

"No, I am fine. At least I can rest my legs for a while, I hope I am not too heavy for you."

"No, no, you are very light, just like the foam on top of the waves."

As they continued their journey, Aliyyah began to notice a kind of shimmer on the horizon. She kept on staring, unable to figure out what it was.

"Aquas," she asked, "what is that up ahead?"

Making excited clicking noises, Aquas replied, "We are approaching the kingdom of the Merpeople. The shimmering light you see comes from the spears of the Mermen guards. You are honoured indeed that they have shown themselves. Normally they do no show themselves to anyone. Of all the ships that pass this way none, of the sailors have seen the Merpeople, not even a glimpse of their tails."

Unsure what this meant, Aliyyah waited in anticipation as they got nearer to the horizon. Before long she could see that the lights were indeed spears, bright golden spears, one after another spreading across the horizon as far as the eye could see.

As they approached they could see that each spear was held aloft by a Merman. Young, strong and muscular, their flowing golden locks gently swayed in the sea breeze. All of them without exception were beardless and wore nothing except a golden helmet, shaped like a stingray, and golden armbands.

A few feet behind the Mermen there was a splendid golden chariot shaped like a giant open clam, pulled by four enormous seahorses, each one a slightly different colour from the rest. Inside this chariot, with one hand grasping the reins of the seahorses and the other his golden trident, was none other than Poseidon, the king of the Merpeople. He was magnificent, taller and stronger than all the other Mermen put together, with jet black hair that curled down to his shoulders as soft and as wild as the waves of the sea. His black beard had been braided with shimmering pearls of the greatest beauty. On his head he wore a light and elegant golden crown that was studded with precious jewels, priceless beyond belief. Upon his chest lay several heavy coral and gold chains. His face was wondrous, fierce and yet at the same time, wise and kind.

When they were within a few feet of the guards, the Mermen lowered their spears and pointed them towards them.

"Who dares cross the kingdom of the Merpeople?" came the challenge.

Aliyyah, without hesitation, replied; "A seeker on the way of the quest. Who dares bar her way?" Silence filled the air as the Mermen seem to be at a loss for words at her reply. One minute, two, three, five minutes passed until a loud chuckling sound was heard from King Poseidon.

"Well said, young Aliyyah, who indeed would want to stop you except for the Dark One and his vassals? Welcome to my kingdom. We were foretold of your arrival by the guardian, who sends you his greetings and hopes that you will be able to answer all of his questions."

Gracefully nodding her head, Aliyyah replied, "Thank you're your Majesty, for if I am not mistaken you are none other than King Poseidon, are you not?"

"Yes, I am," replied Poseidon. "I know that you have very little time, but I wish to invite you to my home for a short while. I have some gifts for you that were entrusted to me by the elder of the Council of Dragons. However, they are locked in a chest in my palace and only the one who has the Keys of Hanaj can open it."

Looking at Poseidon, then at her necklace and bracelet, which remained a neutral white colour, she decided that Poseidon was indeed a friend and was speaking the truth.

"Yes, I will go with you, but is not your palace beneath the waves?"

"Yes, however if I am not mistaken you have already been given some dried mirkweed. You need only to chew one piece and it will enable you to breathe underwater." Turning to stare at Najputih he said, "Unicorn, please wait here with Mantrayini. He will protect you and I will also leave some of the Mermen to guard you. We will not be long."

Urgently Najputih asked Aliyyah, "Is it safe? Can we trust him?"

"I think so," replied Aliyyah. "Anyhow, we cannot afford to offend him."

"Do not worry, Aliyyah" Dark Wing's voice came into their minds. "Poseidon has always been a friend of the dragons as well as being one of the hidden guardians of light. Not even the Dark One has the strength to openly challenge him, not yet anyhow."

"So be it! Dark Wing, please take my bag of provisions and the water flask for me, otherwise the food will be mined."

Taking off the bag containing their food and the flask full of water, she held them out as Dark Wing swept down and gently snatched them from her.

"Aliyyah" called Dark Wing. "Toowooni and I are going to rest on an outcrop of rocks not far from here. When you return, call us and we will rejoin you quickly." Then to Najputih he said,

"Do not worry little one, if you need us just call me and I will fly to your aid, as I would fly to the aid of Aliyyah. The Mermen will keep you company.

I would take you with me, but the rocks are not large or very safe."

With this, he and Toowooni flew out to a small outcrop of jagged black rocks not far away, to rest and wail for Aliyyah to rejoin them.

Aliyyah cautiously removed a piece of mirkweed from its watertight pouch and placed it into her mouth. At first it tasted rubbery and unpleasant, but as she chewed it became softer and the flavour changed, becoming sweeter with each chew. As she finished she began to feel a strange change coming over her. As she looked at her hands she saw soft, rubbery skin beginning to grow between her fingers and felt the same thing happening to her toes. Quickly removing her shoes and stockings as carefully as she could without falling into the sea, she saw that indeed the same thing was happening there as well. As she tied the shoes and stockings together and put them inside her cloak, she continued to watch her hands and feet. Within just a few minutes she had webbed hands and feet, which would make it easier for her to move underwater. At the same time she felt rather than saw gills growing in both sides of her neck, enabling her to breathe underwater.

Startled, Aliyyah felt somewhat afraid that these changes might be permanent. Smiling, Poseidon, who seemed to sense her fear, told her, "Do not worry, Aliyyah, these changes are only temporary. After an hour you will return to normal unless you eat another piece of mirkweed. Now come and join me in my chariot and we will swiftly go to my palace beneath the waves."

Slipping off the back off Aquas, Aliyyah swam the short distance to the chariot of King Poseidon. She was surprised and then delighted with the ease that she could now swim through the sea due to her webbed hands and feet.

As soon as she reached the chariot, King Poseidon reached over and with one hand helped her inside his chariot and bade her sit on the padded bench behind him

"Sit and rest, Aliyyah, our journey will not take long."

Somewhat bemused, Aliyyah did as she was bid, relishing the softness of the cushions that lined the bench.

"Are you comfortable, Aliyyah?" enquired King Poseidon. Nodding her head, Aliyyah waited to see what the palace of the Merpeople would look like.

"Suschi suschi soouuusiii," Poseidon called out in a loud voice, while flicking the reins in his hands. "Suschi netunop merpolis."

Immediately the magnificent seahorses plunged into the sea, pulling the chariot beneath the waves with them. At first the speed of the seahorses and dash through the waters was a bit scary for Aliyyah, but soon she became fascinated so by the passing scenes that she forgot her fears. Fishes of every shape and size were darting this way and that, providing a kaleidoscope of ever-changing colours. As they went deeper the sea became darker and darker and bigger and stranger sea creatures could be seen. As they went even deeper, the fishes changed and seemed to have their own light with them, some in the skin, some near their eyes and one fish even had a light at what seemed to be the end of a very long fishing rod.

Suddenly Aliyyah gasped, for it seemed as if the seahorses were heading straight towards a solid rock cliff. She cringed, fearing that any moment they were going to crash into the side of the cliff covered with long curtains of green and red seaweed. However, just before the expected impact, two of the Merguards swam in front and pulled the seaweed curtain apart to reveal a passageway through the cliff, large enough for Poseidon and his chariot to pass through with ease.

Aliyyah strained her eyes to see where they were going in the darkness of the long tunnel. After a few minutes however, she noticed there was a soft glow ahead and the sound of haunting melodies came from the end of the passage way.

Aliyyah could hardly believe her eyes when they finally came out of the tunnel. Just below her on the seabed was Poseidon's palace. It was a wonder to behold and seemed to be made of living red coral and bright sea anemones growing up from the sand. The twisted towers, shaped like a spiral seashell, rose up like the prongs of Poseidon's trident. Each of the nine towers was capped with exquisite giant glowing pearls that bathed the palace in a soft yellow light.

Surrounding the palace were immaculate gardens of sea urchins, anemones and other strange yet beautiful sea flowers and creatures. The paths that lead through these gardens were covered with small white pearls, much like the gravel paths at home.

Merpeople swam around in groups and pairs, happy and serene in this watery paradise. The singing she had heard came a group of young mermaids swimming in a circle playing a game somewhat like Ring a Ring o' Roses. As the chariot carrying Poseidon and Aliyyah descended, the Merpeople bowed before them. At the same time she noticed that on the cliff walls surrounding the palace there were many Mermen on guard. Some were stationary, alert with sharp spears and tridents, while others were patrolling around astride dolphins and porpoises.

"Why are there so many guards?" asked Aliyyah as they passed beneath the portals of the palace gates.

"We have many enemies now, creatures of the Dark One, sea witches, even the giant congo eel has declared his enmity against us. That is why at all times we must be alert and ready to defend ourselves. It was not always like this. Years ago, I ruled over the seven seas and all the creatures living in it. However, the Dark One has slowly been poisoning the sea with his evil. You must succeed in your quest and reverse these changes or we are all doomed sooner or later."

"Suu suu suchi," called Poseidon to the giant seahorses while pulling the reins tightly. "Suu suu suchi." As they stopped in the palace courtyard, two Merguards grabbed the reins of the seahorses while King Poseidon and Aliyyah swam out of the chariot.

As they entered the palace five beautiful young mermaids came flying down one of the spiral staircases straight into their father's open arms. Laughing, King Poseidon embraced his daughters and then gently chided them to behave.

"Girls, where are your manners? We have a guest. This is Aliyyah, the seeker that we have all been hoping for."

Shyly the young princesses came forward one by one and introduced themselves.

Making an elegant curtsey, the eldest princess said, "I am Melody.

I am the one who sings all the songs into the seashells."

"I am Warna," said the second Mergirl who had the same black locks as her father. I look after the corals and the sands and sing the colours into them."

The third daughter told her, "I am Tempest and I am responsible for the storms and whirlpools except for one, the Whirlpool of Infinity is no longer under my control."

Blushing a little the fourth princess said, "I am Umpai and I look after the seaweed and other sea plants, but to my dismay I no longer control the great seaweed forest, which has grown wild and dangerous through the evil poisons of the Dark One.

Finally, the youngest of King Poseidon's daughters stepped forward. "I am called Bright Eyes and I look after all the small sea creatures. Welcome to our palace, welcome."

"Thank you," replied Aliyyah. "Thank you very much." Then turning to Poseidon she asked, "You have beautiful daughters, do you have any sons?"

Proudly King Poseidon replied, "Yes, six sons, only one is here at present. I he rest are looking after the larger sea creatures and guarding our borders. There is much work to do."

Smiling, Aliyyah enquired as to whether she would see his son or not.

Yes, replied King Poseidon. "Even though he is my youngest son he has been given the most important job, guarding the chest that was entrusted to us."

Beckoning Aliyyah to follow him, King Poseidon began swimming through a maze of passages, corridors and spiral staircases until Aliyyah had no idea where she was or how she had got there. Finally they entered a great hall, at the end of which were two massive wooden doors made from the preserved timbers taken from a sunken ship.

These doors were guarded by two Mermen who would challenge anyone who came near them, while other Mermen lined the walls. Seeing their king they bowed, before resuming their previous positions.

"Come, Aliyyah, for we have little time."

Swimming to the ancient doors he ordered the Mermen to open them for him. One Merman, who was obviously in charge of the others, came forward and respectfully said, "Oh Mighty Poseidon, what is your password. For you have told me to let no person, even yourself, enter without it."

Smiling, King Poseidon replied, "Yes indeed, come close and I will whisper it to you."

So saying the guard came forward and Poseidon whispered the password.

Nodding his head in agreement the Merman ordered the other guards to open the mighty doors. As the doors swung open Aliyyah gave a gasp of surprise and amazement at the sight that lay before her. This indeed was a store house piled high with treasure taken from all over the seven seas.

Shelf upon shelf was stacked with priceless pearls, precious stones and red corals of every shape and size, marble, bronze, silver and gold statues taken from sunken ships as well as chest upon chest of gold and silver coins, and priceless artefacts and costly perfume salvaged from unlucky merchant ships lay on the floor. The list went on and on.

"This is just a small part of the treasures we have collected over the centuries, but to us it has little or no value at all. Now come let us go and open your chest."

Swimming to the far end of the chamber Aliyyah saw a large silver chest guarded by a young Merman who appeared to be no older than fourteen or fifteen.

"Aliyyah this, is my son Adono. For years he has guarded this chest, waiting for your arrival."

Curious, Aliyyah asked, "How many years have you been guarding this chest?"

Seventy-eight," replied Adono. "I was twenty years old when I first started guarding it."

Astounded, Aliyyah stated, "I thought you were younger than I. Maybe fourteen or fifteen, not nearly one hundred years old!"

King Poseidon and Adono chuckled, "Aliyyah, we Merpeople are like dragons. Our lifespans are long, longer than any human life. I was already old when your teacher Mahin was born."

"What?" exclaimed Aliyyah. "You know Mahin?"

"Of course! Who do you think brought the chest here. I have known him for many centuries, fie and I are from the same origin with lifespans longer than others. We are not immortal though and we can be killed. We were given the gift of long life in order that we can always work to protect truth and peace and oppose darkness and tyranny. Now Aliyyah, before I allow you to open the chest you must answer three questions that only one who has been raised by Mahin would be able to answer. Firstly, where does Mahin stand?"

Aliyyah knew the answer to this question straight away. "Between the light and the dark, protecting one and resisting the other."

"Good," replied King Poseidon. "Your second question, what is Mahin's vocation?"

"To train the seeker who will destroy the Dark One and return peace and truth once more to these islands," Aliyyah replied.

"Thirdly, what is Mahin's favourite meat?"

Aliyyah laughed as she realised that this was a trick question. None, tor Mahin does not eat the flesh of living animals, only vegetables, fruits, nuts, herbs, wholesome bread and wild honey."

"Truly," commented King Poseidon. "You were trained by Mahin otherwise you would not have been able to answer the last question. You may now open the chest."

Slowly Aliyyah approached the antique chest made of silver and decorated with strange emblems and ancient writing. The chest was held closed with strong metal bands that were locked together with an old and solid padlock. Taking the Keys of Hanaj out of the deep pockets of her thick travelling cloak she stared first at the padlock and then the seven keys on the thick metal keyring. Each key was a different shape and size, the first key being large and the last, small. Taking the largest key she inserted it into the lock and slowly turned the key. With a loud clunking noise the padlock dropped to the floor. Then, with great effort, Aliyyah, with the help of Adono, pulled aside the metal bands and lifted the heavy lid of the chest only to find another smaller, but otherwise identical, chest sitting snugly inside. There was just enough space between the chests for a second key to be inserted and turned.

"Thank goodness for that," sighed Aliyyah as she inserted the second key into the second padlock. "We would never have been able to lift it out. It would have been much too heavy."

When the second chest was opened yet another chest was found inside, identical to the other two except for its size and colour. Whereas the first two were obviously silver this one was made of a reddish metal.

"Well, this is like playing with a Russian doll," laughed Aliyyah. "As there are seven keys on this ring I am sure there must also be seven chests." And so it was.

Finally, after opening the sixth chest, there lay inside a chest made of pure gold, slightly larger than a jewellery box, nestled in a bed of red silk. Lifting the chest out carefully, Aliyyah and Adono placed it on a small table adjacent to the open chests. A stillness filled the air as Aliyyah took the seventh and smallest golden key and inserted it into the lock. Once more there was a clunking noise as the small padlock opened and sank to the ground. Moving aside the bands that covered the chest, she opened the lid to find inside three treasures lying on a bed of blood-red velvet.

The first object was a small but strong pair of sharp golden scissors upon which were engraved the words: 'No tree or plant on land or sea can hinder me'.

The second object was a golden spoon shaped like the great soup spoons the cooks use. It too had words engraved on it, which read:

The whirlpool and the tempest
The storm and the tide
All will break and become harmless
When I am put inside.

The third and final treasure was a potent and sad one for Aliyyah, for it was none other than a golden portrait of her father. However, it too had writing engraved around the edges of the frame, which read. 'The answers to the questions of the one who guards the city dead, are within the heart of the one you love the most'.

Puzzled, Aliyyah read this several times before noticing a small star like a medal above the place where his heart would be. Resisting the urge to examine it further there and then, Aliyyah took the three objects and put them into the deep pockets of her cloak.

Praise be, Aliyyah,' said Poseidon. "With these priceless gifts in your possession you should have no problems with the seaweed forest or the Whirlpool of Infinity."

Nodding her head in agreement, Aliyyah realised that her hour was almost up. Not wanting to use up too much of the mirkweed she asked King Poseidon to return her to the surface so she could continue with her quest.

"Very well, but what shall we do with these chests?" he enquired.

"Please keep them, for I cannot carry them nor do I need them," replied Aliyyah.

"As you wish. However, as you are taking three treasures out of our store room, by the laws of the Merpeople you must leave three behind to replace those you have taken."

"What treasures can I possibly leave? All I have I need to complete the quests."

King Poseidon gave her a playful smile before asking, "How did you avoid the voices in the Castle of Mirrors?"

"By blocking my ears with wax from a candle to prevent me from hearing them," she replied.

"Then the first treasure I demand of you is a small piece of wax."

Bemused, Aliyyah broke off a small piece of her candle wax and handed it to King Poseidon, who reverently place it into the empty seventh chest.

"Now for the second treasure. What gift were you given by the Dryads?"

Worried, Aliyyah replied, "The Day Bloom but this I feel I will need to use this again."

"No, no," interrupted King Poseidon. "All I want from it is a small piece from the stalk, not the flower, as we know what is and is not."

Not understanding what King Poseidon meant she nevertheless did as she was bidden and a sliver of the stalk, hardly noticeable, was added to the chest.

"Finally, the third treasure I ask for is one hair from your head to replace the picture of your father." Seeing the doubt on her face he added, "Do not worry, for we will not use it for any evil purposes."

Still uncertain, Aliyyah looked at both her necklace and her bracelet, which remained a pure white colour indicating there was no harm in this request.

Asking King Poseidon and Adono to turn away, she removed the hood that always kept her hair hidden from sight, pulled out one of her black-red hairs and placed it herself in the chest. Quickly replacing her hood she told King Poseidon that the hair was already in the chest.

Looking at the hair in the chest, King Poseidon asked her to relock the chest and place it back inside the sixth chest. As soon as she had done this he asked his son to help her relock all the chests so no one, not even the Dark One, could open them again.

When it was done, Aliyyah returned the Keys of Hanaj back into her pockets before following King Poseidon and Adono back through the maze of passages, corridors and stairways to the courtyard, where Poseidon's chariot was waiting.

Turning to his son, Poseidon told him, "Follow us in your chariot. As your job here is finished you are to accompany Aliyyah to the home of the green turtle and aid her in whatever way you can. I charge you to protect her with your life if needs be."

Then assisting Aliyyah into his chariot he ordered the Mermen to release the reins of the seahorses. To the sound of King Poseidon s daughters bidding her farewell, Aliyyah left the magical palace of King Poseidon as the seahorses swiftly pulled them up to the surface one more.

"Aliyyah, I am sorry you were not able to stay longer and enjoy our hospitality. There are many wonders in our kingdom that I would be honoured to show you, however, at least accept this small gift from me," said Poseidon, as he gave her a golden ring crown with a perfect black pearl. "Any time you need my help, use this ring to call me, just rub the surface and I will come to your aid as swiftly as I am able. But I can only help you in the watery realms."

"Thank you," replied Aliyyah. "I will treasure your gift and maybe one day, if I am successful, I will return to visit you and see all the wonders in your kingdom."

When they reached the surface Aliyyah felt the webbed skin between her fingers and toes disappearing, as were the gills in her neck. Relieved at this she turned to see Adono in his chariot rise up beside his father. His chariot was not as magnificent as his father's but was slightly bigger, big enough for both her and Najputih to travel in as well.

As if reading her mind, King Poseidon informed her, "We thought you would be more comfortable in one of our chariots than on the back of Aquas or Mantrayrini."

Thanking King Poseidon for his help, she swam across to his son's chariot. Adono helped her into the chariot before pulling up as close as he dared to Mantrayrini, to allow Najputih to jump the small distance between them.

At first Najputih was hesitant, but with Aliyyah's encouragement he easily cleared the distance between them, rocking the chariot slightly when he landed. Relived to be off the back of the manta ray, Najputih knelt down in the chariot next to where Aliyyah was seated on a bench that was something like a dais.

King Poseidon then addressed Mantrayrini. "Thank you for carrying Aliyyah and her unicorn, and you too Aquas," he added as the dolphin started to make clicking noises. "You may go with Aliyyah if you wish or you may return to your homes with my blessing."

Mantrayrini made his funny bow once more and slowly and gracefully glided back to the deep sea that was his home.

Aquas on the other hand, swam close to the chariot, clicking, "I will follow, I will follow, I will help if I can."

Chapter Seven

The Whirlpool of Infinity

Sitting on the padded bench, Aliyyah stared at the golden picture of her father, whom she had never known. A single tear slid down her cheek as she recalled the stories that Mahin had told her of her father. "He was a good man," he would say. "A wise man who loved your mother deeply and cared for his people as a father cares for his children. When you were born, he looked into the Mirror of Dirtaq and saw his fate and your future. After that he swiftly did all he could to protect you and help you on your quest. Understand, not even I know all the steps he took to ensure your future and, I hope your success."

Wondering at the likeness of her father that even though it was in gold was so real and lifelike, made her heart ache for what could have been. Slowly she lifted the star, like medallion that was positioned above where her father's heart should be. As she did so she heard a click then a whirling sound and before her eyes a rolled up waterproof piece of parchment was gently pushed out of the frame. Aliyyah took the piece of parchment and carefully, so as not to damage it, she unrolled the yellowing manuscript. Once the parchment was open she saw lines written in her father's firm and graceful handwriting:

My clearest daughter, if you are reading this I am no more and you have already started your quest. The things that I have left you will help you on your journey, use them wisely. You will he questioned by the guardian and you must remember that all is not what it may seem. Be careful of your answers for often one word is all that is needed. Remember your training and you should pass the guardian's test. Goodbye my beloved daughter. Although you never knew me, I love you and your mother deeply. I pray to the Creator that he will permit us to be together once more in the life after this one.

Your loving father,
          King Dor.

Aliyyah read the letter several times, ignoring the questions from Najputih as she savoured every word her father had written. Finally she wrapped it up carefully before placing it along with her father's picture into one of the deep pockets of her travelling cloak.

"The letter was from my father," said Aliyyah at last to an impatient Najputih. "He gave me some advice and told me that he loved me very much."

"What else did he say?" thought the unicorn.

Nothing, nothing at all," replied Aliyyah before lapsing into silence. Najputih was wise enough to leave it at that and they sat in silence for some lime as Adono drove the seahorses on as fast as they could go.

As they travelled onwards across the azure seas, the midday sun beat down upon them, drying Aliyyah's clothes quickly. Despite the cool sea breeze that was blowing, both Aliyyah and the unicorn began to feel very thirsty. Looking at Adono who was holding the reins of the seahorses tightly, she could see that the sun was having a much worse effect on him than her. After all, he was used to living under the waves, not on top of them.

Concerned, she asked, "Adono, are you alright? You have been above the sea for some time now, are you sure the sun is not harming you?"

Smiling faintly he replied, "My father commanded me to aid you in whatever way I could, no matter what. So whatever discomfort the sun is causing me is of little consequence."

Aliyyah shook her head, not liking the idea of anyone suffering on her behalf. Quietly she tried to think off a way to make things easier for Adono and his beautiful seahorses.

"Adono," she suddenly exclaimed as a wild idea entered her head. "Will the seahorses allow anyone else to command them or just you?"

"Normally they will only obey myself or my father. Why?" asked Adono.

I was thinking that if they would allow me to drive the chariot for a while, you could return to the cool wetness of the sea. I can't bear to see you suffer like this under the sun's burning rays."

"But how would you know where to go?" interrupted Adono.

"That's simple, you could swim in front guiding the horses. Actually, all I would be doing would be holding the reins, no more than that. You would still be leading them, but in comfort not distress."

Looking at her pensively Adono told her he would think about it. "However," he warned her. "The seahorses are very strong and temperamental. Are you sure you can handle them?"

Laughing, she answered, "I think that between the two of us we can control them."

While she waited for Adono to make up his mind she called both Dark Wing and Toowooni down from the skies where they were shadowing them from above. "Dark Wing I need my water flask please."

Carefully Dark Wing flew as close as he dared with his right leg extended, on which Aliyyah's water flask hung precariously. Cautiously Aliyyah reached out and snatched her water flask. Sinking back on the padded bench she opened the stopper before taking a few sips of the cold water. Turning to Najputih she poured some of the water into his parched mouth.

"Thank you, Aliyyah. Thank you," thought Najputih as the cold water eased his burning throat.

Dark Wing's melancholy voice to drifted down from the skies above. "Aliyyah, do you need any food?"

"Not yet, Dark Wing," replied Aliyyah. "Later. Toowooni," she called, "how much further?"

Fluttering down Toowooni landed on the bench next to her. "Princess, we should reach the Whirlpool of Infinity soon. At any rate we must pass it before nightfall or we will never reach the Island of Mists in time."

"Adono what do you know about the Whirlpool of Infinity?" enquired Aliyyah.

"There are many stories concerning it," replied Adono. "What my father told me is this. Many years ago, before the rise of the Dark One, there were already some creatures that preferred to follow the path of darkness rather than the path of light. Among them was a sea witch by the name of Serenara. She was very beautiful as well as extremely powerful. After my mother died in mysterious circumstances, she aimed to take her place as the queen of the seven seas. She did everything possible to try and make my father fall in love with her. She pretended to be good and kind, publicly helping the Merpeople in all sorts of ways. However, in secret she was practicing black magic of the worst possible kind. When my father found out her true nature and the fact that she was probably responsible for his wife's sudden death, he drove her out of his palace and banished her to the depths where no Merperson dares to go. She became so angry with my father that, using her evil powers, she turned herself into a giant whirlpool determined to smash my father's palace and the homes of the Merpeople to bits and kill as many of us as possible. My father however, proved to be more powerful than her and in the ensuing battle he defeated her. My father's fury was so great that, using the ancient magic, he cursed her to remain in the form of a whirlpool for all eternity, never to change back to her original form. Our father placed her under the control of my sister, Tempest whom you have already met. However, when the Dark One's poison started corrupting our oceans, my sister lost control of her and she is now devouring, in her vengeance, all the boats, Merpeople and sea creatures that are blown near her. She cannot yet break free of my father's curse, so she must remain where she is and in the form she is in."

How sad," exclaimed Aliyyah. "Is there no way to return her to normal form, but without her powers?"

I do not know, answered Adono. "However, the dipper you have been given will stop her from sucking us down to our deaths. Whether or not it will return her to her normal form or destroy her completely, I do not know! But know this. She is so evil that even without her powers she would still remain a dangerous enemy."

"Where did she come from? Is she a Merperson as well?" asked Aliyyah.

"As to where she came from, no one really knows; some say she came from the island of the evil sirens while others say she came from the darkness of the Atlantic trench. However, she is definitely not a Merperson." Then laughing, he added, "For one thing, she has no tail!"

From up above Dark Wing's voice was heard. "Do not pity her Aliyyah, for her heart is blacker than the Dark One's although her true form is fairer. She only lives to control and destroy. Not only has King Poseidon had dealings with her, we dragons, too!"

"How is that?" exclaimed Aliyyah. "I thought that except for Err, the dragons could not enter the oceans."

"True enough, but she was not always confined to just the oceans."

"What do you mean, Dark Wing? I don't understand."

"Serenara was not always a sea witch," answered Dark Wing. "She was born a long time ago on the island of Gamic.'

"The island of the sorceresses," interrupted Adono.

"Yes, that is correct," continued Dark Wing. "Her mother was Inasu, a great and powerful woman, queen of all the other sorceresses. She was a good and powerful ruler who used her magic for the benefit of others. Her daughter, as befitting the child of the queen, was trained in the secret ways of white magic. It was expected that one day she would be as good and as wise as her mother and replace her when she passed away. However, Serenara was not satisfied with the ways of white magic and in secret started studying the forbidden books of black magic."

"But why weren't they guarded?" exclaimed Aliyyah.

"They were," said Dark Wing. "But Serenara stole the keys from her mother's chamber. Then each night she prepared a potent sleeping draught that would make the one who drank it tall into a deep slumber, only to wake when the first rays of the morning sun fell upon them. It was so cleverly made that the person who drank it would not even realise that they had been asleep and would believe that they had been awake the whole night. This potion she would put in fresh fruit juice and give it to the guards just before they went on duty. No one suspected the daughter of the queen of doing any evil, they all thought that it was just the act of a kind-hearted young woman. However, within an hour the guards would be in a deep slumber and Serenara would sneak down to the dungeons and open the doors of the forbidden library, where she would study the black books all night long. Just before sunrise she would slip out of dungeons, locking the doors before returning the keys to her mother's chambers. This went on undetected for many years as Serenara learnt the ways of evil. Soon she became more and more powerful as she began using the black magic she had learnt. Strange things started happening on the islands, students disappeared, unexplained accidents occurred and dark creatures began to be seen on an island which had always been known as the home of white magic.

"Distressed and puzzled, Kinasu realised that someone must have been studying the ancient forbidden books, but who, and how did they get past the guards and open the doors? Unaware that it was her own daughter, Kinasu set a trap for the culprit. Using a long and powerful enchantment, she bewitched the keys to the dungeons where the books were kept so that the next time that they were used, the thief s hand would stick to the keys and a loud shrieking sound would be heard throughout the island. That night Kinasu waited and just after midnight she heard the shrieking sound, as did all the people on the island. Rushing to the lower levels of the castle with her personal bodyguards, she saw the men who were supposed to be guarding the books in a deep, enchanted sleep. No matter how hard they were shaken they would not wake up and Kinasu realised that whoever was responsible had probably used the potion of Ghint, which could only be broken by the sun's rays.

"Cautiously going down the steps that lead to the dungeons she was horrified to see that the one responsible was none other than her own daughter. Heartbroken, she ordered her guards to remove Serenara and imprison her in the castle cells where no magic could work. Ignoring her daughter's pleas, she removed the enchantment on the keys and watched sadly as her daughter was led away. At her trial, Serenara was found guilty not just of the study of black magic, but also of practicing it. She was condemned to imprisonment for the rest of her life. Many of the other sorceresses had demanded her death, for they knew if she were to ever escape she would become a terrible enemy to the light. However, her mother could not bring herself to kill her only child.

"As Serenara was being taken away, some of the dark creatures that she had summoned came to her aid and in the ensuing battle she managed to escape, killing many of the other sorceresses. Where she fled to no one knows, but a few years later she returned to the island with an army of dark creatures determined to destroy the island along with all the remaining sorceresses. Kinasu sent an urgent message of help and we all flew to her aid, including Ne'alder. However, when we reached the islands Ne'alder showed her true colours and joined with Serenara against us. The battle was long and the losses on both sides were great, Greenthor lost three of his sons, two of them killed by their own mother, Ne'alder.

"Eventually, after many hours of fierce battle, we got the upper hand and Ne'alder and the remaining creatures of the dark fled, leaving Serenara to face the vengeance of her mother and the other sorceresses. As her mother raised her arms to send her daughter into oblivion, Serenara hit her with a dark curse so strong that it drew all her life force from her. We dragons were able to save her soul from being destroyed, but were unable to save her life.

"The spell that Kinasu had been reciting was uncompleted, so instead of destroying her daughter it turned her into a sea witch and condemned her to live under the sea, never to walk on the land again. She cannot even raise her head above the waves as the fresh air will kill her. The spell pulled her down to the darkest pits in the Atlantic trench where she was imprisoned.

"She swore vengeance on the dragons and all those who follow the ways of the light. She remained chained in the cold darkness for many centuries, plotting her escape and revenge, but her mother's dying enchantment was too powerful. However, when the Dark One's poison began to flow into the oceans, she somehow managed to escape her bonds. The Merpeople, not knowing her story, allowed her to stay among them. Knowing that Poseidon was one of the guardians of the light she first tried to enslave him with her beauty and when this failed she tried to destroy him."

Aliyyah remained silent, thinking about how anyone could kill their own mother or child. It seemed a crime without reason. "I understand now," she said finally. "It seems that Serenara and Ne'alder are truly evil, but I still wish we could help them. Surely there must be some spark of goodness left in them?"

"You must be careful to guard your heart Aliyyah, for they will use your pity to destroy you. They are cursed beyond all redemption for the acts they have committed. They live only to destroy and rule with tyranny. Do not feel sorry for them, for they will have no mercy on you," cautioned Dark Wing.

Aliyyah said nothing as the long hours of the day slowly ticked by. From time to time Adono allowed Aliyyah to hold the reins of the magnificent seahorses while he returned to the cool waters of the sea, unable to bear the burning rays of the sun any more. Aliyyah had no difficulties with the seahorses, for although she was holding the reins, in reality Adono was controlling the powerful creatures from beneath the waves.

Later on in the afternoon Adono returned to the chariot while Aliyyah and Najputih ate a simple meal of bread, fruit and water. After they had eaten, she asked Dark Wing to once more take the bag to look after, as she did not want the provisions spoiled by the salty seawater.

Shortly after they had finished their food, Aliyyah heard a kind of roaring, crushing sound in the distance. "Dark Wing," she cried urgently. "Fly ahead and see what is in front of us. Is it the Whirlpool of Infinity?"

Dark Wing slowly reeled upwards and flapping his powerful wings he was soon lost to sight. About ten minutes later he returned and told Aliyyah, "My Princess, it is indeed the Whirlpool of Infinity. A truly terrible sight to behold. From the air it looks like an angry, all- seeing eye swirling around and devouring even the birds that try to fly overhead. Even I felt its terrible strength. If I had gone any nearer I would have had great difficulty in escaping its pull. It is truly evil and destructive. Be very careful how you approach it or you will be pulled under before you can even use the dipper."

Aliyyah nodded her head in understanding as she thought of the best way to deal with Serenara. She did not like to risk the lives of her travelling companions, but how was she going to get close enough to use the dipper. Finally, she decided that she would have to use another piece of her precious mirkweed. Turning to Najputih and Adono she explained what she was going to do, while an anxious Toowooni, Aquas and Dark Wing listened on.

"I do not wish to risk any of your lives so I am going to use one piece of mirkweed to give me speed and manoeuvrability in the water. Then as soon as we near the whirlpool I will enter the water and allow myself to be drawn towards the centre. At the moment I feel that the whirlpool is going to swallow me, I will use the dipper. At that moment, Dark Wing and Aquas, you are to come to my aid as fast as possible, for I do not know what will happen when I use the dipper."

Straight away all her companions protested that it was much too dangerous.

"I will drive my chariot as close as I can. This is foolhardy. My father would never permit it!" protested Adono.

"It is too dangerous," pleaded both Aquas and Najputih. "There must be another way."

Only Dark Wing remained silent and pensive until finally his deep voice was heard. "Although I do not like her plan any more than the rest of you, I can see no better way of success. The mirkweed will give her the speed and agility of the Merpeople as well as the ability to breathe under water for an hour. It is a good plan and I will aid her as must all of you."

Grateful for Dark Wing's support, Aliyyah prepared herself for the coming trial. It was not long before the skies darkened even though it was still early afternoon. The clouds seemed to be drawn to the whirlpool, where they were sucked down into the dark depths of the unknown seabed. Lightning and thunder filled the air although there was no rain, only a feeling of terrible doom, a foreboding, heavy, oppressive heat that threatened to suck love, joy and happiness from the heart, leaving only despair and desperation.

Aliyyah, remembering the berries, called Dark Wing to fly low once more so she could take her bag. No sooner had she got her bag then she removed the berries before giving the bag back to Dark Wing.

"I am getting quite expert at this," she quipped as once more Dark Wind snatched the bag and bore it upwards. Aliyyah then insisted that everyone, including Aquas and the seahorses, eat one of the berries, leaving just three on the branch.

"Aliyyah," called Dark Wing, "eat all three berries, you above all of us need the strength they can give you."

Nodding her head, Aliyyah ate the berries one after another, relishing the happiness and joy that came flooding through her veins with each berry she ate. After she had eaten all three berries she felt she could defeat the Dark One himself had he been there.

Despite the terrifying roar of the angry whirlpool, Aliyyah remained unafraid as she removed her shoes and stockings. Taking a small piece of mirkweed, she placed it into her mouth and began to chew. As before, it tasted bitter and rubbery but soon became sweeter. Slowly she felt rather than saw the gills growing once more and saw that her hands and feet were now webbed. Taking the dipper from deep within her pockets, she placed it on the padded bench before removing her cloak.

"Najputih," she thought, "look after my cloak with all its treasures, please. I dare not wear it in case I lose any or the weight pulls me down."

Najputih nodded his beautiful, white head, while Dark Wing's deep voice entered Aliyyah's mind. "We will both protect it, good luck Princess."

With a determined look on her face, Aliyyah placed the dipper between her teeth before lowering herself into the turbulent waters, and started swimming boldly towards the whirlpool.

Anxiously her companions looked on as she struggled through the waves that battered her this way and that. Nearer and nearer she got and soon she felt the pull of the whirlpool reaching out to grab her and pull her down to a watery death.

Dark Wing hovered nearby, determined to pluck her from the waves if she failed, even if it meant his own death. Aliyyah waited to the last possible moment, when she felt the whirlpool grip her waist, before taking the dipper from between her teeth. With one swift movement she raised her hand up high and brought the dipper down into the whirlpool, like a samurai warrior bringing his sword down upon his enemy. A loud scream that threatened to burst the eardrums of all those near was heard as the whirlpool increased in speed before slowing down.

"Quickly, Dark Wing, Aquas, quickly, I need you," pleaded Aliyyah as she struggled to remain above the waves. The dipper suddenly seemed to weigh more than a hundred pounds as she held it close to her, fighting with all her might to prevent it from being dragged out of her hands. As she struggled she saw the whirlpool change until once more Serenara regained her original form

Pleading, the evil sea witch begged Aliyyah, "Young one, thank you for releasing me from the Dark One's spell. Now give me the dipper so I may aid you in your fight."

"No," screamed Dark Wing. "Do not listen to her lies, Aliyyah! Do not let go!"

Aliyyah held the dipper even tighter as she tried to ignore the pleading of Serenara. As Aliyyah stared at the evil witch, her features seemed to merge and change so that it appeared to be her mother pleading to her to release the dipper. When Aliyyah refused to listen, the face changed to resemble first her father, then Mahin, pleading for her to release the dipper. As the fight continued Aliyyah felt her strength, physical and emotional, begin to weaken. Mentally, she pleaded to her companions to help her.

Determinedly, Najputih and Dark Wing joined their strength together and let Aliyyah use their combined power to fight Serenara.

At the same time, Aquas and Adono made their way as swiftly as possible to where Aliyyah was fighting for her life. The battle seemed to go on for ages even though in reality it was only a few minutes, good against evil, dark against light, each struggling to defeat the other.

Finally Serenara took her terrifying dark form and began to threaten Aliyyah and all those she loved. However, Aliyyah could see she was weakening.

"No," Aliyyah suddenly declared. "I will not fall for your lies or threats. In the name of your mother whom you murdered, I banish you into the empty oblivion."

No sooner had the words left her mouth than the dipper grew red-hot in her tired hands. Unable to hold it any more she dropped the dipper, which seemed to explode into a thousand golden pieces. At the same time Serenara gave an agonising scream as she too dissolved into a thousand dark pieces and was sent to the empty void of oblivion.

Aliyyah, her strength drained, found herself slipping into unconsciousness. Before she could sink beneath the waves Aquas swam beneath her and lifted her onto his back. A few minutes later Adono arrived and he gently took Aliyyah from Aquas and laid her on the padded bench of the chariot, before covering her with her cloak.

When Aliyyah regained consciousness a few minutes later she saw all her companions around her, with Dark Wing worriedly circling above her. As she looked around she saw all traces of the whirlpool had disappeared. Both the sea and the sky were an azure blue, calm and cloudless.

"Is it over?" asked Aliyyah. "Has she gone?"

"Yes," replied Dark Wing from above. "Serenara is no more. But tell me, how did you know the way to destroy her?"

Smiling, Aliyyah replied, "Just as my strength was fading, Kinasu appeared before me and told me what words to say to send her daughter to oblivion. It was her mother's blood that she shed that was her undoing."

Dark Wing gave a grim chuckle. "It seems to me that any disobedience to your mother will be punished sooner or later."

Toowooni then hopped up. "Toowoo toowoo, if Aliyyah has recovered we must continue as quickly as we can. We still have far to go and little time to reach the Island of Mists."

Turning to her companions Aliyyah asked if they were ready to continue their journey. Nodding their heads, they prepared to restart their adventure.

Sitting back on the padded bench, Aliyyah, with Najputih by her side, let Adono take the reins of the giant seahorses, for now more than ever, speed was needed.

With Aquas swimming alongside them and Dark Wing and Toowooni flying above, they set off once again to face the seaweed forest and whatever evil lurked within it.

Chapter Eight

The Deception of King Err

The sea stretched on endlessly, mile after mile, with nothing in sight except a few wisps of white clouds in an otherwise brilliantly blue sky.

As the afternoon passed and the temperatures slowly dropped, Aliyyah found it difficult to keep her eyes open. The rocking movement of the chariot and the after effects of her fight with Serenara lulled her into an uneasy sleep. As she slept she dreamed, a horrible nightmare that she had dreamt so many times before. Again and again she saw her father lying dead at her feet his stiff fingers pointing to an unnamed danger that was creeping up behind her, ready to destroy her as it had her father.

As she slept she felt a deadly cold creeping through her until it reached her heart, like an icy hand ready to squeeze the life out of her. Slowly she turned and just as she was about to gaze upon this unknown evil she woke up with a terrible scream.

"Aliyyah, Princess," cried Adono in concern. "What is wrong?" From above came the anxious voice of Dark Wing, "My Princess, are you alright?"

Shaking herself awake, Aliyyah saw the concerned faces of her companions staring at her. "I'm alright," she quickly replied. "It was just dream, a nightmare in fact."

"Are you sure?" thought Najputih. "You seemed so frightened." "Don't worry," thought Aliyyah, so that Najputih and Dark Wing could hear her, but not the others. "It's just a nightmare I keep having. I see my father lying dead at my feet and he is trying to point to some evil behind me. As I turn I feel a deadly cold creeping through me and just as I am about to gaze on this evil, I wake up. It is like this every time and I don't really know what it means."

"But you never knew your father," thought Najputih.

"I know," replied Aliyyah. "That's what makes it so strange."

"Not really," commented Dark Wing mentally. "Even though your father died just after you were born, his spirit is still with you, watching over you and trying to protect you. I believe that these dreams are warnings from your father's spirit whenever you are approaching or are near danger. Be careful, my Princess, be very, very careful."

No sooner had Dark Wing finished these words, they saw in the distance a strange sight. A magnificent castle made of mother-of- pearl, coral and precious jewels taken from numerous wrecks rose up from beneath the blue-green waves. From the top of each sparkling tower, large black flags were flying lazily in the gentle breeze. Each flag was embroidered with a silver dragon holding a white pearl in one hand and a scroll in the other.

"It looks like the palace of King Err," said Dark Wing. "But why is he showing himself like this? Normally he is very secretive."

Unsettled by the uneasiness in Dark Wing's voice, Aliyyah glanced at her bracelet and pendant. To her horror they were flashing a bright red colour, warning her of approaching danger.

"Dark Wing," cried Aliyyah. "I thought Err was a friend of Greenthor? So why are my bracelet and necklace warning me of danger?"

"I don't know, Princess, but many creatures have fallen to the power of the Dark One. I pray King Err is not one of them for he is one of the most powerful dragons living at this time. Even though Greenthor said he was the most powerful of us, none can actually compare with Greenthor."

"In my heart I knew that already," said Aliyyah. "But what should I do now?" she asked.

"Conceal all the treasures you carry in the invisibility cloak you have, then hide them deep in the pockets of your cloak. Your necklace and bracelet, conceal them underneath your garment, that way Err will not be able to see our gifts. If he recognises any of these he will know that not only are you a seeker, but also that you have passed our tests. Whatever you do, tell him nothing directly or indirectly about the reasons for your journey until we know for sure what is going on and whether Err can still be trusted."

"Very well," agreed Aliyyah. "But what shall I tell him if he asks me what I am doing in the middle of the ocean in Adono's chariot with an owl, a unicorn and a dragon for companions? It is, to say the least, a little bit unusual!"

Laughing, Dark Wing replied, "I see your point. Let me think." After a few minutes he said, "You must tell Err that you were travelling in a ship when a terrible storm destroyed your vessel. The only survivors were you and the unicorn. As you were floating on a piece of wreckage, King Poseidon rescued you. He then asked one of his Mermen to take you and the unicorn to the nearest inhabited land and safety."

Then addressing himself to Adono, Dark Wing said, "Adono, I know that you cannot lie, but you must not tell King Err at the moment that you are taking Aliyyah to the Island of Mists. All you are to say is that you have been ordered to ensure Aliyyah's safety. Can you do that?"

Nodding his head, Adono replied, "If that is all, I will do as you say as it is the truth, if not the whole truth. However, no more than that, for you know that I am honour bound to always tell the truth."

Satisfied, Dark Wing continued, "Toowooni and I will fly up high into the cloud cover so we are concealed from sight. Err being a sea dragon cannot communicate telepathically, nor does he know when others are. So when you need me, call me that way. Now we must fly higher before we are spotted. Come Toowooni, quickly, come!"

Apprehensively Aliyyah watched as the palace stopped rising and floated on the top of the waves themselves. A few minutes later a loud fanfare was heard as the drawbridge, made of glittering gold and silver, was slowly lowered revealing a double door made of solid silver and embedded with priceless pearls and sparkling jewels. Slowly the doors opened and a guard of strange creatures, which seemed to half glide, half swim out of the palace, appeared. Their bodies resembled humans, but their heads were those of fish and other sea creatures. As Aliyyah looked on, fascinated, she saw a giant chariot made of pure gold and drawn by seven small silver grey dragons leave the palace and make their way towards the chariot she was in. Inside this chariot was King Err himself.

He was a brilliant-looking dragon covered with silver scales that glittered and winked in the sunlight. He was obviously very old and unlike the other dragons he had a long thin beard and moustache, which gave him a rather oriental look. His wings were small unlike the large powerful wings of the other dragons, but living underneath the sea he did not really have any use for wings larger than he had.

Sitting in the chariot with him was a beautiful young woman with long black hair that flowed down her back and shoulders and was braided with pearls and small jewels. Her eyes were big, black and deep, as deep as the ocean she lived in. She had a kindly face with generous lips that naturally smiled gently. She was dressed in a long flowing robe of rich silk, but when the chariot came closer Aliyyah saw to her utmost amazement that only the top half of her was human. From the waist down she was a dragon!

Dark Wing," thought Aliyyah quickly. "Who is this woman who is half human and half dragon?"

Sighing deeply Dark Wing replied, "Then it is as we dragons had secretly feared, Err has broken the dragons' law."

"What do you mean?" queried Aliyyah. "I don't understand."

A short time ago some of the sea creatures who work secretly for the Council of Dragons told us that many years ago Err saw a beautiful princess travelling on a magnificent ship with her entourage. She was on her way to be married to a prince of a distant country. However, Err became infatuated with her and kidnapped her along with her entourage. He forced the princess to marry him and changed her entourage into the creatures you see now, so that they could never return to their homeland to inform their king of what had happened. Now they are forced to serve him. This woman you see now must be the result of this unnatural union and the reason why we dragons have had no news from Err for many a long year. It is also why your bracelet and necklace warned you of danger."

'I still don't understand," thought Aliyyah. "How can Err have a relationship with this woman and what danger?"

"Aliyyah, a dragon as powerful as Err also has the ability to take human form for short periods of time. However, it is forbidden under our laws and by the ancient magic to marry a human, willingly or by force. If a dragon breaks any of our laws they cross over to the dark side and lose their goodness. The only acceptable punishment is exile or death. Obliviously Err has chosen neither, so I fear that he has chosen to follow the Dark One. Be careful what you do and say. Remember, however, you still know his secret name and he will have to obey you, but in the case of a dragon who has rebelled you can only use his name three times. Use this weapon wisely. I don't know what he wants you for, but be wary, he is clever and cunning, do not let him trap you!"

Dark Wing had just finished his warning when the chariot pulled up in front of them and King Err, in his deep voice, hailed them.

"Welcome, strangers, to my domain. Please tell me, what is a young girl and a unicorn doing in the chariot of one of King Poseidon's sons?" Then he added slyly, "It is Adono is it not?" Err hoped to trap them into revealing that they were on the quest.

Quickly, before Adono could say anything, Aliyyah replied, "We were travelling in a ship when we were hit by a terrible storm and our vessel was wrecked. We would have surely drowned if King Poseidon had not rescued us when he did. Now he has commanded one of his Mermen to take us to the nearest inhabitable land and leave us there.

A strange look entered King Err's eyes as he said, "I see, well the nearest land is the Island of Mists, but no one lives there. You will have to travel on at least two weeks journey to reach the nearest inhabited lands. It is a very long journey."

"It is of no matter," replied Aliyyah. "We have trust in King Poseidon and we know he has ordered that we be brought to our destination safely and swiftly."

"I see," muttered King Err. "Anyhow, I am forgetting my manners. This is my daughter, the Princess Errina, and we insist that you take some refreshments with us before you continue your journey, we have so few visitors."

Aliyyah felt rather than saw both her necklace and bracelet grow hot, warning her of the danger. "We are honoured, but I feel that it is better we continue our journey as soon as possible."

A hard and calculating tone entered King Err's voice. "We insist, only for a short while. You will need our protection in these waters for there are many hidden dangers here."

Unwillingly Aliyyah was forced to accept. Err had made it quite clear that if she refused his hospitality he would make sure some terrible things would happen.

"Very well," she replied. "But only for a short while as we are anxious to reach our destination."

"Good, very good," said Err as he rubbed his claws together. But wait, you have not told me your name, or the unicorn's."

Aliyyah was not going to reveal either her name or the unicorn's, for it seemed obvious now that Err was indeed their enemy.

"I have many names, but most people just call me Princess. As for the unicorn, he cannot speak so he cannot tell me his name," replied Aliyyah, not lying, but not telling the whole truth.

King Err seemed to realise this and with a hint of frustration in his voice he commanded, "Well then, please follow me as the food is all prepared. Come, enter my chariot for I am sure that the unicorn and the Merman will not be offended if I ask them to wait outside the drawbridge for you."

"They are not invited?" enquired Aliyyah.

"My dear," explained Err. "The Merman needs water and as my palace is now above the waves, how would he enter? And if I take it below the waves how would you breathe? As for the unicorn, I know from experience that they do not like dragons. However, I will order my servants to pack a basket of the most delicious food for you to bring back and share with them."

Looking meaningfully at Adono she asked him to wait for her. As she stepped carefully from one chariot to another Najputih begged Aliyyah, "No Aliyyah, no, don't go."

"I have no choice," thought Aliyyah. "Don't worry, I will be very careful. As soon as we have entered the palace, call Dark Wing and ask him to be ready to carry me away from the palace as soon as I call him. Then ask him to tell Adono to get as far away from the palace as possible. I want both of you out of harm's way. We will rejoin you as soon as we can and please, Najputih, do not argue with me, I know what I am doing."

As she entered King Err's chariot she saw a deep sadness in the eyes of his daughter

"Please, sit next to my daughter, it will only take a few minutes to reach the palace."

Sitting next to Errina she politely answered as many of the princess's questions as she dared. To her dismay Aliyyah realised that Errina was very clever and knew almost certainly that she was a seeker. Dread entered her heart, but at the same time she was determined to find a way out of her present situation.

As they entered the palace and the chariot came to a stop, King Err asked her to follow him to the banqueting hall. Errina looked at her directly, and she could see that some sort of battle was going on in Errina's heart. As she stared at Aliyyah it seemed that suddenly she had come to some kind of a decision.

As Aliyyah got up to leave the chariot, Errina gently touched her arm and quickly whispered to her so her father could not hear. "Do not eat any of the food or you will be turned into a servant like the entourage of my mother. Instead, as soon as you come to the banqueting hall, ask my father if there is somewhere you can tidy yourself first."

Nodding her head slightly in understanding, Aliyyah made her way into the palace behind King Err. Surprisingly, for a building that less than half an hour ago had been underwater, the palace was dry with orbs of luminous light floating above their heads. Everywhere she looked the walls were richly decorated with pictures made of embedded jewels telling story after story as they walked deeper and deeper into the palace. At last, after walking up a grand flight of marble stairs, they entered the grand banqueting hall. It was truly a magnificent sight. The room was round with full sized French windows made of coloured glass running along three sides of the walls. These windows had been flung open so a pleasant sea breeze blew in keeping the room light and cool. From the ceiling hung a great chandelier, no doubt taken from some grand ship that had sunk to the bottom of the sea. The table was long and made of red coral that had been painstakingly carved into intricate and detailed panels. Each panel told its own story. The chairs were made of the same red coral, beautiful, but hard and cold. The table had been laid with a multitude of sumptuous foods served on platters of solid gold and silver. Also on the table were tall golden flasks of some strange drink waiting, ready to be served. At the head of the table stood a magnificent chair that was more like a throne and which was obviously intended for King Err.

In the corner of this grand room was a small dais on which stood a group of musicians ready to serenade the king as he ate.

113

On the fourth side of the room were several small doors, which led to washrooms where one could refresh and tidy oneself before eating.

Motioning Aliyyah to the table he asked her to be seated and partake of the food and drink that had been prepared.

"Thank you, King Err," replied Aliyyah graciously. "But is there somewhere that I could wash and tidy myself up first?"

Amused, King Err ordered one of the servants to show her to a washroom. Silently a servant who had the head of a porpoise took her over to a washroom and opened the golden door for her. Slipping inside she found Errina already inside waiting for her.

"Quickly," she said, "for my father will not wait long. You are a seeker, are you not?"

Cautiously Aliyyah replied, "And what if I am?"

"Answer truthfully," demanded Errina. "For if you are, we may be able to help one another."

"What do you mean?" asked Aliyyah.

"My father," explained Errina, "has very powerful magic, which for many years he used wisely and for the benefit of all. Then one day he saw my mother standing on the deck of the royal ship and fell deeply and uncontrollably in love with her. Ignoring the ancient law of the dragons he forced my mother to marry him while he turned her advisors, maids and guards into the servants you see here."

"Is your mother still alive?" asked Aliyyah.

"It depends on what you mean by alive," sobbed Errina. "After she tried to escape so many times my father imprisoned her in the tallest tower in this palace. No one except her personal maid, my father and myself are allowed to see her. My mother, sadness and longing for her homeland and her freedom from her forced marriage with my father is so great that it is slowly killing her. Every day I feel my heart will break as I watch her slowly fading away. I have pleaded so many times with my father to allow her to return to her own people, but he refuses to listen and becomes enraged whenever I mention her sadness."

"I see," said Aliyyah gently. "But how can I help you and what does your father want with me?"

"My father says he knows who you really are and he wishes to enslave you then trade you to the Dark One, in return for a powerful potion that will make my mother forget her past and fall deeply in love with him. He is also demanding that in return for your capture, the Dark One must help him to defeat King Poseidon so that he can become the master of all the oceans. Even that is not enough for him, as he is also plotting to extend his kingdom above the waves and is willing to destroy all those who stand in his way. He has no fear of the consequences as he knows that under dragon law his punishment is death for what he has done. I cannot support him in this madness and secretly I have been trying to help King Poseidon. No one knows about this, not even his sons, for my very life would be forfeited if my father knew what I was doing. I can help you escape from this palace, but in return you must free my mother and her entourage and make sure they return to their home. I ask you again, are you a seeker?" Sensing she could trust Errina she finally replied, "Yes, I am." Heaving a sigh of relief, Errina continued, "And as a seeker you must also be a dragon friend?"

Nodding her head, Aliyyah replied, "That I am."

"Do you know a dragon called Greenthor, the greatest of all dragons, even more powerful than my father?" asked Errina.

"Yes, I do," Aliyyah said.

"Did he by any chance reveal to you my father's secret name or give you some kind of token?" continued Errina.

"He gave me both," replied Aliyyah.

"Thank goodness," exclaimed Errina. "We may yet succeed! Now listen carefully and do exactly as I tell you. I have arranged that some of the dishes are not affected by my father's magic and are quite safe to eat. These dishes will be served by the servant who has a head like a dolphin. Do not eat the food that is served by any other servant or we are lost. When you have finished your meal you are to ask permission to continue your journey. Knowing my father, when he sees that you are unaffected by his magic he will lose his temper and try to harm you. The moment he turns to attack you must call him by his secret name. He will be shocked and enraged, but by the ancient magic he will be forced to obey you three times. Firstly you are to command him to release my mother and all of her entourage, turning the back to their original forms. Secondly you are to command him to return to them their ship, fully provisioned and seaworthy, and to allow them to return to their homeland unharmed. Lastly you are to command him to swear an unbreakable oath that he will never try to topple King Poseidon in any way, or aid the Dark One or any of his creatures.

My father will be forced to obey you as even he cannot fight the ancient magic. At first he will be overcome with sadness at losing my mother and he will watch her as she disappears into the horizon. While this is going on you must flee the palace as quickly as you can, for my father, once he can no longer see my mother, will pursue you, determined to destroy you in revenge. Show me, what token did Greenthor give you?"

Aliyyah removed the small piece of bark that Greenthor had given her, covered in strange writing, and showed it to Errina.

"Good," commented Errina. "Greenthor is very wise. He must have suspected that something was wrong while hoping that everything was still alright. When my father chases you, throw this in the water behind you and recite 'hamdan ruguni hamdan lasani'. It will grow and form a magical wall that my father will not be able to pass through, and you will be safe. However, you must never return this way again unless my father is no more, as he will never forgive you and will remain your enemy for the rest of his life."

Thanking Errina, Aliyyah turned to leave the restroom. Half way across she stopped and turned to face Errina once more. "What about you? Will you be safe?"

"Don't worry about me," replied Errina. "If all goes as planned my father will not suspect me at all and he will need someone to comfort him."

"I suppose so," commented Aliyyah. "But is there anything I can do for you in return for your help?"

"Setting my mother free is payment enough, but if you do get to see the wise turtle, ask him if there is any way that I can be changed from the form I have now. Tell him it does not matter which, either to become human or dragon, but not half and half. However, if possible I wish to become human and leave the seas and live with my mother above the waves."

From outside the door Aliyyah and Errina could hear King Err calling Aliyyah to hurry up. "Go now and I will join you in a few minutes," said Errina as she left the washroom by a hidden door.

Stepping out of the washroom, she saw King Err waiting impatiently for her.

"Please be seated, you must be very hungry by now. Let us eat and talk, we do not have very many guests here. Now, where is my daughter? She should be here to entertain you as well."

No sooner had King Err finished his sentence then his daughter glided into the room accompanied by two of her handmaidens - both had heads shaped like dolphins. Errina had quickly changed her clothes and was now wearing a rich robe of Chinese brocade embroidered with bright yellow flowers, the centre of each flower being a glittering, bright, blood-red ruby. The robe was so long it had to be held by her handmaidens and completely covered her dragon body. In her hair was a bright red sea flower, a kind Aliyyah had never seen before, and strings of white, perfect pearls hung around her slender neck.

Aliyyah looked at her in amazement. How on earth did she manage to change so quickly? Surely her father could never suspect that she had been talking to her.

"I am sorry if I am a little bit late," she said sweetly. "But I thought in honour of our guest, I would change my dress."

Smiling at his daughter, King Err replied, "No matter, you look very beautiful, my daughter." Errina sat down and smiled gently at Aliyyah.

King Err clapped his hands and the servants stepped forward, each carrying a different dish on a golden platter, which they showed to the diners before serving it. The first course served to Aliyyah by a dolphin-headed servant, was a soup, rich, golden with an aroma something like chicken. Looking towards Errina she saw her nod her head ever so slightly to indicate it was safe to eat.

Cautiously Aliyyah took her spoon and, taking a small sip, she found that the soup was as delicious as it looked. Watching King Err, she slowly finished her soup while she listened to all he had to say.

After the soup came a salad made from seaweed, shrimps and vegetables Aliyyah did not recognise. Once more she looked at Errina before daring to eat even one mouthful. As they ate Aliyyah did her best to avoid answering, as carefully as possible, any questions that King Err asked, while at the same time trying not to appear rude or offend the dragon king. Course after course was served until finally the dessert arrived. It was some sort of sea trifle shaped like King Err's palace and made of many multi-coloured layers.

"Ah, you must try this, Aliyyah," commented King Err. "This is truly a culinary masterpiece."

Aliyyah quickly glanced at Errina to see her shake her head warningly.

"I am sure it is, but I have eaten so much that I could not eat any more."

Disappointed, King Err said, "Are you sure? It is really the most delicious trifle you will ever eat, one that would change the way you are forever."

"I am sure," replied Aliyyah. "I don't wish to offend you by being sick, and that is what will happen if I eat another mouthful."

Nodding his head, King Err watched Aliyyah intently as if he expected something to happen to her any minute. As the seconds slowly ticked by Aliyyah waited to see what was going to happen. Finally she said, "Thank you so much for your hospitality, but I must continue my journey, so with your permission I will return to the chariot."

No sooner had she finished talking than a change came over King Err. His eyes darkened, his nostrils flared and small flecks of fire seemed to dance within, while his whole body looked ready to pounce on Aliyyah like a cat waiting to jump on a cornered rat.

"What magic have you being using? How come you have not been affected by the food?" he snarled. "Now I will have to deal with you the hard way."

Aliyyah waited for Err to move and the moment he seemed ready to spring, she quickly stood and in a loud voice declared, "Err, by your secret name, I command you to obey me in three things!"

Infuriated, Err challenged Aliyyah, "I do not believe you know my secret name."

"Oh yes, I do. It was entrusted to me by Greenthor, for I am a dragon friend. Come closer and I will whisper it to you, unless you wish me to say it out loud for all to hear and command you."

Frustrated and fearfully, King Err came close to Aliyyah and bent his magnificent head down so that she could whisper into his ear. The colour drained from his face as he realised that Aliyyah did indeed know his secret name and by the ancient magic he would be forced to obey her.

"Well, it seems I have no choice but to do as you say. I underestimated you, you are much cleverer than I anticipated, but I think you must have had some help as well."

Seeing that she must be very careful how she answered or risk putting Errina in mortal danger, she pulled back the sleeve of her garment to reveal her bracelet and pulled the necklace out from under her cloak so it once more lay across her chest, before saying, "I am a seeker who has passed the test of the dragons. As a reward for answering all their riddles correctly, each dragon gave me a gift to help, protect me and warn me of any and all dangers. If that is the help you are talking about, then yes, I had help."

"None of my servants helped you?" Err asked slyly.

"When have I had the chance to talk to any of them?" retorted Aliyyah. Still not satisfied, King Err was about to ask another question when Aliyyah said in a firm voice, "Do not waste any more of my time. Now you must obey me or be destroyed. The first thing I command you to do is to release the princess you kidnapped along with her entourage, making sure you remove all your spells on them first so that they return to normal."

King Err began to tremble, partly from anger and partly from a sorrow so great it was threatening to break his heart into pieces. "Do not command me to this, I beg you. It was because of the princess that I broke the dragons' law in the first place. If the Council of Dragons find out what I have done..."

"They already know," interrupted Aliyyah.

"Then you know that now if they catch me either my life will be forfeited or I will be exiled! Do you know where they exile dragons, especially sea dragons?"

"No," said Aliyyah, "it is not my business to know such things." "There is a valley hidden between two mountains. A black, barren valley where nothing can thrive. It is guarded by the ancient magic, which will prevent any dragon who has been condemned to live there from ever escaping. For any dragon confined there it is a fate worse than death and death is the only escape."

Out of curiosity Aliyyah asked, "Then how did Ne'alder escape?" Wearily King Err explained, "Ne'alder is a wild dragon and although she is still bound by the ancient magic, she is not bound by dragon law, so the valley would never be able to hold her. She was imprisoned instead in the stone caverns used to punish the wild dragons who break the laws of men and dragons, and cause problems and trouble to others."

Firmly, Aliyyah said, "Still, you must do as I command or face the consequences of your actions."

"Princess, have pity. If you force me to release my wife you will break my heart and I will have no reason to go on living."

Although she felt sorry for Err's distress she nevertheless replied, "I am sorry, King Err, but I have sworn to release all those imprisoned by magic. What you did was wrong. I cannot help you. Now do as I order or face your own destruction."

Not daring to disobey Aliyyah, commands' he ordered one of the servants to bring the princess down from her locked room in the highest tower of the palace. As they waited, King Err continued to plead with Aliyyah not to take his wife away from him. After about ten minutes the princess, who was dressed in rare and expensive silks and adorned with priceless pearl and diamond necklaces and bracelets, appeared before them in the banqueting hall. As Aliyyah looked upon her she realised where Errina got her great beauty from, but she was also struck by the great sadness and hopelessness in her eyes

"You summoned me," said the princess without raising her eyes and with a voice that was devoid of all emotion.

"My love, this young girl has ordered me to release you and all your entourage and I have no choice but to do so, unless you agree to stay with me of your own free will."

At first, the princess kept quiet, then slowly she raised her head and, looking at Aliyyah, she asked in a voice that had just a hint of hope in it, "Is this true?"

"Yes," replied Aliyyah. "I know King Err's secret name so now he has to obey me three times and I have commanded him to release you and your entourage."

Turning to King Err the princess said, "All these years, although you have treated me well, I have hated you for what you have done in me and my people. That is why I tried to escape from you so many times, and when you confined me to my rooms in the tower I wished only for death to come quickly and release me from the nightmare you have forced me to live. I can never forgive you for what you have done and I hope that you will be punished for your acts. Neva would I agree to stay here for even one minute more than I am forced too,"

King Err's body shook as he heard these words, but before he could say or do anything Aliyyah reminded him he still had to remove the spell he had placed on her entourage and release them as well from their bondage.

In words that Aliyyah could not understand or even hear properly, King Err began the incantation to set the servants free. As before when Greenthor released the failed seekers, one colour after another appeared until a blinding white light filled the room. When Aliyyah could see properly once more she saw that all the servants had been returned to normal and there were no longer any fish-headed servants left. Looking at each other and at their beloved princess they began to cry with joy as they embraced each other, before turning to Aliyyah to thank her for breaking the evil spell on them.

Nodding her head Aliyyah once more turned to face King Err. "My second command is that you return them to the ship they were on when you captured them, make it seaworthy and provision it fully and let them return to their homeland safely without any harm. Do it now, for I know that you still have very powerful magic and it will be no difficulty for you to do this straight away."

"No!" screamed King Err. "No, please, no, you will kill me."

"Do it or die," replied Aliyyah firmly. "Now!"

In a voice that betrayed his sorrow he commanded the ship to rise up from the bottom of the sea. As they watched from the banqueting windows the saw the ship appear. At first all they could see was the top of the masts, but before long the whole vessel was floating merrily on top of the sea. The ship was, as Aliyyah had ordered, seaworthy and frilly provisioned. Turning to the princess, she told her, "You are free to go, return to your homeland in safety with your entourage. However, I advise you never to travel across the oceans again."

Embracing Aliyyah with tears in her eyes, she thanked her again and again before bending close to her and whispering, "What about my daughter? Can you help her?"

"I do not know," replied Aliyyah truthfully. "For the time being she must stay here and if I can help her, I will, that I promise."

Nodding her head in understanding the princess said goodbye to Aliyyah, before going over to Errina to say goodbye to her as well. As the princess left the palace with her entourage, King Err call her name again and again only to be ignored by her.

Desperately he called her as she embarked on the royal ship, but not once did she turn back to look at him or answer his cries.

Aliyyah knew that King Err would soon turn on her so she quickly said, "King Err, my third command to you is that you, here and now, swear an oath that you will never try to attack King Poseidon or leave the sea to attack anyone on the land. You must also swear never to aid the Dark One or any of his servants."

"You are wise but cruel, Aliyyah," replied Err. "Not only have you robbed me of my love, but also destroyed all my plans. I swear to do all you say."

Laughing, Aliyyah replied, "Do not think I am a fool, King Err. You must say, 'by the ancient magic I, King Err, swear never to attack King Poseidon or anyone on the land above. I also swear never to aid the Dark One or any of his servants in any way'! Say it now!"

King Err was looked at her. Aliyyah could see a cruel gleam enter his eye, as he repeated the words that Aliyyah had commanded him to say. As he finished, he turned to her and said, "You are a fool, I have sworn not to harm others, but you forgot to ask me to swear not to harm you. Now I will destroy you for what you have done."

At that precise moment a cannon shot was heard and Err turned to see the ship carrying his beloved wife slide away from the palace and begin its journey back to where it came from. This was the chance Aliyyah had waited for. Running quickly to the open window she cried out mentally, "Now, Dark Wing, now. Quickly!"

As King Err turned once more towards Aliyyah, Dark Wing swooped down from the skies and snatched the young girl out of danger's way. "Hold on tight, Aliyyah. We must fly far and fast to get away from King Err."

"Where are Adonis and Najputih?" thought Aliyyah.

"They are safe, but we must flee now. We will rejoin them when we are out of King Err's reach. Now hold on," he finished as he soared up into the blue skies with Aliyyah holding on for dear life.

Chapter Nine

The Seaweed Forest

The waves seemed to rush past as Aliyyah dangled precariously from the talons of Dark Wing. Even though she knew that the dragon would not drop her, she began to feel her arms ache while her shoulders felt as if they were going to rip any minute.

"Dark Wing," she thought, "I do not know how much longer I can hold on!"

"Do not worry, Princess, just up ahead there is an outcrop of rocks just big enough for you to stand on. I will drop you there as gently as I can and then I will try to land next to you. As soon as you can you must climb up onto my back and sit between my wings, near my neck."

Nodding her head, Aliyyah gazed at the sea beneath her, looking left and right for the outcrop. Within a few seconds she saw the black rocks sticking out of the ocean like sharp pointed needles on a pin cushion. How was Dark Wing going to land there?

"Aliyyah," she heard Dark Wing call. "I cannot land there, but if you look closely at the rocks, in the middle there is a clear space just big enough for you to jump on to. When you have landed, make your way to the edge of the outcrop. There is one rock taller than the others that has a flat top. Climb up to the top and as soon as you are there, I will fly as close to it as I can and you must try to jump onto my back. Be careful, the rocks are sharp. Have you anything to wrap around your hands?"

"Yes, Dark Wing in the pockets of my travelling cloak, I have a pair of leather gloves, they are soft, but very strong!"

"Good! Now get ready," said Dark Wing as he flew as low as he could over the centre of the outcrop. "Jump now."

Without thinking about it, Aliyyah let go of Dark Wing's talons and tumbled into the middle of the rocks, rolling to break her fall. Slightly winded, she was nevertheless unharmed. Standing up she brushed her hands on her cloak before reaching into her pockets for the leather gloves. As she put them on she looked around for the rock Dark Wing had told her to climb. As she stared she saw the rock he was talking about, but at the same time, it looked very difficult to climb being almost sheer. Putting her doubts behind her, she picked her way towards the edge of the outcrop and the tall rock. As she got nearer she saw it was not as sheer as she had thought and that she should be able to climb it, though with some difficulty.

From above came the voice of Dark Wing, "Aliyyah, swiftly, we do not have much time, Err will soon be after us and I cannot match his magic."

With a look of determination upon her face, Aliyyah started to climb. Searching for holds with her hands and her feet she inched her way up until she managed to scramble onto the flat top of the rock.

"Dark Wing where are you?" called Aliyyah, unable to see the dragon.

"Here, just below you," replied Dark Wing as he tried to hover as steadily as he could. "You are going to have to jump again, can you manage it?"

"I think so," replied Aliyyah. "But if I fall, make sure you catch me." Then with a dogged look on her face she backed away to the edge of the rock and taking a few running steps, she launched herself into the air, aiming to land on Dark Wing's back. With a heavy thud she found herself clutching Dark Wing's neck while one leg dangled in the air. Still hovering, Dark Wing waited until she had managed to pull herself up into a sitting position between his massive wings.

No sooner had she settled herself Dark Wing cried, "Hold tight, Princess, here we go." Then beating his powerful wings they quickly rose up into the air and flew in the direction of the Island of Mists. Exhilarated, Aliyyah felt the wind blowing through her hair as they sped forward.

"Dark Wing this is amazing," said Aliyyah. "I've never ridden on a dragon before except for the short ride Wild Wind gave me. I never imagined it could be like this!"

Giving his distinctive laugh, Dark Wing replied, "Yes, Princess, now you can truly call yourself a dragon rider."

Curiously Aliyyah asked, "Have you ever carried a person before?"

Dark Wing remained quiet for a while before replying, "I am not old enough to remember the time of the dragon riders. You are the first person I have allowed to ride me and you will probably be the only one that I will ever allow to ride me."

Humbled, Aliyyah replied, "I am greatly honoured, Dark Wing. Thank you for trusting me enough to allow me to ride you."

"An honour you have earned, Princess. You set us free, saved Wild Wind, rescued Greenthor's last egg - you have more than proved your trustworthiness."

Embarrassed and at the same time happy, Aliyyah said nothing, forgetting everything for the moment as she enjoyed flying through the air on Dark Wing's back. However, they were not out of danger, as before long they heard a loud rushing sound behind them, like the strong wind that precedes a tropical storm. Turning her head she saw King Err pursuing them in his silver chariot drawn by the seven small dragons. Behind him the clouds were darkening as he muttered an evil incantation. As she watched, the sea behind her rose up like a giant hand ready to swat them as if they were a pair of flies.

"Faster, Dark Wing, faster," cried Aliyyah.

"I am flying as fast as I can," he replied. "I am afraid I cannot out- fly Err. Only Wild Wind is fast enough to do that."

"Never mind," said Aliyyah. "I will use the charm that Greenthor gave me. Errina told me that it would protect us from her father."

Quickly but carefully she removed the wood from her pocket and recited, "Hamdan ruguni hamdan lasani," before throwing it behind her into the dark green wave. No sooner had the wood hit the water than the wave froze before dropping back down to its normal level. At the same time the sky was filled with one light after another, each one more brilliant than the next. As the colours faded Aliyyah saw a shimmering wall like a rainbow stretching across the sea as fast as the eye could see. It was beautiful, but at the same time, it seemed so fragile she wondered how it was going to stop King Err.

As she watched, fascinated, King Err reached the barrier and as he tried to ride through it he was thrown back, almost as if he had been struck by lightning. Charging at the barrier a second time the same thing happened. Again and again Err charged the barrier only for the same thing to happen. Infuriated, he threw one spell after another at the barrier trying to break through, but to no avail. He could not cross the magical barrier at all.

As Dark Wing and Aliyyah sped away she heard King Err shouting, "I will get you, Aliyyah. Somehow I will get you! I will make you pay for what you have done, just you wait and see."

"Well done, Aliyyah. How did you know the light spell?"

"The light spell? What is that?"

Laughing, Dark Wing replied, "What you just did, Aliyyah, what else? It is an ancient magic that prevents anything or anyone who has evil intentions from passing through, while letting everything else pass."

"It was Errina who taught me. She has been helping Poseidon without her father knowing and she has asked for my help as well." replied Aliyyah.

"In what manner?" enquired Dark Wing.

"Errina is unhappy being half dragon, half human. She has asked me to find a way to change her to either a full dragon or totally human, not half and half. She would prefer to become human so she can live with her mother on the land, but she would be satisfied to be a dragon if she must."

"I have never heard of this being done before," commented Dark Wing. "But if anyone knows the way it will be Greenthor, Mahin or the wise turtle, but I know for sure that neither Greenthor nor Mahin will ever tell you as it is against the laws they swore to obey."

Concerned, Aliyyah asked, "Does that mean I cannot help her?" "No, Aliyyah, you can still help her if you find the way. Greenthor and Mahin are guardians of the light and have great powers, but in order to protect themselves as well as others from misuse of these powers, there are strict laws they observe. The Dark One was also, at one time, one of the guardians of light, but he broke their laws and allowed himself to be corrupted by evil."

Relieved, Aliyyah said, "That is good as I have promised to try and help her and so far I have never broken a promise."

"Good, that is very good, Aliyyah," continued Dark Wing. "But I fear that even if you find the way you will have to fight with her father and defeat him before you can aid her. Remember, next time will not be so easy, you no longer have the advantage of knowing his secret name. Not just that, but you have freed his wife and her servants and forced him to make promises he knows he cannot break. His heart will be filled with hatred towards you and he will live daily in sorrow and anger waiting for any chance to take his revenge upon you. The only way you can help his daughter in the long run is to kill her father, but that may also backfire and turn her against you, for no matter what, he is still her father."

"Is there no other way?" asked Aliyyah.

"Unless you can trap him in the valley where the dragons who break the law are imprisoned, I do not know. Maybe the wise turtle will be able to answer that question for you." Then Dark Wing saw the chariot of Adono below. "Aliyyah, the chariot is below, do you wish to join Najputih or do you wish me to carry you further?"

Smiling, Aliyyah replied, "I really should join Najputih, but if you will carry me I would like to fly with you for a while longer."

In reply, Dark Wing did a sudden dive, almost touching the waves before pulling out and raising up into the sky again.

Laughing, Aliyyah said, "Dark Wing, if I did not know better I would think you were playing!"

Chuckling, he replied, "Really, even we dragons have a sense of humour, despite rumours to the contrary. I just wanted to give you a taste of what it is like to be a real dragon rider. I would have done a somersault, but you have no saddle to hold on to."

"Don't you dare," exclaimed Aliyyah. "I have to face enough danger without falling off the back of a somersaulting dragon."

"Don't worry, Princess I will never drop you, there is no jewel more precious than you."

Alarmed, Aliyyah quickly replied, "Dark Wing do not give your heart to me, please, I don't want any harm to come to you."

Firmly Dark Wing replied, "I am not that young a dragon, Aliyyah. I am older than Wild Wind and wise to the ways of the world. I do love you, but not in the way that Wild Wind has fallen into, but as a father loves a child. I have had many eggs and my love for you is the same as my love towards my hatchlings. I would give my life for you, but I will not die as you must one day long before me, as my heart is still very much my own. You have no need to worry, Princess."

Relieved, Aliyyah smiled once more. "Thank you, Dark Wing, thank you. Now I had better tell Najputih and Adono that I am travelling with you for a while. Can we fly nearer the chariot so I may talk to them?"

Without replying Dark Wing swooped down and flew alongside Adono and Najputih. Toowooni was there as well, perched on the bench next to the unicorn, half asleep.

"Adono," shouted Aliyyah. "How much further is it to the Island of Mists?"

"Not far now," replied Adono. "But we still have to pass the seaweed forest."

"Aliyyah," interrupted Najputih. "Are you coming back into the chariot?"

Laughing, Aliyyah replied, "If you don't mind, I prefer to fly for a while. I never knew that it was so exhilarating and I don't want to get wet again just yet. Don't be upset, I will join you again soon."

Najputih remained quiet, almost as if he was sulking, but in his heart he rather envied Aliyyah at that moment. Dark Wing seemed to know what the unicorn was feeling for he said, in a teasing voice that made the others laugh, "Najputih, don't be jealous. After Aliyyah I can give you a ride as well, but in your case I will have to carry you in my talons. I don't think that you can stand on my back without falling off!"

With a snort and a toss of his beautiful white mane, Najputih replied, "If unicorns were meant to fly they would have been given wings, thank you!"

"Najputih," declared Aliyyah. "Don't be upset, we still have a long journey to go and I won't be flying the whole way."

Dark Wing then soared upwards again. They flew sometimes in front of the chariot and sometimes behind. As they travelled Aliyyah asked Dark Wing if he knew anything about the seaweed forest.

"Not much Aliyyah. It is said that long ago in ancient times there was a was a woman whose hair was a mass of living, writhing snakes. She had been cursed for telling the people what was going to happen in the future without permission to do so. Anyone who looked at her would be turned into stone forever. She was said to be the sister of another creature called Suraya. However, she lived in the sea where as her sister lived on the land. Do not get confused with Medusa, who was slain by one of the Greek heroes, although their stories are quite similar. Eventually the creatures who lived in the sea complained to King Poseidon, who sent his son Aquaisa to slay this creature. After a long and tierce fight, Aquaisa managed to separate her head from her body, but as soon as the head touched the ground the snakes turned into brown seaweed and rapidly spread along the seabed. These weeds grabbed Aquaisa, trying to squeeze the life out of him. They would have succeeded if his father had not intervened.

"By the power of his trident he freed his son, however, the seaweed kept growing until it formed a great forest. Anything that went near it would be ensnared and slowly pulled down and strangled. Even the great ships had no chance of escape once the weeds had hold of them. Eventually, Poseidon and some of the guardians used a powerful spell to prevent the forest from spreading and destroying any other beings. The forest was then placed under the control of one of his daughters. For many years she kept the forest under control, but when the Dark One rose to power and his poison started spreading in the sea, she lost control of the forest, although the seaweed has not yet started to spread as the spell has not been totally broken."

"I see," replied Aliyyah. "What was the name of this unfortunate woman?"

"Her name is Saragossa and the place where her head lies is called the graveyard of the ships," replied Dark Wing.

"Was she always evil?" asked Aliyyah.

"No, she was once a beautiful young woman who liked to help people, but she was also rather foolish."

"What do you mean by that?" interrupted Aliyyah.

"Well, one of the people she helped was, unbeknown to her, a powerful wizard who, as a reward for her kindness, offered her anything she wished. Without thinking of the consequences she asked for the gift of seeing into the future. The wizard asked her if this was what she truly wanted. When she replied that it was, the wizard told her he would give her what she wanted, but she must remember that although she would be able to see the future, she must never tell anyone what was going to happen, Saragossa promised, but she broke her word. Whenever she saw that something evil was about to happen to someone she would quickly go and warn them. It was not long before the wizard angrily returned and without a word he turned her hair into a nest of swarming snakes. 'Now,' he told her, 'you will not be able to tell anyone what you know as they will all fear you and be afraid to come near you. Furthermore, anyone who is still brave or foolish enough to try and talk to you will be turned to stone the moment they look at your face. I also banish you from the land that you love and command you to live below the waves where you cannot harm your family and friends. Never will you be free of this curse until the daughter of a slain king cuts the snakes from your head and restores life to your dead heart or separates your soul from your body'.

"Saragossa was then forced by the wizard's powerful magic to enter the deep oceans, but as she left her home her youngest and most beloved of all her sisters ran after her. Saragossa refused to turn around despite the frantic calls of her sister, for fear of turning her into stone. However, the young girl was determined to catch up with her elder sister and at last she managed to overtake her. No sooner did she look upon Saragossa's face than she was turned into stone.

"Heartbroken, Saragossa could not even stop and weep as the spell compelled her to enter the sea straight away. At first Saragossa kept herself away from all living creatures in fear of harming them, but as the years passed, the sorrow in her heart became like a cancer turning sorrow to anger, then haired and finally a desire for revenge took root in her heart. After that she deliberately turned to stone anyone that happened to chance her way, until there was a landscape of frozen figures adorning the reefs and the seabed where she had been forced to make her home."

"What happened to the creatures she turned to stone?" interrupted Aliyyah.

"When Poseidon and the other guardians defeated her and placed her under their spell, they released all creatures she had turned into stone from their cold prisons."

"So," commented Aliyyah. "There is still hope for her, she is not totally evil."

"About that I do not know, maybe, maybe not. It depends on how diseased her heart has become. Although her head was severed from her body, she was unable to die and lies there, her head the centre of the seaweed forest with her motionless body next to it. As long as her head survives, so does her body."

"So there is still a chance of saving her?" asked Aliyyah.

"In this I cannot advise you, but maybe it is better to end her misery that risk the chance of restoring to life someone whose heart has grown truly evil," still Dark Wing insisted.

Aliyyah said, "I have sworn to aid all those imprisoned by magic regardless of the danger to myself."

With a grim chuckle Dark Wing replied, "I know, Aliyyah, but I thought that your vow only applied to black magic, not white. After all, it was the ancient white magic that forced King Err to obey you and protected you from him when he pursued us."

Confused, Aliyyah could say nothing. Was the wizard's spell white or black magic? Did she have a responsibility to help Saragossa or not? Suddenly a thought occurred to Aliyyah.

"Dark Wing, you have explained to me how Saragossa became the way she is, but what about Suraya?"

"Suraya," replied Dark Wing, "was with her sister when the wizard returned to curse her. She tried to prevent him from casting his spell, for she too was skilled in magic. However, she was not as powerful as the wizard and he turned her into a creature like her sister. He then banished her to live alone in a deep cave on the top of the Broken Mountains away, from all living creatures, in a barren and lifeless wasteland. There she remains to this day and can only be released from her misery when her sister is either dead, or restored to what she once was."

"I see," said Aliyyah. "It truly seems that knowledge is sometimes a deadly gift. It is like a two-edged sword that cannot only destroy one's enemies, but destroy oneself at the same time."

"Well said, Aliyyah," replied Dark Wing with a touch of pride in his voice. "You are growing wiser every day, but remember that knowledge is also the source of all power as well as the root of wisdom, understanding and compassion. Knowledge in itself is not evil, but depends on the way that it is used."

For a while they flew in silence, both deep in thought, until Toowooni flew up beside them.

"Aliyyah, Dark Wing, look ahead, look!"

As they looked in front of them they saw they were nearing the seaweed forest. Thick fronds of dark brown waving seaweed, as tall as trees, could be seen menacingly beckoning them to come nearer. Hundreds and hundreds of fronds writhed and tangled with each other like a nest of life-snatching snakes.

"How are you going to deal with so much seaweed, Princess?" asked Toowooni in great concern. "There are too many fronds. For sure, as you cut one the others will ensnare you!"

Thinking for a few minutes, Aliyyah said to Toowooni, "Tell Adono, Najputih and Aquas to stay away from the forest, for I have an idea."

Nodding his head, Toowooni flew down to the chariot to tell them to wait there for a while and not to go any further.

"Dark Wing, can you fly to the very centre of the forest? We must find where the head is. Only then do we have a chance of destroying the seaweed forest."

As they flew over the forest of tangled, swaying fronds they searched to see where the centre of these malevolent weeds was, until finally, after searching for about half an hour, Dark Wing noticed a spot where the weeds were rotating in a thick circle upwards from the seabed, then spreading outwards and splintering off into many different branches.

"Aliyyah, look down there! I think that is where the head must lie."

Squinting her eyes to get a better look, Aliyyah had to agree with Dark Wing. With concern showing in his voice, Dark Wing asked Aliyyah, "Princess, how are you going to cut the fronds from her head? Surely you will be strangled before you can reach it? We could just fly over the forest and onwards to the Island of Mists!"

Taken aback, Aliyyah sharply replied, "Dark Wing, how could I abandon our friends, Najputih, Aquas, Adono and Toowooni?"

Laughing, Dark Wing replied, "Abandon! Of course not! I will carry them over the forest one by one, except for Toowooni of course. He can fly.

Feeling a bit ashamed of herself Aliyyah said, "I am sorry, Dark Wing, I should have known better than to think that you would leave them. However, I am still honour bound to free the sea from this menace and release Saragossa from her misery one way or another."

"Are you sure, Princess? Sometimes it is wiser to run rather than fight."

"Maybe, but if I break my promise once, how many times after this will I break it as well? I have been given the tools to do the job so I would be a fool not to try."

Dark Wing remained silent for a few minutes before asking, "Princess, how do you intend to get close enough to use the scissors? Have you got a plan?"

"Yes," replied Aliyyah, "but let us return to the others so I can explain what I intend to do and prepare myself."

When they reached the others, Aliyyah asked Dark Wing to fly low and she jumped back into the chariot. Sitting on the bench she told them, "I am going to eat another piece of mirkweed so I do not drown under the water. Dark Wing will fly me back to where we think the head lies and I will jump into the water, cutting all the fronds that come near me until I reach the head and cut the seaweed at its source. Dark Wing, I will need your help in distracting as many of the fronds away from me as possible."

"What do you mean, Aliyyah?" asked "Dark Wing.

"I want you to fly low over the seaweed so that the fronds try to catch you, but every time they try to ensnare you must make sure you quickly fly out of their reach. That way, at least some of the fronds will not attack me. But make sure you do not put yourself in too much danger."

"Very well, Princess, but are you sure you want to do this?"

"Yes, Dark Wing I must, I really have no choice, I am a seeker." "Very well then, Princess, prepare yourself."

Aliyyah took out the golden scissors and taking a strong, thin piece of cord, she tied one end of it to the scissors and the other end to her wrist so that she would not lose them in the coming fight. She then removed her stockings and shoes placed them on the floor of the chariot near the unicorn, and after taking one piece of her precious mirkweed from its bag she placed the rest back in the pocket of her travelling cloak, before removing it and all its treasures. Folding it neatly, she placed it on the bench for Najputih to look after. She placed the mirkweed in her mouth and began to chew the bitter plant. As the mirkweed softened and changed flavour she felt the webbed skin growing once more between her fingers and toes, as well as the gills that could now be seen each side on her neck.

Turning to Najputih and Adono, she said, "When you see that the forest is destroyed, come swiftly and pick me up for I'm sure I will be exhausted as before. However, if I do not succeed, you are to return to your own homes as quickly as you can, but first you must return this cloak and all it contains to the elder Mahin, and Mahin alone. Do you understand?"

Nodding their heads her companions agreed to her wishes, but Najputih could not help interrupting her mentally, "Don't say that, Aliyyah, you must succeed, you must!"

Smiling, Aliyyah called Dark Wing who had been hovering over the chariot while she prepared herself.

"I am ready, Dark Wing, let's go."

Dark Wing flew as close to the chariot as he dared and Aliyyah gracefully leapt onto his back.

Rising up, they flew back to where they thought the head lay. As they watched the swirling nest of dark brown fronds, Dark Wing once more asked Aliyyah, "Are you ready, Princess? There is still time to turn back, you know!"

Shaking her head she replied, "No, I must do this. Fly as low as you can without touching the seaweed and I will jump!"

Slowly and carefully, Dark Wing skimmed across the seaweed fronds making sure he touched none of them and none of them touched him.

Looking intently, Aliyyah grasped the scissors, opening them ready to start cutting as soon as she hit the water. Dark Wing felt her body go rigid just before she leapt into the tangled mess of seaweed.

She had not even touched the water when she felt her ankles and waist entwined by the seaweed, which seemed to have an iron grip, trying to drag her down to a watery death. Twisting, she snipped the fronds encircling her and felt herself hit the water before more seaweed bound itself around her. Snipping furiously, Aliyyah twisted and turned this way and that as she tried to swim down to the bottom of the seabed where the head lay.

Minutes passed as she fought her way down further and further. She could see nothing but brown seaweed in all directions, seaweed that was trying to squeeze the life out of her. Protecting the scissors with one hand she continued cutting until, finally, she saw the head of Saragossa directly below her. With a determined look on her face, Aliyyah forced her way down next to the head and fought to cut off all its thrashing fronds. As the first strand fell, Aliyyah was shocked to see Saragossa's eyes suddenly open and stare at her, eyes that were empty, void, full of despair like a deep well of depression falling down into eternal darkness. At the same time, a terrible, piercing scream vibrated from the decapitated head. Ignoring the screams that threatened to shatter her mind Aliyyah continued with her grisly task and as the last frond fell from Saragossa's head, a final unearthly scream was heard followed by an even more unnerving silence, total and absolute.

As Aliyyah watched, the thick fronds of the seaweed forest shivered then melted into a shower of brown mush, which floated down to the bottom of the sea and dissolved into the sand without leaving a trace. A morbid mockery of the pristine snow that melts into the earth after a long and bitter winter, heralding the arrival of spring, new life and new hope.

Aliyyah could now see clearly not just the head, but also the body of Saragossa, and realised that at one time she must have been a maiden fair to behold, for her beauty could still be seen on her ravaged head and body.

Urgency filled Aliyyah's thoughts as she stared at the unfortunate Saragossa, for she knew she must return to the surface soon before the effects of the mirkweed wore off. However, what was she going to do about Saragossa? She could hardly leave her lying there, for although she appeared lifeless, Aliyyah knew that she was not dead, but somewhere in the shadowy realm between the two worlds of life and death.

As she pondered, she heard Saragossa's voice within her head.

"Aliyyah, you must now choose whether I live or die."

"You know my name?" replied Aliyyah.

"Of course, have I not been cursed with the gift of being able to see into the future."

"Then what choice should I make?" asked Aliyyah.

"Whatever choice you make," came the reply, "you will live to regret it!"

Confused, Aliyyah asked her what she meant by this.

"Part of my curse is that I must always tell the truth regardless of the consequences. If you kill me, my sister Suraya will be released from her curse, but she will become your bitter enemy seeking revenge on you for my death. On the other hand, you cannot allow me to live as my heart has already grown cold and black and all the goodness in it has been destroyed. All that is in my heart now is the desire to destroy anything and everything that crosses my path."

"In that case," interrupted Aliyyah, "it seems my only choice is to leave you lying here."

The head gave a morbid chuckle. "You cannot escape your destiny that way either. Look carefully, see where you cut the fronds from my head. Already they are growing back. Within a few days the seaweed forest will be as thick as it was before you came and my anger will be twice what it was."

To her dismay Aliyyah could indeed see the greenish brown shoots of seaweed peeking their way out of the top of Saragossa's head.

"It seems I face an evil choice no matter what," said Aliyyah. "As you are cursed to always tell the truth, advise me as to what path I should take."

"Aliyyah, it seems that my goodness from the beginning is to be repaid with evil. Do not ask me this, for I can see what would happen in all three cases."

"You are mistaken, Saragossa," said Aliyyah. "Your fate, that you brought down upon yourself by asking for a gift that none of us have the wisdom to hold. After that you broke your promise and the trust placed upon you. Even though your intentions were good, the results were bad. Only the Creator has the right to decide what will happen in the future, so when you betrayed your trust in reality you were trying to betray the Creator. Now tell me what I should do with you. Quickly, for my time is short!"

With a gasp that was also a sob, Saragossa replied, "In order for you to succeed in your quest you must destroy me, but this will also in the long run cause the death of my sister as well."

"I do not seek her life, nor do I wish to harm her," protested Aliyyah.

"Nevertheless," replied Saragossa, "you will have no choice, it will be you or her."

"But how do I destroy you and the magic that keeps you alive in this condition?"

Sadly, the reply came, "Look carefully, you will see a thin thread of light that connects my head to my body. Cut that and the magic is destroyed and I may at long last die and, I hope, find peace once more. I was not always evil and maybe in death I will find salvation from my actions."

Nodding her head Aliyyah looked and saw the thin thread of light that ran from her head to her body. It pulsed rather like a heartbeat as it flowed from the head to the body of Saragossa. Taking the scissors she prepared to cut this fragile thread and so end the life of the tragic Saragossa.

"Are you ready?" asked Aliyyah.

"Yes," came the reply.

"Please forgive me," sobbed Aliyyah. "I do not wish to do this, but I cannot permit the other two choices."

"I forgive you, but remember this, my death is on your hands. As recompense I demand that when you kill my sister you are to bring her body here and bury her beside me. Only then will we be able to rest in peace."

Shaken by Saragossa's words and realising the immensity of what she was about to do, Aliyyah steeled herself, then, closing her eyes, she snapped the thread of light before moving back to see what was going to happen.

This time, however, there was no flash of light or change of colours. Slowly the head and the body joined together as if they had never been separated. The face of Saragossa changed revealing all the beauty of her youth and the softness of her heart before she turned cold and evil. Opening her eyes, she sighed, "Thank you for ending my misery, Aliyyah, thank you, goodbye!" The light in her face dimmed as her life force seeped out of her body, leaving a cold shell on the seabed.

Realising that she had been under the waves for almost an hour Aliyyah frantically kicked upwards as the effects of the mirkweed began to wear off. Up, up, up she swam, desperate to reach the surface before she reverted to her normal condition. Bursting into the bright sunlight she saw her companions searching for her.

Dark Wing was the first one to spot her and he quickly flew to where she was tiredly treading water. At the same time, Adono and Najputih saw her and sped towards her. Aquas, who was still following them, swam swiftly to Aliyyah, allowing her to rest her tired body against him until the others could arrive, while Dark Wing hovered anxiously above them.

"Are you alright, Princess," he said. "Shall I lift you out of the water?"

"It is alright, Dark Wing, I am just tired, the effects of the mirkweed always drain my energy." Then half heartily she joked, "It is not easy being a fish."

By this time Adono had arrived and he carefully helped Aliyyah to climb aboard the chariot where she gratefully sank down on the soft bench. Leaning back, she closed her eyes and remained quiet.

"Aliyyah," said Dark Wing, "you seemed more than tired, what happened down there?"

Aliyyah ignored Dark Wing at first while a few tears slipped down her cheeks, then she told all her companions what had happened!

"Aliyyah, do not feel bad," said Dark Wing. "You had no other choice and you have released her from her living death."

"Yes, but what about her sister? I have no wish to harm her!" cried Aliyyah.

"Your destiny awaits you," said Adono. "But it does not necessarily mean you will be forced to kill Suraya. Many things can change before then."

"Adono is right," added Dark Wing. "Even what seems so certain may not happen, but if and when the time comes, you will know what path to take for sure. Now you should rest, for Toowooni has informed me that we will soon reach the Island of Mists."

"Yes," replied Aliyyah. "But first we must bury Saragossa, she has suffered too much and it's not right that we just leave her body there to be eaten by the fish."

"Do not worry about that," said Adono. "Aquas and I will make sure she is properly buried. Now rest while you can for soon we will reached the Island of Mists."

Nodding her head Aliyyah wearily snuggled down next to Najputih and quickly fell into a deep slumber.

Chapter Ten

The Island of Mists

Aliyyah slowly opened her eyes as she felt Najputih gently nudging her, while at the same time she heard Toowooni twittering, "Aliyyah, look, look ahead, the Island of Mists." Shaking herself awake she stared ahead of her to where an island could just be seen in the dim of the failing light.

The island, or what she could see of it, seemed to be quite large although it was surrounded by rolling clouds of swirling white mists. The island was neither hilly nor mountainous, at least from what they could glimpse through the misty curtains that hid it.

"I understand now why they call it the Island of Mists," commented Aliyyah. "Has it always been this way?"

"As far as I know," replied Toowooni, "the mists have always been here. Maybe Dark Wing, who is the oldest of us here, knows more?"

"Not really," answered Dark Wing. "However, it is said the greater the treasure the more it is hidden by veils of mystery, which only one with a pure heart can penetrate."

Smiling, Aliyyah replied, "An answer that is not an answer, Dark Wing. Is there any danger there?"

"As I said, Princess, it depends on your heart what you will find there, it holds the secrets of the gateways to more than one hidden world, but not all of them you would wish to enter."

"Then how do I know which is the right gateway?" asked Aliyyah.

"One of the mysteries of this place is that only the gateway that your heart is truly seeking will open up for you. The rest will remain closed and hidden."

"I see," said Aliyyah. "The island's protection is your own desires. It gives you what you want despite the consequences that may follow."

"Both yes and no, Princess," teased Dark Wing. "For not everyone knows what their heart truly desires!"

Laughing again Aliyyah said, "It seems that I am playing the riddle game once more."

"Not really, Princess! I have told you what we dragons know about this place, no more, no less."

By this time the island was looming directly in front of them. What struck Aliyyah the most about this place was the silence. At first she thought that it was totally silence, but as they got closer she could hear whispering, unclear, indistinct, but definitely whispering voices, many voices talking in a language she had never heard before. At the same time she saw shadowy figures in the gathering gloom, ethereal lights, flicking like human fireflies.

"Dark Wing, what are they?" asked Aliyyah.

"They are the ones who protect and look after this island," replied the dragon. "They are called the Vilena."

"Are they dangerous, Dark Wing?" asked Aliyyah.

"They can be dangerous or harmless it, depends..." Before Dark Wing could finish, Aliyyah interrupted with a laugh.

"On your heart. Am I right?"

"Yes, and what did Mahin teach you?" enquired the dragon.

"To follow my heart," replied Aliyyah.

"That is what you must do in this place. I have no need to warn you again to be careful, what you do and say," cautioned Dark Wing.

"I will be careful," promised Aliyyah.

The chariot was now near enough for Aliyyah to swim the short distance to the shore.

"Aliyyah," thought the unicorn, "how am I going to reach the shore? Unicorn's do not know how to swim and you know that Adono seahorses can go no further in."

Turning to Adono, Aliyyah asked, "Will you wait for us or must you return to your father now that we have reached the Island of Mists?"

"My father ordered me to bring you to safely to the Island of Mists and then return. However, I can wait until after you have returned from the city of Atlantis before following my father command. After all, he made me promise to look after you and protect you for as long as you are in his realm," replied Adono.

"Thank you, Adono. Najputih, you may wait here in the chariot."

"Or," interrupted a voice from above, "I can carry you to the island."

"No, thank you," thought Najputih swiftly. "I may be tired of this chariot and longing to be on solid ground again, but that desperate I am not! I will wail here."

"Aliyyah," said Dark Wing hovering near her. "You have no need to get wet yet again. It is only a short distance, catch hold of my legs and I will carry you there."

Relieved that she would not have to enter the water wearing her thick travelling cloak, Aliyyah waited until Dark Wing was just above her and then she caught hold of his powerful legs.

"Ready, Princess?" asked the dragon as he felt her holding his legs.

"Yes," replied Aliyyah.

Dark Wing rose up with Aliyyah dangling beneath him.

"Hold tight, Princess."

Nodding her head, Aliyyah felt her arms being pulled as she hung on tightly. However, it was not as bad as the first time when they were trying to escape from King Err.

Almost as soon as Dark Wing had lifted her up she heard him say, "Aliyyah, get ready to let go."

Steeling herself she looked down at the ghostly landscape beneath her. When she was only a couple of feet above the ground she let go of Dark Wing's legs and dropped to the ground beneath her, rolling herself into a ball to break her fall. Landing beside her Dark Wing peered into the growing darkness.

"I think we had better rest for the night," said Dark Wing. "Who knows what lies ahead."

Nodding her head in agreement, Aliyyah waited until Dark Wing settled his massive body on the ground before removing her cloak. Folding it into a rough square she put it on the ground next to Dark Wing before lying down her head on her cloak with her body protected by Dark Wing's massive bulk.

"Goodnight, Dark Wing," she said. Then mentally she sent the same message to Najputih who had snuggled down in Adono's chariot for the night, accompanied by Toowooni who was resting next to him.

"Goodnight, Princess," replied Dark Wing. "Sleep well, I will look after you throughout the night."

Gratefully Aliyyah closed her eyes, but sleep did not come easily to her. All around she could hear those ghostly whispers while she could feel the Vilena moving around them silent as a cat, brushing past them, but not actually touching them. Aliyyah did not fear them, but nevertheless it was still very unnerving.

Eventually, however, exhaustion set in and she fell into a deep slumber knowing that Dark Wing would never permit anything to happen to her.

Dark Wing, seeing that the young girl had finally fallen asleep, closed one of his eyes to rest as well, leaving the other eye (a trait all dragons have) to keep watch for any potential dangers.

When Aliyyah awoke, she felt rather than saw, the first rays of the morning as everywhere was still covered with a thick, while mist. Shaking herself awake she felt stiff and cold from the damp earth she had been sleeping on.

Stretching herself, she looked around with her still sleepy eyes. Standing up she looked around her to see if there was any clue as to which direction she should take.

"Good morning, Aliyyah," came Dark Wing's deep voice. "Don't you think that you should have something to eat first?"

"Good morning, Dark Wing, yes, but I have only one small loaf left and that I must share with Najputih."

Chuckling, Dark Wing said, "You must still be sleepy, look at your feet!"

Staring down Aliyyah saw a brown bag woven out of some kind of plant material, delicately and intricately made. Bending down she picked it up and looked inside. To her surprise it contained fresh fruits, nuts and delicious berries. It also contained some wild honeycombs wrapped in leaves and dripping with honey, and a strange looking fruit, one she had never seen before. It was a brownish colour and of an oblong shape, smelling of freshly baked bread. Gingerly she broke off a small piece and ate it. To her astonishment it not only smelt like bread, but tasted like bread too!

"Dark Wing, what is this?"

"That," replied Dark Wing, "is Quazusa. It is a fruit that only grows on this island. You need only eat a little of it to feel full and revitalised."

"But where did all this come from?" asked Aliyyah.

"When you were sleeping, Toowooni watched over you while I searched for food for you and Najputih. I managed to gather enough to fill two bags. One for you and one I gave to Adono and Najputih. When I left them they were happily having breakfast together," answered the dragon.

"But where did you get the bags from? They are beautifully woven, don't tell me you made them?"

Laughing, Dark Wing merely replied, "Let's just say that it is dragon magic and leave it at that!"

But Aliyyah was curious and kept asking Dark Wing where he had got them from. Dark Wing on the other hand, was just as adamant and refused to say another word on the matter.

"Aliyyah," a thought came into her mind. "Good morning, did you sleep well?"

"Yes, Najputih," thought Aliyyah. "How about you?"

"Hmph, I suppose quite well for a unicorn stranded in a rocking chariot in the middle of an unknown ocean."

"Stop grumbling, Najputih," teased Aliyyah. "I know you better than that! Now did you enjoy your breakfast?"

"Yes, but I ate a little too much and now I feel much too full."

"Never mind, Najputih," thought Aliyyah, "you can rest until I return." As she finished speaking she could feel Najputih tense as he replied, "Please be careful, Aliyyah! You don't know what lies ahead."

"Don't worry, Najputih, just rest, I will not be too long."

Turning towards Dark Wing she asked, "Just how do we find the right gateway?"

"In this place," commented Dark Wing, "you do not look for the gateway, rather, the gateway will find you."

Exasperated, Aliyyah was about to be sarcastic when Toowooni flew up and landed next to Aliyyah. "Princess, we must wait until midday, only then will the pillar point the way to the underwater path to Alantis."

"But where is the pillar and how can it point anywhere in these mists?"

"Princess, before you can reach the pillar you must first go through the gateway and then answer the questions of the guardian."

"I thought the guardian lived under the sea?" queried Aliyyah.

"There are many guardians and you must answer all their questions, but until you have passed the first test you will not see the rest."

"So how do I find the gateway?" asked Aliyyah once more in a frustrated voice.

"Ask the Vilena," said Toowooni. "They are the ones that know all the secrets of this island, they are the protectors and keepers here."

"But how do I call them?" questioned Aliyyah. "I don't know their language, nor can I see them."

"You must ask them with your heart, of course," said Toowooni. "And if your heart is true, they will answer you."

Looking first at Toowooni and then at Dark Wing, Aliyyah fixed her eyes on the heart pendant she wore around her neck. Concentrating as hard as she could she sent out the message, 'I am Aliyyah, a seeker, daughter of King Dor, I need to find the gateway to Alantis so that I may see the wise green turtle.'

As she concentrated and sent out the same message again and again, a figure formed from among the mists and made its way towards the three companions. Stopping in front of them, they could see that the figure had taken the form of a young woman. Although she did not open her mouth, all of them heard her speak in a clear, bell-like voice that tinkled like the water in a small brook merrily flowing on to the mighty sea.

"Aliyyah, I am Quasa, the leader of the Vilena. Why do you seek the green turtle?"

"To find the Book of Fazma," replied Aliyyah.

"And why do you want the Book of Fazma?" Quasa questioned.

"To recover the Sword of Ila."

"Why do you need the sacred Sword of IIa," continued Quasa.

"I have the first two treasures of Lamis, I need the other two to destroy the rule of the Dark One forever."

Quasa kept quiet for a while before replying, "Your heart is true, but you are only the Gatherer. It is another's destiny to destroy the Dark One, however, without the Gatherer he cannot succeed in his task."

Shocked, puzzled and confused all at the same time, Aliyyah asked her what she meant.

"It is written that the Gatherer will succeed in recovering all four

treasures, after which a period of time will pass, a time of war and battles long and hard fought, until finally the Gatherer will pass over the sword to one who is dear and close to her. It is this person who will slay the Dark One, this person and this person alone, no one else will be able to."

Shaking her head, Aliyyah said, "I still do not understand?"

"You will, Aliyyah, in time. Now follow me," replied Quasa.

Quasa glided through the ghostly mists. After what seemed to be hours they reached a massive stone gate standing in the middle of nowhere. It consisted of two mighty slabs of stones holding up a third stone, which was covered in some strange and ancient language. Aliyyah was not sure, but she guessed the writing must be in the forgotten tongue of the people of Atlantis.

"Aliyyah, this gate is the pathway to what you desire. The guardian awaits you on the other side, but you must enter alone, none of your companions may accompany you," said Quasa.

"Very well," replied Aliyyah.

"You must also only take with you that which is necessary, the rest you must leave here with your companions. They will look after your treasures until you return."

Nodding her head, Aliyyah removed the small bag containing the brownish pieces of mirkweed from the deep pockets of her cloak. Once more removing her cloak she folded it neatly before handing it over to Dark Wing to look after.

"Take good care of this, Dark Wing," said Aliyyah. "You know what to do with it in case I am unable to return."

"Don't worry, Aliyyah, just concentrate on your task ahead. We will wait for you. Remember what your father said in his letter, remember his advice to you."

"Are you ready, seeker?" asked Quasa.

"Yes," replied Aliyyah.

"Good," said Quasa. "However, you do realise that if you are unable to answer the questions of the guardian you will be trapped between the gateway and the pillar of Atlantis forever, there will be no escape. Do you still wish to continue?"

"What choice do I have?" asked Aliyyah.

"None," replied Quasa.

With a determined look on her face, Aliyyah walked towards the stone gateway shrouded in swirling mists. As she approached she saw a barrier of light filling the front of the entrance, a bluish-white light that hurt her eyes with its intensity.

Shutting her eyes tightly she stepped into the strange light. As soon as she entered she felt herself being pulled swiftly to the other side, almost as if she was sliding down a steep, slippery tunnel, while whispered voices surrounded her, serenading her on her way. All of a sudden the voices stopped as well as the feeling of being pulled. Standing still for a moment without opening her eyes she could feel the heat of the sun beating down upon her skin, while the sound of waves crashing onto a rocky shore filled her ears. As she opened her eyes she saw that she was standing near the top of a green hill overlooking an azure sea.

The sound of the waves was coming from the sea as it broke upon the jagged shoreline at the bottom of the hill. Surprisingly there was no mist here and she could see clearly everything in front of her, including a massive black pylon made of shining marble and engraved with the same strange writing that was on the gateway. This undoubtedly was the pillar of Atlantis, but where was the guardian?

As she looked carefully she thought that she saw something moving behind the giant pillar. Maybe the guardian was waiting for her there. As she neared the pillar the guardian stepped out from behind and revealed himself.

"Sayning," gasped the shocked Aliyyah. "What are you doing? Where is the guardian?"

"Princess," replied Sayning doing a small dragon bow. "I am the guardian."

"You? How? I don't understand! Do the other dragons know?"

"One question at a time please," replied Sayning. "Firstly, yes I am the guardian. I have always been the guardian of this gateway. When we dragons were imprisoned in the dragon chamber by the ancient magic that is stronger than ours, this gateway was closed and no one, not even the Dark One would have been able to find it. However, when you released us, this gateway reappeared on this island and one of my many secret tasks is to question the seeker who tries to pass through it."

"So," interrupted Aliyyah, "you knew I would have to face your questions yet again?"

"At that time I was not sure whether you would be able to pass all the trials that would lead you here. Although I must admit I was hoping you would be successful. However, do not think I will have any mercy on you or give you any help in answering the questions you must answer."

Smiling, Aliyyah replied, "I know that, everyone has warned me about you, but I believe you have a good heart or you would not have been given this task."

"Maybe, Princess, maybe. We will see. As for the other dragons, they do not know, except for Greenthor and he is bound by our laws not to say anything. We all have our secrets and our tasks and no other dragon knows his brother's job, except for Greenthor. If you succeed in this task you are also honour bound as well not to reveal to my brothers what I am."

"You have my word on that, Sayning, for I will never betray a guardian or a friend, even if it means my own death."

"You have not yet earned my friendship, Aliyyah, as I told you before, but I appreciate you honesty and your loyalty. Now prepare yourself, for you have to answer all five questions to continue your quest. If you fail to answer even one question you will be stuck here for all eternity. Not even I could help if that happens."

"I understand," answered Aliyyah. "What is the first question?"

"Of all the gifts given to men, what is the greatest?"

"That is easy," replied Aliyyah. "Wisdom with compassion and understanding."

"Well done, Princess! Your second question, what is the root of all evil and all good, but in itself is pure?"

This question stumped Aliyyah for a moment until she remembered the teachings of Mahin her mentor. "I think, Sayning, that the answer must be knowledge, pure in itself, but it can be used to create great evil or great good."

"Right once more. Your third question. Which is greater, the day or the night?"

"Neither," replied Aliyyah. "They go together. Without the day there could be no night, and without the night there could be no day."

"You have grown wiser, Princess! Your fourth question, what is the purpose of the seeker?"

Puzzled at what seemed to be a simple question, she was about to say to fulfil the quest when she remembered what Quasa had said about her being only the Gatherer and not the one to destroy the Dark One.

"If I am not mistaken, it is to prepare the path for the one who is destined to destroy the Dark One!"

Sayning gave her a strange look before asking, "How did you know that, Aliyyah? If you had said to fulfil the quest you would have failed."

"I remembered what Quasa said about me, that I was only the Gatherer, therefore I must also be the one to prepare the path for the one who will destroy the Dark One!"

Aliyyah was surprised when she heard the normally solemn and cunning dragon chuckle. "Too honest, as usual! You must learn to be more discreet. Do you know who this person will be?"

"No," answered Aliyyah. "Only that he will be someone close to me." Then looking closely at Sayning she asked cautiously, "Do you know, Sayning?"

"What makes you ask that?" he questioned.

"It was the look in your eyes and the tone of your voice when you asked me that makes me suspect that you know who he is."

Frustratingly Sayning told her, "Maybe I do and maybe I don't. However, it is irrelevant whether I do or not, for the only one who has the permission to answer that is the Sand Wizard. Now, here is your final question. Where is all true knowledge and wisdom found?"

"That is easy enough, in the heart, the seat of knowledge, wisdom, compassion and love."

"Well done, Princess now you may take one step further on your journey. Soon the sun will strike the top of the pillar and its shadow will point to the doorway that will lead you to the underwater world of Atlantis. A flight of steps will take you down and at the bottom there is another gate and another guardian."

"Is it another dragon?" interrupted Aliyyah once more.

"No," came the reply. "We dragons cannot live in the water. All dragons are forbidden to enter the watery realm except for King Err and his dragons. You will know this guardian when you see him. He will ask you three questions more difficult than mine and you must answer all, or be trapped between the pillar and the gate of Atlantis. If you succeed, you will be admitted to the lost city and you must straight away go to the great temple in the middle of the city, for that is where the green turtle lives. Remember, there are many hidden dangers in the city so be careful. When you reach the temple there will be one more guardian who guards the entrance. He will ask you one question and if you can answer it you will be allowed to see the green turtle. You may ask the turtle seven questions and no more, so be careful what you ask and do not ask that which you know he is not permitted to answer. Now wait and watch."

Aliyyah nodded her head and watched as the sun slowly rose. However, she was still curious about the island and she asked the dragon, "If it is not against the laws, can you tell me how many hidden gateways there are on this island?"

"Your curiosity is great, Princess and I am permitted to answer this question. There are seventy thousand secret gateways on this island, each one leading to a different world and each having its own guardian, and no two guardians are the same. Are you satisfied now, Princess?"

Musing on this Aliyyah merely nodded her head again. As she contemplated, the sun finally struck the pillar and a long shadow fell on the ground in front of her. As she looked she saw the tip of the shadow touching what seemed to be a small indentation in the ground. "Quickly, Princess, for the gateway will not be open long." Running fast, she saw that the indentation was in fact a sunken staircase leading down into the ground. Whether it had been there all the time or whether it had only appeared when struck by the shadow of the great pillar, she had no idea but without a second thought she plunged down the stairs before they disappeared from sight.

As she descended she could smell the damp earth surrounding her, while green globes attached to the walls lit her way. Down and down she went, deeper and deeper, along the spiral staircase inside the hill until at last she could hear the sound of water just below her. As she turned the next comer she saw the tunnel was

149

flooded with clear water that ebbed and flowed like the sea. The staircase could still be seen clearly descending down into the water, while ghostly globes of yellowish light continued to show the way under the water.

"Well, it seems like it is time to use the mirkweed. I just hope I have enough left." Opening the bag she looked inside at the mirkweed. She knew she had twenty-seven pieces left, but would that be sufficient to last her until she returned? Slowly chewing a piece of the rubbery weed, she closed the bag and hung it around her neck so that she could easily take another piece as soon as she felt its effects wearing off. She waited until the mirkweed had taken effect before stepping down into the cold waters at her feet.

"It is a good thing I left my cloak behind," she thought, "it would have been very cumbersome here."

Following the tunnel down through the waters, she now swam rather than walked and as she did so she noticed that small fish and other sea creatures were to appearing around her. Finally she reached the bottom of the staircase that flowed out onto a golden seabed covered with a garden of sea anemones and urchins of indescribable beauty and colours. Blinking her eyes she saw directly in front of her a massive gate wrought of pure silver and studded with precious pearls and red coral, forming intricate patterns that could, she suspected be some form of ancient writing.

"This must be the gateway to Atlantis," she thought, "but where is the Guardian?"

Looking around she saw a strange figure approaching her. It was not a Merperson or a fish or anything between, but rather it was like a giant squid, a vivid blue colour which had a human face at one end.

Hovering in front of Aliyyah it used the common tongue to demand, "Who are you and what do you want here?"

Unafraid, Aliyyah replied, "I am a seeker who wishes to speak with the green turtle."

"And what name do you go by, stranger? For we do not admit the nameless to Atlantis," replied the strange creature. "Answer quickly and don't fear."

Reluctantly Aliyyah replied, "I am Aliyyah, the daughter of King Dor."

Eyeing her carefully, the squid, if that was what it was, said, "Welcome seeker, I am Diousni of the Suqaqusi. We are the guardians of all the underwater gateways. In order to continue your journey you must answer my questions. If you fail, let us say I will not go hungry today."

Taken aback, Aliyyah nevertheless said bravely, "I think you would find that I am rather inedible, however, as I do not intent to fail the questions, I think you will have to find some other dinner today."

"Bravely spoken, little one. For your sake I hope you do succeed." Then with a glint in his eyes Diousni continued, "I much prefer to eat fish anyway. Your first question, if you are ready. Of all the ancient cities, Atlantis was one of the greatest in all aspects, yet its people were destroyed as a punishment for their sins. Out of all the sins, what was the one mainly responsible for their destruction?"

Aliyyah thought about this for a few minutes as she recalled all the stories that Mahin had told her about Atlantis and how the people had grown proud and arrogant and had tried to challenge even the Creator himself. So, which was their downfall, arrogance or pride? As she thought, she realised that arrogance comes from pride and one who has no pride also has no arrogance, therefore the answer must be pride.

"The answer is pride, Diousni. It was pride that brought down their civilization."

"Yes," said the squid. "You have studied well. Your second question. Of all the weapons of the Dark One, which is greater, fear or hate?"

This question Aliyyah was able to answer straight away. "It is fear, for all hatred grows out of fear and lack of understanding."

"Well it looks like I will be having fish again today!" quipped Diousni. "Your final question, Aliyyah, and think carefully before you answer. The mother you tread upon in your youth and strength will one day embrace you when you are old and tired. Who is your mother?'

Secretly thanking Mahin in her heart for being so strict with her and making sure she learnt all her lessons well, she replied, "My teacher told me that the mother we walk upon is the earth, from which comes all that we need to live - food, shelter and clothing. When we die the earth embraces us when we are buried within her arms."

"Correct, seeker, you may now enter. The green turtle lives in the great temple in the middle of city, but there are many dangerous creatures that still roam there. Do not try to fight them, but use the gifts a dragon friend has been given." Diousni then swam down toward the gate and muttered some words that Aliyyah was unable to hear properly or understand.

Slowly the massive silver gates swung open revealing a marble paved road that led to the sunken city, which could just be seen in the distance.

"Good luck, seeker, I will wait here until the same time tomorrow. If you have not returned by then, the gates will be relocked and you will never be able to leave Atlantis."

Swimming Aliyyah followed the wide marble road towards the sunken city, which was both beautiful and sinister at the same time.

Deserted palaces, grand villas and mighty temples rose up from the seabed like giant tombstones marking the death of a great city. Silence now reigned where once there had been laughter and gaiety, arguments and songs, all extinguished like a candle many centuries ago.

Now the buildings were home to fish and other sea creatures, no humans, not even Merpeople, came here anymore. It was a cursed and sinister place yet at the same time it was the place that the green turtle had decided to make his home.

By now Aliyyah had reached the city's outer walls, made of gleaming white marble, smooth, perfect, except where they had been cracked and thrown down by the massive earthquake that had sent Atlantis to the bottom of the sea.

Swimming over the walls she reached the outskirts of the once mighty city. Clusters of small houses stood like sentinels, watching, waiting endlessly. As she swam past them she swore she could see yellowish red eyes staring out at her sending a shiver of fear down her spine. Hurrying past she was aware of the hungry great white sharks that had begun to circle above her. Slowly one by one they swam past her, nudging her as if they were small children playing with their food before eating.

Realising that there was no way she could out-swim them, she frantically searched for an escape. 'Use the gifts given to a dragon friend', Disouni's words echoed through her mind. Of course, the bracelet Light Chaser had given her. All she had to do was recite the incantation he had taught and all the sea creatures would help her and obey her commands.

Quickly she recited, "Hadsha kani hadsha awelth hadsha dangu hadsha mulase." As before, the stones of her bracelet lit up one by one, each a different colour. However, this time, instead of all the lights shooting up into the sky, only one light shot up, a greenish yellowy light that fell back down into the water, striking all the sharks that were circling around her. After being hit by the lights the sharks continued to circle her, but no longer in a threatening manner, nor did they nudge her anymore, it was as if they were waiting for something.

As Aliyyah too waited, an enormous white shark larger than all the others approached her from the direction of the city. Swimming powerfully, he approached Aliyyah and asked, "Who are you, dragon friend, and what are you doing here?"

"I am a seeker and I wish to talk to the green turtle."

"Do you? Do you now?" mused the great white shark. "Why do you wish to speak to the green turtle, may I ask?"

"You may, but I reserve the right not to answer. I have passed the questioning of two guardians, is that not enough to show I have the right to see the green turtle?"

"Maybe yes, maybe no. My children here," referring to the circling sharks, "are disappointed that they cannot enjoy a tasty titbit for dinner. However, we are bound by the ancient magic and we cannot harm a dragon friend, especially one who wears the Bracelet of Terwa. I am Kara, greatest of all the sharks. Father of many and leader of all. Among my kind, my word is law and I now proclaim that the seeker, Aliyyah, is to be protected and helped by all our kin no matter what sea she is in!"

"But how do you know my name?" demanded Aliyyah. "Who told you?"

"Are you not a dragon friend and a seeker?"

"Yes," replied a bemused Aliyyah.

"Well I know of only one seeker who entered our realm, Aliyyah, the daughter of the slain King Dor. News travels fast underwater and besides, I know Greenthor well. He recently sent me a message asking me to help you in your quest and protect you from the many dangers hidden in the lost city."

"So why did your sharks surround and threaten me?" said a slightly angry Aliyyah,

"Don't lose your temper, Aliyyah! We ourselves had to be sure. The Dark One has many tricks and devices he can use to deceive us as well as being able to take any form he desires. Even the guardians are not immune to his deceits. That is why there is more than one of us. Only when you used the bracelet were we sure who you really were. If truly we had wanted to eat you, you would not have seen us coming. Now, young one, there are many dangers in front of you, but as you have called us we will aid you. Climb up on my back, don't be afraid, and I will take you safely to the great temple where the green turtle lives. That way you will not have to face any more sea creatures. Hurry now, I know you do not have much time. Oh Greenthor also told me to remind you about the mirkweed. How long have you been underwater now?"

Looking at her fingers Aliyyah realised she must have been underwater for almost an hour as the webbing between them was starting to recede. Realising that she must immediately eat another piece of the precious weed before her gills disappeared and she drowned here in the city of Atlantis, she opened the bag around her neck and swiftly fished out another piece of mirkweed. Placing it in her mouth, she quickly ate it looking anxiously at her hands and feet. As she chewed, she was relieved to find the webbed skin had already grown back. Closing the bag carefully she thanked Kara for reminding her in time.

"Thank you, Kara, thank you, I must be more careful in future, but it is so difficult to gauge the time down here."

"In that case, I think I have the answer," said Kara, then, in a strange shrill voice that was more like a whistle than speech, Kara called for one of the younger sharks. After conversing for a few minutes in their strange language, the younger shark swam away towards a cluster of houses nearby. Entering one of the larger houses the shark disappeared for a few minutes before resuming with an ancient sand clock about the size of a small trinket box in his mouth. It had a silver frame containing two glass globes, one on top of the other with a tiny hole leading from one globe to another. The bottom globe was half filled with multi-coloured sand while the edges of the silver frame was engraved with the same writing she had seen on the pillar and the gateway.

"Take this, Aliyyah, it is one of the sand clocks the ancients used to use to measure the passing of time. It takes one of your hours for the sand to run from one globe to another. So now you will know when it is time to eat another piece of mirkweed."

Gratefully she took the sand clock and turned it over so the sand within it started running from one globe to another. She then attached it to the wide belt she wore where she could easily see it each time she looked down.

"Thank you, Kara, for your gift, I am in your debt."

"Think nothing of it," replied Kara. "Despite our fearsome reputation, we have no love for the Dark One and we are always ready to aid those who fight for the light. Now quickly, let us go."

Swimming up, she sat herself on the back of Kara just behind his great dorsal fin. "Hold on tight, Aliyyah," he told the young girl. "Here we go."

Swiftly Kara swam through the water in a zigzag movement. Beneath them Aliyyah could see the houses and streets of the city, leading into squares and larger houses. The streets now were filled with fish, eels, seahorses and many other sea creatures. No longer did the people of Atlantis walked proudly along the roads having been destroyed centuries ago.

There were, however, more sinister creatures that Aliyyah saw lurking in dark comers and peeping out of deserted homes. Creatures with sharp teeth and claws and fiery red eyes.

"Do not worry, Aliyyah, they cannot harm you now, but if you had tried to reach the great temple by yourself they would have surely attacked you."

Aliyyah said nothing, but she began to feel a little bit as if all her moves had already been planned long ago and she was just following a course that had already been plotted. As she mused on her situation she heard Kara say, "Aliyyah, look ahead, the great temple."

Staring ahead of her she saw the great temple, which stood upon a slight hill. Its massive fluted marble columns seemed to grow upwards, on and on, until they were finally capped by a roof of thinly cut marble slates covered by sheets of finely beaten gold leaf so that it shone like a beacon through the sea waters. From where she was, Aliyyah could just see through the pillars at the front of the temple to where lay a huge courtyard leading to an inner temple and the home of the green turtle. In front of the temple and leading up to it was a great flight of steps made of black marble, which contrasted with the brilliant white of the temple.

Kara stopped at the steps that led up into the temple and said, "I will leave you here and return in three hours time to take you back to the gate. If you are not waiting I will assume that you have failed the test of the last guardian and I will return to my home. Good luck seeker and remember the mirkweed."

Swimming from the back of the great white shark, Aliyyah made her way up the steps and into the vast courtyard. Looking around she could almost imagine how it would have been during the time of the people of Atlantis. The noise, colours and hustle and bustle that must have taken place every day and even more so on the many grand festival days, yet now it was silent with no sign of life at all. How far the great have fallen, the old saying flicked through her mind while an unaccountable sadness filled her heart at the demise of such a great civilization.

As she looked around she wondered who the guardian would be this time. No sooner had that through entered her mind than she glimpsed a shape coming forward from inside the great temple at the far end of the courtyard. At first the shape was not clear, but after a while she could see it was a young woman wearing a pristine white toga after the fashion of the ancient people of Atlantis. As she came closer Aliyyah could see that although her face was very beautiful, it was also cold and proud, almost arrogant, as if she believed that everyone else was far beneath her.

"I am Alaneai, the guardian of Atlantis. I carry within me all the memories and secret knowledge of this city. Who are you and why do you dare enter here?"

Aliyyah stared at the haughty young woman for a few moments wondering whether she was a ghost, a living memory or a real flesh and blood person, before asking, "You have told me who you are but not what you are. Before I answer your question, you must answer mine."

With a toss of her head, which was crowned with locks of raven black hair, Alaneai replied, "I am neither human nor ghost, but a living memory of everything that ever happened or was invented in this city. The elders of this city created me and placed me as a guardian here. For as long as even one building remains, I will exist. When everything here is destroyed I too will cease to exist, along with all (he knowledge I carry within me. Now answer my question who are you and what do you want here?"

Realising that she would have to introduce herself formally to Alaneai, she said, "I am Aliyyah, the daughter of King Dor, true ruler of the nine sacred Islands of Lamis. A seeker on a quest to bring about the destruction of the Dark One and restore peace, harmony and justice once more. I entered here in order to speak to the wise green turtle."

"Hmph, a princess no less," commented Alaneai. "But so young for one to be on such an important mission. However, as you have reached this far there must be more to you than meets the eye. Now before you can go any further you must answer my question or join my ancestors in their watery graves."

Nodding her head in understanding Aliyyah replied, "What is your question?"

"What is nobler, the peasant, the warrior, the priest or the princess? Think carefully, for this question is not what it may seem."

Puzzled, Aliyyah tried to remember everything Mahin had ever taught her. She knew that it was the heart that counted and not who they were. At the same time she remembered the words of her father, sometimes the answer is just one word. What did he mean? Who is nobler, no wait a minute, she had said what is nobler, not who. Frantically now, Aliyyah searched for an answer until it dawned on her what it was. Oh so simple, yet so difficult at the same time.

"The answer is truth," Aliyyah stated firmly.

"Truth?" queried Alaneai.

"Yes," Aliyyah replied. "The most noble of people is the one who has the truest heart no matter what their social status."

"Well done, young Aliyyah! You may pass and ask the green turtle your questions. First, turn round and look on the alter in the middle of the courtyard, you will find a seashell there. Contained within it is the knowledge of our people, take it, for you have earned it. Use it wisely to help others and do not suffer our fate."

"Thank you," said Aliyyah. "But are you sure? It is a great gift!"

Smiling slightly Alaneai replied, "It has been written that with the coming of the seeker the green turtle will leave here and return to his home in the deepest part of the ocean, where no other creatures can survive. When that happens this city will sink beneath the seabed and I will exist no more. The gateway will then be closed forever and all our knowledge will be lost unless you take the shell with you. You must realise though that the gift I give you is a dangerous one, for the knowledge within can be used for good or bad depending on the owner and many will try to steal it if they know you possess it. Now go, for time is short."

Glancing at the sand clock she realised Alaneai's words were true in more than one way, for the sands were running out. Quickly she took out another piece of mirkweed and ate it, before swimming over and picking up the shell, which was surprisingly light, and attaching it to one of the hoops on her bell, she swam towards the great temple and the green turtle.

As Aliyyah entered the grand temple she saw that the walls were lined with massive white marble statues of the elders of the ancient city, so carefully and lovingly made that they seemed to be sleeping and could wake up at any moment. The delicate carving made it seem that their robes were actually rippling in the wind. Each statue seemed to represent some different art, sport or sphere of knowledge that had made Atlantis such a wonder of its time. At the far end of the temple was a flight of steps leading up to a dais, which had a screen of the finest and most delicately engraved marble depicting the many aspects of daily life in the city.

Aliyyah guessed that the wise green turtle must be beyond the screen.

Swimming towards it, she searched for a way around it. Looking carefully she saw that there was a dark passageway that led behind the white marble screen. Feeling her way along with her hands, Aliyyah followed the passageway until it opened up into a large round chamber that was lit by the same greenish yellow lights that had lit the passageway down from the Island of Mists.

The chamber was plain except for the detailed and intricate scenes that had been carefully painted on all the walls. Each scene told part of the story of Atlantis so that in this chamber the complete history of the city was displayed for the chosen few who could see and understand. The ceiling overhead was smooth and plain, unadorned save for a golden star with nine points. This took Aliyyah somewhat by surprise for this was the same design on the

158

flag of Lamis. A golden star upon a white background with nine points, one for each of the nine sacred islands and symbolising all that was good and holy.

In the middle of this chamber, staring at Aliyyah with round, unblinking eyes, sat the green turtle. Aliyyah knew that he was the oldest and wisest of all living creatures, but she was unaware of how enormous he was. Even though the chamber was bigger than the audience room in the royal palace of Lamis, it seemed almost too small for the turtle.

The turtle's face was old, so old drooping with wrinkles like an ancient dried prune. Its long moustache was not grey, but a pure white like virgin snow that has just fallen. Its body was covered with a series of hard interlocking plates, smooth green and polished as if they were made of the finest living emeralds. It was from beneath this shell that the turtle's head and feet peeked cautiously.

However, it was his eyes that held Aliyyah's attention. They were deep, dark pools of mystery, which seemed to see right through you and into the infinity beyond. At the same time they were also filled with so much pity, sadness and compassion as well as untold wisdom, that Aliyyah almost choked on the tears that sprung up from within her and flow unchecked down her cheeks.

"Princess Aliyyah, welcome! Long have we awaited your arrival. We are glad to see you have survived all the dangers placed before you. I am Ethos, the green turtle, as you know, I am the keeper of all knowledge both good and bad. The ancient ones of all the worlds entrusted me with the task of preserving all knowledge known to mankind and all other creations. They also bestow upon me the wisdom and compassion to use it for the purpose of helping those who strive to protect the light from the darkness and preserve peace and justice in all the worlds."

"Greetings, Ethos!" replied Aliyyah. "But why do you hide here where those who desire knowledge cannot come?"

Chuckling, Ethos answered, "Princess Aliyyah, knowledge is a treasure and the greatest treasure that anyone can have, for it is a power beyond comprehension. As it is such a great treasure it must therefore be both protected and hidden. Only the ones who are sincere and seek knowledge for the truth and light will endure all the hardships necessary to be given it. Even then, if We do not deem them worthy We will reveal nothing to them.!"

Nodding her head in understanding, Aliyyah waited for the green turtle to continue.

"You have earned the right to ask seven questions, no more, and I will answer all your questions except for the ones you must ask another. First, however, you must pass one more test. Come forward and you will see between my front legs three chests. Each one contains a different gift. Choose one. If you choose the wrong gift then you will be trapped within that chest forever."

In between the turtle's legs there were three large, polished, wooden chests such as sailors use on board their ships, bound with thick strips of gold and silver. Cautiously she opened the first chest to see a blue diamond of incredible beauty and size set into a gold ring covered with ancient runes. The second chest contained a ruby necklace of equal beauty. Each stone had been breathtakingly carved into the shape of one of the many sea creatures that lived in the watery depths. The third and final chest contained a single white feather lying on top of a small leather bound book. The feather had been cut to form a pen and had delicate drawings painted on it, while the leather book was bound by straps that were locked with a small gold paddock.

Without any hesitation Aliyyah exclaimed, "Ethos, the gift I choose is the quill and book."

"Are you quite sure?" asked Ethos.

"Yes," replied Aliyyah. "I have no desire for the ring or the necklace, despite their great beauty. The gifts the dragons have given me are more than enough. I do not desire to amass riches, but only to somehow end the reign and tyranny of the Dark One and restore peace, harmony and light once more."

"Well said, young Aliyyah. Take the book and the quill. I assume that you have already obtained the Keys of Hanaj before you searched for me. The smallest key will open the book for you."

"I have the keys," confirmed Aliyyah. "But I left them in the care of my companions until I return as instructed by the guardian on the Island of Mists."

"Who is waiting for you on the island?" interrupted Ethos.

"Dark Wing, one of the nine dragons, and Toowooni of the island of the Screeching Owls."

"Are there any others who are accompanying you?" questioned Ethos.

"All the dragons have travelled with me at one time or another, but only Najputih the unicorn has been my constant companion since I freed him from his imprisonment in the Castle of Mirrors."

"Najputih, a good companion to have. Please send him my greetings and best wishes. Tell him that when he has paid his debt his powers will be restored."

Taken aback, Aliyyah asked, "You know Najputih? He has never told me he knew about you at all."

"Aliyyah, do not get offended, for he is bound by the ancient magic not to reveal to anyone, including you, what he knows about me. Najputih is much older than you think and he, like Mahin, is one of the protectors of the light. His long imprisonment has weakened him and if the Dark One had managed to kill him and absorb his powers it would have been a hard blow for the light," said Ethos.

When Aliyyah made no comment Ethos continued, "The book contains all the protective spells known to the elders and was written by your ancestors thousands of years ago. Your father brought it here for protection just before his death and entrusted it to my keeping. If I recall correctly there is also a letter inside, which may be for you. I am not sure as I have never opened the book."

"A treasure indeed," exclaimed Aliyyah.

"Now look into the other two chests once more," commanded Ethos, "and see what is truly in them."

In the first chest now there was nothing but a black swirling mist from which the most heinous of screams were coming, while the other chest contained a mirror showing the gaunt faces of young men and women filled with despair and fear. Full of pity, Aliyyah asked, "Who are they and what is that black mist?"

"They are seekers from different worlds who failed their test here and were trapped within these chests, as would have been your fate if you had chosen wrongly. The mist is their ignorance and fear, which caused them to choose wrongly, and that is what is now tormenting them."

Full of compassion, Aliyyah asked, "Is there no way to set them free from this torment?"

"Do they deserve to be set free?" questioned Ethos.

"Yes," replied Aliyyah firmly. "They must have been chosen in the first place to set out on the quest and to reach here they must have already passed many tests and dangers. Furthermore, they must have been sincere to pass the questioning of the guardians. They should be forgiven for failing your test and sent back to their home worlds unharmed."

"You truly are a seeker," exclaimed Ethos. "But how should they be returned?" he asked quizzically.

"I think they must have been imprisoned by the same magic as the seekers in the dragon chamber were. I am sure you know how to release them and send them back to their own worlds, with all memory of the quest removed from their memories to protect them and the true seekers of the light," replied Aliyyah.

'You have grown wise, young Aliyyah, and indeed I do know how to release them, but only after I have answered your questions and you have left this city and returned to the Island of Mists," said Ethos.

"Why must you wait?" queried Aliyyah.

Chuckling, Ethos explained, "Once I release them this city will be destroyed and buried beneath the seabed. Then I will be able to return to my home in the underwater mountains in the deep trench of Cepa at the very bottom of the sea. Now, what is your first question, Aliyyah?"

With Ethos's permission, Aliyyah sat down at the feet of Ethos. Compared to the size of Ethos she appeared as small as an ant. Composing herself, she asked her first question.

"I came here to ask you where to find the Book of Fazma. Can you please tell me its hiding place?"

"Well said, Princess. A polite question will nearly always get you the right answers. The Book of Fazma is hidden in a chest in the nest of the king of all the giant eagles, high in the Cantun Mountains, beyond the lands of the whistling winds, a three-week journey from the Island of Mists."

Thinking about this, Aliyyah asked her second question. "Flow do I retrieve the book from the chest while protecting myself and my companions from the eagle king and his subjects?"

Chuckling once more, Ethos replied, "A wise question, Aliyyah. Swift Wing, the king of all the eagles, is a friend of Mahin and Greenthor. He has no love of the dark and possesses great powers. No one, not even the Dark One would be able to take the book out of the chest without his permission. So the answer to your question is you ask him politely for the book and then you prove to him who you are. You can do that by opening the chest to which you already have the keys."

It took Aliyyah a moment to realise that Ethos was referring to the Keys of Hanaj.

"It seems the keys open more than one treasure," she said to herself.

"Your third question, please," demanded Ethos.

"I have promised Errina, the daughter of King Err, that I would help her," began Aliyyah. "She is filled with sorrow at being half human and half dragon. She wishes to become either human or dragon. She would prefer to become human so that she can be reunited with her mother, but she would still accept becoming a full dragon if that is the only choice. Dark Wing said the only one that might be able to help is you. So my third question is, how do I help her to become human?"

"A difficult question to answer, for you may not like to hear what you have asked for," replied Ethos.

"I have made a promise to help if I can and I cannot break it now, especially as she risked her life helping me. I have a debt to pay."

"Very well," said Ethos. "But you must swear to me that you will only try to help her after you have recovered all four treasures and you know what your next task is."

"I swear upon my honour as a seeker and a dragon friend," Aliyyah said solemnly.

"Very well, in order for her to be reborn she must first die and let her old body be burnt away like the phoenix. You must take her to the legendary city of Zinavry in the land of the Sand Warriors. In this city there is an ancient temple guarded by a multi-coloured serpent by the name of Zuzu. After you have passed all his tests you must ask him for the elixirs of life and death and pay him whatever he demands without question. Do not fear, for he is a creature of magic and does not eat any form of flesh, but his price may be high. When you have fulfilled his terms he will give you two glass phials, one red and one white. Errina must drink the red one first, making sure that she concentrates fully on obtaining a human form. You must be prepared for a raging fire that will spring up around her and start to bum away the dragon half of her body. Wait until not one scale of her dragon body remains and then quickly pour the white phial into her mouth. Do not be late or the fire will destroy her completely. Do not fear the flames as they will not harm you, however, Errina will fear the pain a real fire causes. You must be strong and not listen to her pleas and screams, but wait until the right moment. Too soon or too late and you will kill her. After drinking the white phial, the flames will disappear and Errina will appear to be dead. You must cover her with the white cloth that Zuzu will give you and wait until Errina sits up by herself. Do not be tempted to remove the cloth before that or her transformation will be incomplete."

"You are sure that she will become totally human?" interrupted Aliyyah.

'That depends on Errina and which side of her nature is stronger. If her human side is stronger than the dragon part will be burnt away forever and she will become human like her mother. However, if the dragon side is stronger, when you cover her with the cloth she will revert and be transformed into a full-blooded dragon with no human form at all. What will happen I cannot predict, but you must explain fully to Errina these things before you take her to Zinavry. Now, your next question, please."

"Errina's father has sworn to destroy me if he has the chance, for freeing Errina's mother and forcing him to promise never to aid the Dark One or oppose King Poseidon again. So how do I rescue Errina from her father's palace without getting into a fight with King Err or harming anyone in the palace."

"That is simple, Princess," retorted Ethos. "You must ask the dragons to take you to the island of the healers far away from here. As soon as you arrive you must ask to see Kathir, the oldest and the leader of all the healers. You must ask him for the strongest sleeping potion he has, one that can be used on sea creatures, especially sea dragons. He will ask you what you want with the potion. Do not be afraid to tell him the truth for he is a friend of the light. Do not forget to ask for the antidote as well, for if the sea creatures fall into too deep a sleep or they sleep too long, they may actually drown. As soon as you have the potions you must ask at least two of the dragons to accompany you back to King Err's palace. Do not worry about the magical barrier, for it will not stop you if your heart is pure. Once you are above the palace you must pour the sleeping potion into the sea waters and wait for it to take effect. As soon as you see any sea creature floating on the water's surface you must dive down and search for Errina. When you find her, pour a little of the antidote into her mouth and wait for her to wake up. Once she has recovered you must, with as much speed as possible, leave the palace and return to the surface where the dragons will be waiting. Ask one of them to take Errina to the nearest land and wait there for you. Once you see that Errina is out of sight, release the rest of the antidote into the water before you leave on the other dragon. Fly swiftly, for the first to awake will be King Err himself. You must pass through the magical barrier before he catches you or there will be a bloody battle. After that, make your way to the city of Zinavry if you can. Remember, however, that you are responsible for any adverse consequences of helping Errina, no matter what they are, so be wary and careful in all you do. That is four questions, what is the fifth?"

Aliyyah thought for a minute before asking, "I know that Mahin is one of the guardians of the light and has great powers, but why does he not use them to defeat the Dark One and set the islands free?"

"This question I am not permitted to answer, except to say everything has an opposite that complements it, as day and night follow each other and life comes from death and death comes from life. You still have three questions left."

"I know that my father is dead, but what about my mother? Does she still live, and if she does, where is she now?"

Ethos looked curiously at Aliyyah before asking, "Mahin never told you?"

"Told me what?" replied Aliyyah.

With a great sigh Ethos asked, "Do you really wish to know something that will only bring you pain?"

"Yes," stated Aliyyah firmly. "I need to know what happened and why Mahin would never tell me anything about my mother."

"Very well," replied Ethos resignedly. "Your mother was a beautiful and intelligent woman who loved your father dearly, however, shortly after your birth she had to travel to her mother's city far away. Your father could not accompany her and on the way back her entourage was attacked by the Dark One and she was taken prisoner. After a few months, she either escaped or was released and made her way back to your father. Overjoyed, your father took her back to the royal palace unaware that she had been bewitched by the Dark One to kill your father. On the next hunting trip she insisted on going with your father. After a long chase, she and your father were separated from the rest of the party as they pursued a particularly beautiful stag. On and on they went, your mother leading your father further into the deep forest. Finally they reached a glade where they were surrounded by the servants of the Dark One. Your father tried to protect your mother, but she pulled out her knife and stabbed him, driving the blade deep into his arm. At the sight of your father's blood the spell was broken. Shocked at what she had done she started weeping as she pulled her blade out of your father's arm. Ripping the hem of her dress she swiftly bandaged the wound then stood beside her husband, blade in hand, and waited for servants of the Dark One to attack. The battle was long and many of the enemy fell beneath the blades of your mother and father. Eventually one of the Dark One's servants ran straight at your father from behind. Your mother saw the danger and shouted a warning to her husband. Seeing that your father would be unable to defend himself from this attack as he was being attacked by two men in front of him, she threw herself between there attacker and your father, taking the stroke that was intended for him. Turning round he saw your mother collapsing with a dagger stuck deep into her chest. At that moment the rest of the shooting party arrived and the enemy was driven off. As your mother lay dying in your father's arms, she begged him to forgive her and to look after you. Heartbroken, your father took her back to the palace and had her placed into a glass coffin in the crypts of the palace, where you have never be allowed to enter. Shortly after that your father too was murdered and laid to rest next to your mother in the palace crypts. Your birth had been kept a secret from the other elders, so Mahin ghosted you out of the palace and, keeping his promise to your parents, raised and trained you the best he could."

Weeping, Aliyyah was unable to say anything. For a while Ethos watched and waited for her to calm herself, but eventually said, "Aliyyah, you have little time, what are your last two questions?" Taking a deep breath Aliyyah said, "The Dark One has a lot to answer for! I need to know if he has any weaknesses. How can he be destroyed forever?"

"A difficult question Princess Aliyyah. Firstly, as I am sure you know by now, you are not the one to defeat the Dark One, but someone close to you. I am not permitted to tell you who that person is, but if you succeed in your quest to recover all four treasures, who it is will be revealed to you. As for the Dark One's weaknesses they are many, but he is aware of them all and is careful to keep them in check. He is proud and arrogant and tends to underestimate some things that he should pay more attention to, so that these weakness, we can use to our advantage. He is also somewhat hasty, acting when he should perhaps wait, but his greatest weakness is his belief that he is invincible and all powerful. While it is true his powers, both spiritually and magically, are great, he tends to forget that he can be destroyed as all creations can."

"But how?" interrupted Aliyyah. "How."

"Simple, Aliyyah, there is only thing that can destroy the Dark One and that is the Sword of IIa, that sword and that sword alone can take his life and only one person can wield it. Who that person is, only the Sand Wizard can tell you. One more thing, Aliyyah, even if the Dark One is destroyed, it does not mean that evil is destroyed as well. Even if the light triumphs and we achieve peace once more, sooner or later evil will return in one form or another. Not until every bad thought and action has been removed completely from the hearts of all the creations will evil be destroyed forever. You have two more question, use them wisely!"

Glancing at her sand clock Aliyyah realised it was almost time for her to eat another piece of mirkweed. "Forgive me," said Aliyyah. "I must eat another piece of mirkweed or I will lose the ability to breathe underwater."

Ethos smiled and waited while Aliyyah chewed the bitter mirkweed.

Finally, after she had swallowed the last little bit of the rubbery weed, Aliyyah said thoughtfully, "Of all the nine dragons only Sayning has remained aloof and suspicious. He is so different and cunning that not even the other dragons trust him, yet I feel that he would be a true friend if only I could gain his trust. Tell me, how do I gain the trust and friendship of Sayning?"

"A difficult task, Princess Aliyyah, for Sayning is not what he seems to be. To gain his trust you must first prove yourself worthy and to gain his friendship you must first be a true friend to him. Remember too that friends take each other as they are and don't ask questions or doubt each other, but love and protect one another. Take special care with Saying for a truer friend you will never find, but remember as well that if you betray him in any way, a greater enemy you will not find. Your last question please."

Although Aliyyah was not satisfied with Ethos's answer she knew even if she pressed him about Sayning he would say no more. One question left, but she had so many questions to ask. She had to be careful and choose wisely.

Thinking furiously Aliyyah finally decided what her last question would be. "Ethos, I feel in my heart that the quest and the eventual defeat of the Dark One is going to take many years, therefore tell me what thing will not only be my greatest protection against the Dark One, but also my greatest weapon."

Chuckling once more, Ethos replied, "You are cheating, Aliyyah! That is in reality two questions, not one, but as the answer is the same I will tell you. Your greatest protection and your greatest weapon is your heart. The Dark One cannot control a heart that is pure and sincere, he fears a truthful heart more than he fears anything else. He knows that the only thing that can kill him is the Sword of IIa and that only a person with a truthful and pure heart can wield that sword. Now I have answered all your questions you must leave this place. Go with my blessings and do not look back. I will give you time to reach the gate leading back to the Island of Mists before setting the other seekers free. Make sure you are no longer here when that happens. Tell Kara, I am going home, he will know what to do. Farewell, Princess Aliyyah, may you succeed where others have failed."

Looking at the ancient turtle, Aliyyah made a slight bow before saying, "Thank you for your wisdom and knowledge. May you live for many more years, Ethos."

The turtle gave her a funny look, both sad and pitying, which made Aliyyah feel slightly uneasy. She wanted to ask Ethos what was wrong, but she realised that Ethos valued his privacy and it would be bad manners to intrude by asking him what was the matter.

Swimming as quickly as she could, Aliyyah left the inner chamber of the temple and swam out into the great courtyard. It seemed to be even more deserted now, not a single fish could be seen anymore. It was almost as if all the sea creatures knew some disaster was about to befall this city once more. Hurrying out of the temple she found Kara still waiting for her at the bottom of the stairs. Swimming as fast as she could towards the great white shark she grabbed hold of his dorsal fin before saying, "We must return to the gate as swiftly as possible."

Kara nodding his head began to swim as fast as he could towards the underwater gate and passage that led up to the Island of Mists.

As they swam, Kara asked Aliyyah, "Did the green turtle give you any messages for me, Princess?"

"Yes," replied Aliyyah. "He told me to say to you that 'he is going home'. Although I do not understand what he meant by that."

Sighing Kara asked, "You asked him to release the trapped seekers did you not?"

"Yes," replied Aliyyah. "Why, did I do something wrong by that? I have sworn to set free all those imprisoned by magic, so I had to fulfil my vow."

"Do not misunderstand me, Aliyyah. Truly you are a seeker, but I think that you do not know what Ethos truly meant by going home."

"What do you mean?" pleaded Aliyyah. "Please explain."

"Ethos is old, so old that there is no creature who is as old as he is and he is tired, very, very tired. He has carried his burden for untold centuries waiting for the right person to come along before he could return to place he came from. Aliyyah, he is going home to die and at last find peace. Did he by any chance arrange for a shell to be given to you?"

"Yes, he did," answered Aliyyah. "Why?"

"You have been given a great honour and an even greater responsibility. Ethos has chosen you as his heir, for in that shell is all the knowledge, wisdom and understanding he has guarded all these long centuries. Use it wisely and protect it with your life."

Aliyyah remained quiet for some time, overcome by the action of Ethos. Never in all her life had she even dreamt of such an honour and responsibility falling upon her. It was also rather frightening as she realised that many people, especially the Dark One would do anything to get their hands on this knowledge. Suddenly a thought crossed her mind, "Kara, what about you and your people? Where will you go?" "Do not worry about us, Princess Aliyyah! As soon as you entered the great temple I ordered all the sharks under my rule to leave this city and swim to the open sea where they are waiting for me to join them. As soon as I have left you at the gateway I will swim swiftly to our rendezvous and then lead my kind to the far eastern seas, where another lost city lies on the ocean seabed."

As they approached the gateway to the underwater passage leading up to the Island of Mists, they felt the seabed begin to tremble as buildings started to shake, threatening to collapse around them.

"Quickly, Aliyyah," said Kara. "You do not have much time, you must reach the island before the city is totally destroyed or you will be trapped between the two gateways! Hurry."

Aliyyah was relieved to see Diousni still waiting for her and as she approached she saw the gateway was still open.

"Quickly, Princess, you have little time! Good luck and may you succeed in your quest!" cried Diousni. "Send our greetings to Greenthor and Mahin, goodbye."

By now, the trembles had grown even stronger and some of the buildings had started to collapse as the seabed cracked and moved. Swimming as fast as she could, Aliyyah entered the tunnel and pushed herself upwards. Frantically she swam up and up until she reached the turn where the water ended. Pulling herself up she realised she was still not safe as breathlessly she ran up the remaining steps to the surface. Behind, she could hear the falling buildings and, as she glanced backwards, she saw the glow-lights going out one by one as water raced up the tunnel after her.

Running now as fast as she had ever run, she looked ahead hoping to see the exit of the tunnel. Just as she thought her lungs would burst and her legs collapse beneath her she saw bright sunlight flooding down, illumining the tunnel. With a final effort, she ran up the last few steps, to collapse exhausted and out of breath on the grass of the cliff overlooking the sea.

As she lay there she felt death throes of the ancient city of Atlantis and her heart was filled with sadness at what it meant. She hoped that Kara and Diousni had got away safely and that maybe one day she would see them again. Now, however, she needed to rejoin her companions and continue the quest.

As she rose to her feet she heard a familiar voice behind her. "Well, Princess, what have you been up to this time?"

"Sayning," exclaimed Aliyyah as she turned round to face him. "I know where the Book of Fazma is!"

"Well done, Aliyyah, well done. I will lead you back through the gateway so you can rejoin your companions, but remember you must never tell them that I am one of the guardians here."

"But I thought Atlantis was destroyed, Sayning. Is not your work here finished?"

Looking at Aliyyah firmly, Sayning replied, "There are many gateways to many worlds, more gateways than there are guardians. There is still much work to be done here, but I will see you again soon, maybe sooner than you think," he added cryptically.

Chapter Eleven

Swift Wing

As they walked towards the gateway, Sayning noticed how sad Aliyyah was. "What is wrong, Princess?"

"I have the information I needed, but the city of Atlantis is now destroyed and Ethos.

"Ethos," interrupted Sayning, "has returned to his home. In this world you will see him no more. Come we must hurry, for the gateway will not remain open long. As soon as we pass through it will be closed forever, never to be reopened. If we stay here we will be trapped between the two gates."

Hurrying, they quickly reached the gates. Just before they passed through the portal, Sayning told Aliyyah, "As soon as we reach the other side I will disappear in the mists before anyone, especially Dark Wing sees me."

"Are you sure that there will be a thick enough mist to conceal you?" asked Aliyyah.

"Of course there will be," replied Sayning. "This island protects its secrets, as you must now know, and I am one of its secrets."

Side by side they passed underneath the great stone portal and as before Aliyyah felt herself being pulled through the void, while whispered voices once more surrounded her, talking softly in a language that she could not understand. As she stumbled through the portal on the other side she heard Sayning's voice, "Remember your promise, Aliyyah, tell no one, not even Dark Wing about me."

As she emerged from the stone gateway she saw the landscape was indeed covered with a white mist so thick she could not even see her own hand when she held it out in front of her. However,

172

after a few minutes the mists disappeared and she saw Toowooni and Dark Wing waiting anxiously for her return. Toowooni was the first one to see her and he flew over to her twittering excitedly. Dark Wing waited for Aliyyah to come over to him before asking, "Princess, you were successful?"

"Yes," replied Aliyyah, "but unfortunately the city of Atlantis no longer exists."

"It is as we excepted," replied Dark Wing. "There is a time and a place for everything and when that time is finished then we must return from where we came from." Then looking at Aliyyah squarely he asked, "Ethos?"

"You know his name?" asked Aliyyah.

"Of course I do, all dragons know who Ethos is and many of us have studied with him or from his students, as your own teacher Mahin did."

"He has returned home," said Aliyyah sadly.

"May he find peace at last," said Dark Wing. "Now, where do we go from here?"

"We must go to the Cantun Mountains in the lands of the whistling winds and search for the king of all the eagles Swift Wing, as the Book of Fazma is in his possession."

"That is a three-week journey from here," said Dark Wing. "We can travel by sea and then by land until we reach the foot of the mountains. Once we are there, Najputih and Toowooni must stay behind as the road is too steep for Najputih and too high and cold for Toowooni. I will carry you up to the eagles' nests, but we must approach them very carefully or they will attack us without asking any questions first."

"Surely they will not attack a dragon?" asked Aliyyah.

"Well that depends on who the dragon is," laughed Dark Wing. "Some of the younger and more foolish dragons have on occasions been known to try and steal eagle eggs for their breakfast, but they soon learnt the hard way not to disturb the eagles!"

"What happened to them?" asked a curious Aliyyah chuckling.

Dark Wing replied, "Let's just say that a dragon's nose is very sensitive and eagles are very fast. Now, I think we had better rejoin the others and continue our journey."

"Wait a few minutes," said Aliyyah quickly. "There is something I have to do first. Please hand me my travelling cloak."

Dark Wing, who had been guarding the cloak, passed it to Aliyyah who put it on before taking out of one of the pockets the Keys of Hanaj. Next she removed the small leather book she had been given by Ethos from inside her dress pocket. Taking the smallest key, she placed it in the lock and turned. Click, the lock opened and Aliyyah was able to remove the straps that kept the book shut tight.

"What is that, Aliyyah?" twittered Toowooni in excitement. "What is it?"

"This," replied Aliyyah, "is a gift from Ethos, the green turtle. It contains all the protective spells and amulets known to the elders."

"A priceless gift, Princess," commented Dark Wing. "One you must look after with your life and use with great care."

"I know, Dark Wing, but inside it is something that to me is even greater and more precious," replied Aliyyah.

"And what could that be, Aliyyah?" questioned Dark Wing

"Ethos told me that it contained a letter from my father."

"I see," replied the dragon. "We will give you time to read it, but please do not be too long as the others are waiting for us and they must be very worried by now."

Nodding her head Aliyyah started turning the pages of the book one by one looking for her father's letter. As she turned each page she glanced at the inscriptions and diagrams that covered the paper. Some of them she could read with ease while others remained a mystery to her to be solved at another time and place. After a short while she found what she was looking for. Tucked into the middle of the book was a yellow envelope, which had the royal seal stamped in candle wax on the back, sealing the letter. On the front was written 'To my beloved daughter'.

With trembling fingers she gingerly broke the seal and opened it. Inside she found a single sheet of paper, a golden key and a colourful headband made of eagle feathers, taken from the first fluffy feathers that drop from the baby eagles as they grow their adult wings. It was soft and warm to the touch, and light, hardly weighing anything at all. Each feather had been dyed a separate colour and then sewn together on a thin piece of cloth. Picking up the piece of paper, she read:

My dearest daughter, if you are reading this then you have already spoken with Ethos. He would have told you where to find the Book of Fazma. However, he would not have given you the key that fits the lock of the chest, as unbeknown to him it is in this letter. The Keys of Hanaj, although they can open many things, cannot open the chest containing the Book of Fazma. You must wear the headband when you approach the nests of the eagles so they recognise you as a seeker and do not attack you, and whichever dragon carries you there. After you have taken the book, place the headband in the chest, lock it and give the key to Swift Wing for the headband is an ancient treasure of the eagles and long have they waited for it to be returned to them.

Once you have the book you must seek out the Sand Wizard, who lives in the empty quarter of the desert of the singing sands. It is he and he alone who can tell you what you must do after you have retrieved the four treasures, as it is he and he alone who holds the Sword of Ila. However, the dragons cannot help you here as they are bound by the ancient magic, which makes this place forbidden to them. If they try to enter it they will be destroyed. Only a companion who has to repay a debt to you may accompany you here.

Farewell, my daughter, and give my greetings to Swift Wing and his subjects, they were good friends to me and I am much indebted to them.

With trembling hands, Aliyyah read and reread the letter before carefully putting it back in the envelope, along with the key and the headband. Then she placed it into one of deep pockets in her travelling cloak and told Dark Wing and Toowooni what her father had written.

"The headband of Kumus," piped Toowooni. "No eagle would dare attack the one who wears it.

"Why is it special, Toowooni?" inquired Aliyyah curiously.

"Each king of the eagles has a very long life, eight times the life span of a human but they only ever have one male hatchling. When the hatchling grows up it loses its baby down before growing its adult feathers. The first downy feather to fall from the hatchling is kept and then added to the headband when the old king dies. It is at this time also that the hatchling receives its name from the eagle elders. Each feather is dyed a different colour so that the eagles know from which king the feather came. It has great ancestral value as well as being endowed with certain magical properties. What they are I do not know, as it is a secret kept closely guarded by the eagles. I also do not understand how it came to be in your father's possession, for I can think of no reason why the eagles would allow it to be taken from them, unless by some strange chance your father had actually succeeded in becoming an eagle friend."

"An eagle friend?" asked Aliyyah. "What do you mean by that?" "I can think of no other reason why they would trust him with their most precious possession. However, if he was an eagle friend he would be only the second person the eagles have trusted. He must have done something very great to gain their trust," explained Toowooni.

"Who was the other person?" asked Aliyyah.

"The other person was Aliyyah the Pure, your namesake. She cured their king after he was shot by a poisonous arrow fired by one of the Hodglings. These vile creatures resemble large rats that walk on two legs, like humans. They speak a language similar to the speech of other dark creatures and are very cunning. Living underground in damp, dark places, they thrive wherever there is death and disease. They are totally corrupt and evil and consumed with the desire to destroy their ancient enemy, the eagle."

"I see," replied Aliyyah. "I think I will have to ask Swift Wing about the headband and my father and hope that he will tell me the full story about them." Then turning to face Dark Wind, she asked, "Dark Wing, is it true that no dragon can enter the desert of the singing sands?"

"Yes, my Princess," replied Dark Wing. "Our magic and the magic of the singing sands are like fire and water. One will always destroy the other. We cannot even fly over the desert, but must always fly around it. I am afraid that once you enter that desert we cannot help you at all. Not even Greenthor will dare risk the consequences of the clash of magic."

"I see," said Aliyyah. "I must enter the desert alone then?"

Dark Wing chuckled, surprising Aliyyah. "I think you have forgotten about Najputih! Although he is a magical creature, his magic has been drained from him. Not only that, he is still in debt to you for rescuing him from the Castle of Mirrors. I think, as well, he would definitely refuse to be left behind again."

Smiling, Aliyyah replied, "I guess you're right, and we had better go and rejoin him before he gets too worried. Will you carry me once more, Dark Wing?"

"With pleasure, Princess," said Dark Wing, as he lowered his body to make it easier for Aliyyah to climb up. With as much dignity as she could manage she climbed up onto the dragon's back, avoiding the sharp spikes that ran all along his side, and settled herself just behind his neck. Bracing herself she felt a surge of exhilaration as Dark Wing slowly opened his massive black wings and rose up into the air, followed by Toowooni.

Flying high above the mists, Aliyyah could see the mysterious island beneath her. As she flew back to Adono and Najputih she could just hear the guardians bidding her goodbye.

Almost as soon as they had left the island Aliyyah could hear Najputih frantically calling her telepathically. "Aliyyah, where are you? What's happening? Answer me!"

"Don't worry, Najputih, we are on our way, everything is alright!

I will explain it all in a while."

"Just like a mother hen," mused Dark Wing. "Don't worry so much, Najputih, I will look after her!"

"And who will look after you?" retorted Najputih.

Laughing, Aliyyah saw the chariot just below her where Adono, Aquas and Najputih were restlessly waiting. Flying as low as he possibly could, Dark Wing hovered while Aliyyah half scrambled and half dropped into the chariot below.

After picking herself up as gracefully as she could, she settled herself down on the padded bench before telling the others most of what had happened, being careful to make sure she did not mention Sayning.

When she had finished Adono told her, "I can take you and the unicorn to the shores of the land of the whistling winds, but from there you will still have a two-week journey."

"Thank you," replied Aliyyah. "You have been a great help to us."

"It is nothing, Princess, we are in your debt. Already you have freed us from Saragossa and the threat from King Err. My father will be overjoyed with what you have accomplished. We only hope that you will succeed in your quest and the Dark One will be vanquished."

Warily Aliyyah replied, "If it is my destiny then I pray that I can fulfil what is written."

Adono looked at her before enquiring, "Shall we go, Princess?"

With a small nod Aliyyah settled back and rested her head against the back of the chariot, as the giant seahorses swiftly began to pull them towards the land of the whistling winds.

From above Aliyyah heard Dark Wing say, "Rest, Aliyyah! I am going to search for some fresh water and fruits for you and Najputih. I will return soon."

"Thank you, Dark Wing," said Aliyyah. "Thank you so much!'

As soon as Dark Wing was out of sight, Aliyyah opened her thoughts to Najputih. "Najputih, why did you not tell me that you were one of the guardians of the light? You do not trust me?"

"Who told you that?" replied Najputih.

"Ethos," answered Aliyyah. "He asked me to send his greetings to you as he is going home to rest."

Najputih understood straight away what was meant by that. "He deserves his rest. Long has he served the light, but it saddens me that he will no longer be there to aid us in our fight. He passed his knowledge to you I presume?"

"Yes," replied Aliyyah. "But you have still not answered my question. It seems you still do not trust me!"

"It is not a question of trust, Aliyyah," said Najputih. "Yes, I am one of the guardians of the light and that is another reason why the Dark One was trying to destroy me. I am also one of the elders. I am as old as Mahin, having reached maturity when the council of elders was first set up. However, I, like all the other elders, am bound by the strict laws of the ancient magic. I may tell no one who I am except for those who already know what I am, and even then I cannot reveal more that I have just told you."

"So," thought Aliyyah, in such a way that Najputih knew she was very hurt. "You have many more secrets that you have not yet told me?"

"Yes," replied the unicorn. "As do Poseidon, Mahin, Ethos and even the dragons, but it is for your own safety and good that you do not know these secrets. Sometimes to have a little knowledge is more dangerous than not knowing at all. Each of us has our own job and responsibility to take care of and we are given the knowledge we need to perform these tasks. Only a few of us are entrusted with great knowledge, as to carry the weight of it is very great. Even I do not know who all the guardians and elders are and I suspect the only two who may know are Mahin and Ethos. You must know, however, you can trust any one of us and we would willing give our lives to protect you, so do not feel hurt, my Princess!"

Aliyyah said nothing as she sat thinking about everything she had just learnt. It was true they had always tried to help and protect her, so why should she feel hurt or angry with them if they did not tell her their secrets. Najputih was right, after all, even she had her own secrets.

As she sat there she could feel Najputih trying to read her thoughts, even though he knew he could only communicate with her when she opened her mind to him and not read every thought that passed through her mind.

"You are right," she eventually thought. "Sometimes it is better not to known that which in itself may become a great burden to oneself. Keep your vows and my friendship. I will never desert you, dear friend, no matter what! However, after this I will not be surprised about anything I hear in the future."

Before long Dark Wing returned, bringing Aliyyah's water flask filled with fresh cool spring water and her provision bag, full with fresh fruit and nuts.

"I am sorry that there is no bread," said Dark Wing as Aliyyah took the flask and bag from the hovering dragon. "But the nearest land is uninhabited and I did not want to fly far away and leave you without my protection for too long."

"Do not worry," replied Aliyyah. "This is fine." Opening the bag she took some of the fruit out and shared it with Najputih. She offered Adono and Aquas some as well, but they both declined, saying, "Thank you, but we prefer fish or seaweed and flowers." Finishing their meal with some water, Aliyyah placed the flask and bag on the seat and closed her eyes. Before long the rocking movement of the chariot and the warmth of the morning sun had lulled her into a deep sleep.

When Aliyyah awoke it was mid-afternoon and the sun was beating down mercilessly, however she had not suffered any harm except for feeling very thirsty, as her companions had rigged a piece of thick sail cloth over her head so the sun did not bum her. As she reached for the water flask by her side she wondered where that piece of sail cloth had come from. After taking a few mouthfuls of water to slake her thirst, she rubbed her eyes sleepily before looking around.

To her greatest surprise, she saw that Dark Wing was pulling the chariot along using a piece of thick, twisted rope, obviously taken from some long, lost forgotten wreck. Of Adono and the seahorses, there was no sign. What had happened? Where were they? Not wanting to awaken Najputih, Aliyyah called out gently to Dark Wing, asking him what was going on.

"Do not worry, Princess, they are fine. The heat of the sun was torturing them so I took pity on them and told them to swim beneath the waves until it becomes cooler and I will pull the chariot for a while."

"I see," said Aliyyah. "But does the sun not bother you?"

Giving his now familiar chuckle, Dark Wing replied, "I am a dragon, we breathe fire. The heat of the sun is nothing to me. In fact, the hotter it is, the happier I am!"

Laughing at Dark Wing's words, she settled back underneath the canvas to escape the sun's rays. Before long Najputih awoke and told her how Toowooni and Dark Wing had arranged the shelter after Adono had swum deep to the bottom of the sea to find the sail cloth from an ancient wreck.

Looking around she could not see the owl anywhere. "Where is Toowooni?" she asked.

"I do not know," replied the unicorn. "But he said he was hungry so I assume he has gone hunting."

On and on they travelled and as the sun began to sink Adono and the seahorses surfaced not far from the chariot.

"Dark Wing, they are back!" cried Aliyyah, pointing to them.

"Good," replied the dragon. "They can take over, I need to go and find myself some food. Do you need any more water, Princess?"

Looking into her flask she saw that there was a little less than a third left, taking a few deep swigs she fed the rest to the unicorn before replying, "Yes Dark Wing the water flask is now empty."

Waiting for Adono to harness the seahorses once more, Dark Wing then dropped the rope he had been pulling, letting it fall back into the sea where Adono got it and hooked it to the chariot. Flying down low over the chariot, Aliyyah passed him her water flask to be filled up.

"I will not be very long, rest while you can as soon we will reach shore and you will have a long way to walk then." Then adding, with a sly chuckle, "that is, unless Najputih would like to be carried?"

"No," thought Najputih, "not unless I have no other choice at all! If Aliyyah is tired I can always carry her. She has not yet ridden a unicorn!"

"Touche," said Dark Wing as he disappeared into the gathering gloom, leaving Aliyyah and Najputih in the capable hands of Adono.

A few hours later Dark Wing returned, accompanied by Toowooni. Both of them looked well fed and happy. Dark Wing gave the water flask to Toowooni before flying up and away to find a place to rest for a few hours.

Gliding gently down, Toowooni dropped the flask next to the sleeping girl before perching himself on the edge of the chariot and also nodding off to sleep.

For the next few days they followed the same routine. Adono and the seahorses pulled the chariot throughout the night and into the early morning until the sun became too hot for them. After which, Dark Wing would lake over until the evening. Even Toowooni tried to pull the chariot, much to the amusement of the others, but gave up after a few tries, it was much too heavy for him.

Finally, on the eighth day, Toowooni, who had gone out hunting again, came flying back breathlessly. "Land, land ahead, not more than an hour's flight. Land!"

Searching the horizons, both Aliyyah and the unicorn strained their eyes to see where the land was.

"There," exclaimed Aliyyah. "Over there, it is land, at last." Then looking up she noticed Dark Wing had a rather amused look on his face. "Is that the land of the whistling winds?" asked Aliyyah.

"Yes, my Princess, it is! We should reach the shore within the hour."

181

"At last," thought Najputih. "I will be able to feel firm ground beneath my feet once more."

As they neared the shore, Aliyyah could understand how the land got its name. The trees all seemed to be bent down towards the ground and a whistling sound could be heard playing amongst the foliage.

When they had reached the shallows where the seahorses could go no further, Najputih finally consented to being carried the short distance to the shore by Dark Wing, after realising that although the waters were shallow for the seahorses it was still too deep for him. Najputih, like all unicorns, had no idea how to swim and had a greater fear of drowning than of dragons.

Chuckling all the way to the shore, Dark Wing carried the complaining unicorn as gently as a mother carries a newborn baby.

Aliyyah on the other hand preferred to swim. Handing her cloak, flask and provision bag over to Dark Wing to carry to the shore, she slid into the water and said goodbye to the giant seahorses. Stroking each one gently, she thanked them for bringing her so far away from their homes. Tossing their heads, they nudged her as if to say, 'It is our pleasure'.

Then, as she trod water, she said goodbye to Adono. "Thank you Adono for all your help. I will always remember you and what you have done for me."

"It is nothing, Princess. It was an honour to help you. I will miss your company on the way back."

"Thank you and please thank your father for me as well. Tell him I will return to visit him and see his kingdom as I promised, but I do not know when that will be."

"We understand," replied Adono. Then asking her to wait for a few minutes, Adono disappeared into the ocean, to return with a necklace made from dainty and beautiful sea flowers. "This is a gift from us, I hope you like it. It will dry out on land, but blossom again each time it is returned to the sea. And now," he added mischievously, "let's see who can reach the shore first."

Aliyyah knew she had no chance of beating Adono, but nevertheless she tried her best, swimming as fast as she could. As she expected, Adono reached the shore long before her and sat in the waves that were lapping the shore, his tail lazily flapping up and down.

As Aliyyah stood and walked towards him, he turned himself with a quick flip so that he was now facing back out towards the sea. "Goodbye Aliyyah," he called as he swam into the deeper waters. "Goodbye. Remember me until we meet again. Take care!"

As Aliyyah waved goodbye to him, he dived back into the sea so that all could be seen was his tail and the sea chariot slowly disappearing beneath the waves with him.

As she left the sea, she headed to where her companions waited for her.

"Well, there are just four of us now," she said as she sat down on the sands.

The sun had only just started to rise up high in the sky and the sands where still cool, although in a short while they would become warm as the sun heated them.

As she sat there, Toowooni hopped over to her. "Princess, I am afraid that there will be only three of you continuing this journey for I must return to my own islands. I have gone as far as I dare and I have many duties and responsibilities to attend too among my own people. I dare not go any further, please forgive me."

Looking at the contrite owl, Aliyyah smiled. "Go in peace, my friend, and thank you for all your help and guidance. Send my greetings and thanks to your kind. If I can, I will return to your islands one day and learn some of your beautiful songs."

Toowooni brightened up at Aliyyah's kind words. "Thank you, Princess. We will wait for that day." Then hopping up closer he did a clumsy little bow before turning towards the unicorn and dragon and saying goodbye to them as well. Flying up into the air he cried out, "Goodbye, goodbye, until we meet again, goodbye."

Aliyyah and the others watched until he was out of sight then started walking towards the woods that lined the hills. Taking her cloak from Dark Wing, she put in back on as she was now feeling a bit cold in her damp clothes. She then slung the water flask and provision bag over her shoulders as they began their long trek to the Cantun Mountains.

Aliyyah soon realised that more than one wind was playing around them, it seemed that there were several. She could hear different kinds of whistle as the winds playfully tugged at her clothes and tried to blow her cloak off. Some whistles were loud and short while others were like soft whispers, long and mysterious. As they travelled, Aliyyah marvelled at the magnitude of the landscape, but at the same time wondered when they would reach a village or even a house in this strange land.

"Dark Wing, is there no villages or houses here at all? Does no one live here?"

"My Princess, no one can stand the whistling winds. At first you will be able to tolerate them, but after some time most people would go mad. The winds never stop nor do the whispers. The only creatures that live here other, than the eagles and the Hodglings, are some wild animals. Sometimes, but not very often, you may find a traveller, but they never tarry long and leave this land as soon as they can."

"I see," said the young princess. "How far are the mountains from here?"

"By foot, a two-week journey, however, if we flew it would only take five or six days."

Alarmed, Najputih quickly protested. "I do not want to dangle beneath Dark Wing like a floppy toy for five to six days. I will walk, thank you!"

Laughing, both Aliyyah and Dark Wing assured the irate unicorn that they would not force him to fly.

"I need the exercise anyhow," added Aliyyah. "After all that sitting down in the chariot."

"But it would be faster," said Dark Wing slyly.

Day after day they travelled, getting closer to the mountains. As they journeyed the countryside began to change. The woods gave way to great plains of grass that rippled like the sea as the winds, stronger now, blew backwards and forwards across them in an endless game of catch-me-if-you-can. By now Aliyyah could understand why no one dared live here, even she was beginning to find the constant whistling extremely annoying. Even at night she found it difficult to sleep with the non-stop whistling everywhere, and as a result she was getting irritable and bad tempered. Her only comfort, other than her companions, was the fact that every day she could see the mountains getting closer.

After twelve days of constant blowing and whistling they approached the middling marshes that lay between them and the mountains.

Dark Wing suddenly stopped and looked carefully at both Aliyyah and the unicorn. "In front of us are the middling marshes, a foul, black, stinking land full of pits that can suck you down to your death. They writhe with poisonous snakes, scorpions, spiders, bugs, biting insects and other evil creatures. They stretch right back to the foot of the Cantun Mountains. At the base of the mountains there are many dark and damp caves. This is where the Hodglings make their homes. Anyone who nears these marshes are in danger of being attacked and killed by these obnoxious and evil creatures. Probably they already know that we are approaching, but they will not attack yet, they are cunning, but also very cautious. They will not make a move until they are sure they can capture us without any difficulties."

"If that is the case, what do you suggest we do?" asked a concerned Aliyyah.

"I have a plan," replied Dark Wing. "One Najputih will not like and one that is not without danger, but to try any other way would be even more dangerous."

"What is it?" thought Najputih.

"Halfway up the mountain there is a wide ledge that juts out. It cannot be reached except by creatures that fly. Often the eagles use it for some of their ceremonies, but most of the time it is empty. The Hodglings have never been able to reach it from below and of course if they tried to reach it from above, the eagles would pull them off the mountains and smash their bodies on the jagged rocks below. As we cannot leave Najputih here, I suggest that he allows me to carry him up to that ledge, where he can wait in safety until we have retrieved the book."

"Not again," cried the distressed unicorn. "Is there no other way?"

"None that I can see," replied the dragon. "Even now I can sense we are being watched. We must move swiftly before they make their move."

"You said that there was some danger," interrupted Aliyyah. "What do you mean?"

Sighing deeply Dark Wing replied, "The Hodglings are excellent archers and dip all their arrows in a poison that kills slowly and painfully. Anything that moves they shoot at, especially anything that flies over them. The eagles always fly high, way out of their reach, but when I carry Najputih I will be

185

forced to fly slowly to avoid the jagged rocks that surround the mountain and prevent the Hodglings from climbing."

"Why can't you just fly up high from here like the eagles?" questioned Aliyyah.

"Because, Princess I need to land on the ledge and the wind currents are too dangerous to fly any other way with such a burden."

"I am not that heavy," thought an offended unicorn.

"I did not mean it in an offensive way, Najputih even the eagles are careful when trying to land there, but you must realise that while I am flying you will be vulnerable to their arrows. Aliyyah will also be at risk, but less so than you as she will be riding on my back. Are you prepared to take the risk?"

"Do I have any choice?" retorted Najputih. "Stay here and be captured and maybe killed by evil rats or dangle from your claws again as a target for their archers!"

Putting her arms around the distressed unicorn, Aliyyah hugged him close. "I will not let anything happen! You know that. Anyhow, don't forget I carry the Day Bloom and if by chance an arrow did hit one of us, I could quickly cure it."

"Still," protested Najputih, "I am going to be the most obvious target."

"Do you have any other plan?" queried Dark Wing. "We can leave you here to wait for us, of course, but I don't know whether we will find you or roasted unicorn when we come back!"

Reluctantly Najputih had no choice but to agree to Dark Wing's plan.

"Don't worry too much, I will protect both of you," said the dragon.

"Hmph," thought the unicorn, "that is a great comfort, I must say."

Shaking her head in amusement and concern, Aliyyah once again climbed onto the back of Dark Wing and settled herself as comfortably as possible, just behind his scaly neck.

"Remember, Najputih, if everything goes as planned I will gently drop you on the ledge and take Aliyyah up to see Swift Wing. I will not land there unless one of us has been injured." Then, before the unicorn could make any protest, Dark Wing continued, "I cannot carry you up to the top, the air currents are too dangerous and there is a good chance the eagles would attack you before realising you were a friend. Not only that, there is no place to land at the peaks except for narrow shelves of rock or the nests of the giant eagles themselves. I will have to hover and although I am strong, you are heavy. I am afraid you must wait where you will be safest."

Without another word, Dark Wing opened up his mighty wings, gently clasped Najputih in his claws and lifted the trembling unicorn off the ground.

"Aliyyah," called the distressed unicorn. "You should have asked Ethos how I could grow wings, it would be much easier than this."

Feeling once more the exhilaration of flying, Aliyyah laughed before replying, "Relax and enjoy yourself, feel the sun and the wind!"

"I would rather feel the ground beneath my feet," complained Najputih.

By now Dark Wing had reached the middling marshes and as his powerful wings bore them, they looked down at the dark and desolate ground beneath. The earth itself was black, an evil, unnatural black, darker in some places than others. Aliyyah realised that these must be the places where the 'Quick earths' lay. Tough, shaggy bushes dotted the landscape, their curved, razor-sharp thorns ready to ensnare and tear the clothing and skin of anyone who tried to penetrate them. What few trees there were appeared more dead than alive, their stunted twisted branches looking like the deformed limbs of a crooked man whose back was bent with some unseen burden.

A putrid sulphur-like stench rose up from the fermenting ground, making Aliyyah want to gag and vomit on its foulness. Despite all this though, Aliyyah could still see that there were in fact creatures who seemed to be at home in these marshes, other than the foul Hodglings. Small, reddish lights appeared and then disappeared only to reappear a few minutes later. Eyes, evil, red eyes that stared at them with hate and malice as they flew overhead.

Although the marshes only covered an area of ten square miles, it seemed to take ages to cross them and by the time the mountains loomed up ahead, Aliyyah's head was dizzy and spinning from the obnoxious and poisonous gases.

"Get ready," warned Dark Wing. "We are nearing the homes of the Hodglings."

Looking down, Aliyyah could see hundreds of small and large caves that dotted the base of the mountains. Fires flickered in many of these caves and she could see small figures running here and there in chaos. As she stared she could see vaguely that many of them had bows and arrows and were now aiming at her and her companions. Suddenly the sky seemed to be full of arrows singing their way towards them.

"Faster, Dark Wing faster, hurry up!" Beating his massive wings, Dark Wing flew at the steep slopes of the mountain, avoiding the arrows while trying to negotiate the treacherous air currents that threatened to smash them to their deaths against the jagged spikes that girdled the mountain. As they climbed up higher and higher, Aliyyah caught her first clear glimpse of a Hodgling sentry, which made her shudder in disgust.

The Hodgling was about four and a half feet in height, rather plump and covered in dirty, grey, rough hairs. It was wearing rough breeches made of out of some kind of black leather. Its long, bald tail sneaked out of a hole in the back of the breeches and twisted and turned like a deformed snake, ready to attack anything that came near it. It also wore a ragged, sleeveless jacket tied together with cross strings. Its face was small and pointed with a sharp nose from which long whiskers poked. Its eyes were small and beady, dark red, almost black, alive with cunning and reeking of evil. Over its shoulder was a pannier of arrows and in its hands there was a bow, drawn ready to release its poisonous arrow. With one swift movement it released the arrow, which sped upwards toward Dark Wing.

'Look out," cried Aliyyah, but Dark Wing had no need for her warning as he had seen the danger and quickly veered to the right, causing Najputih to call out in fear.

"The rocks. Don't dash me against the rocks!"

Dark Wing made no reply, but concentrated on getting Najputih and Aliyyah out of the reach of the malevolent Hodglings. Finally the ledge came in sight and Dark Wing gently dropped the trembling unicorn on the ledge, which was larger than Aliyyah and Najputih realised. Dark Wing then, to Aliyyah's surprise, landed himself, instead of continuing up the mountain.

"Are you both alright?" he said in his deep voice.

"Yes," they replied together.

"But why did you land?" asked Aliyyah in a concerned voice. "Are you hurt?"

Dark Wing did not reply, but lay his head wearily on the ledge and remained silent.

Jumping lightly off the dragon's back, Aliyyah began to examine the prostrate Dark Wing.

"Oh no," she exclaimed as she looked at his long tail. It was covered in dozens of black, tipped arrows. "Oh no, Najputih, help me! We must remove these arrows and apply the Day Bloom water before the poison reaches his heart!"

Quickly taking the Day Bloom out of her cloak she dipped it into her drinking flask as she had no bowl and there was no other water nearby. No sooner had the flower been submersed than the water changed colour and a marvellous fragrance filled the air. Then, with the help of the unicorn who pulled the arrows out with his teeth, she began pulling the arrows out of Dark Wing's tough hide. It was not easy, for the arrowheads were barbed and embedded deep within the flesh, so that each time they pulled out an arrow the wound gushed with blood, while pieces of Dark Wing's flesh and scales clung to the arrowheads. Aliyyah realised that the pain must have been almost intolerable for the dragon, but she was racing against time to save his life. She had no other choice. As each arrow was removed they threw it over ledge, careful not to touch the poisonous head.

"I hope some of them fall upon the Hodglings themselves," exclaimed Aliyyah. "I hope they kill many of them!"

As each arrow was removed, Aliyyah poured a little of the water of the Day Bloom over the wounds. As the water covered them the bleeding stopped and miraculously the flesh, skin and scales grew back before their eyes without leaving a trace of injury. Working as fast as they could, Aliyyah and the unicorn pulled out all the arrows that had embedded themselves into Dark Wing's tail, but it still took more than an hour before the last arrowhead was removed and the wound treated with the last few drops of water.

Aliyyah and Najputih then waited anxiously to see if they had been in time or not. For a while Dark Wing did not move and they began to fear that they had been too late.

After a while though the dragon opened one eye before slowly lifting up his tired head. "Thank you both, thank you."

Almost crying with relief, Aliyyah asked, "Are you alright, Dark Wing? There are no more injuries, are there?"

"I am fine now, Princess, no other injuries. However, I will not recommended you as a nurse, you are much too rough." Then with a weak chuckle he added, "You make a good battle nurse though."

"I am sorry I hurt you so much, but I had to remove the arrows quickly before the poison reached your heart."

"I know, Princess," said the dragon. "I am grateful, I owe you my life."

"But how did you get hit so many times? I don't understand!"

"Hmph," grunted Dark Wing. "I promised Najputih that he would not be harmed so I used my tail to protect him from the arrows. I did not think that the Hodglings were such good shots."

"I did not realise," exclaimed Najputih, feeling rather guilty. "I was too scared to notice anything much. Thank you, Dark Wing, how can I ever repay you?'

"No need, my friend," replied Dark Wing. "However, next time I have to carry you, do not complain so much," he added slyly. "I will not drop you!"

"Are you ready to continue or do you need to rest a while?"

"I am sorry, Aliyyah, but I must rest and regain my strength. Do you have any water?"

"I am sorry, Dark Wing, I used it to heal your wounds."

"No matter, Princess, we will have to find some later. I think you had better put the headband on, for the eagles will have heard the commotion and for sure they will come down to investigate."

Aliyyah quickly did as he said. It would not do to be mistaken for an enemy and attacked here on the ledge where they had little chance of defending themselves.

True to Dark Wing's words, Aliyyah soon saw several giant eagles circling overhead, looking at them with their keen eyesight.

Eventually one of the eagles glided down and landed gracefully on the ledge to where Aliyyah was standing. "Hail, who are you and why do you wear the headband of Kumus?"

Aliyyah remembered Ethos's advice and politely said in the high language of kings, "Hail to you as well, great eagle of the elder race. I am Princess Aliyyah, daughter of King Dor, and the

190

true heir to the Kingdom of Lamis. I am also a seeker who needs your help to find the Book of Fazma."

"Well said, Princess, but what makes you think that we can help you?"

"I sought the advice of Ethos concerning the book and he informed me that it was in the possession of your lord and king, Swift Wing. That is why we travelled far to your lands, seeking the guardian of the book."

"We know Ethos well, how is he?"

Sadly Aliyyah replied, "He has returned home."

The eagle stared her at a while before saying, "That is how it should be. He has laboured long and deserves his rest. What gift did he give you?"

"Is it not enough I wear the headband of Kumus?" replied Aliyyah cautiously.

"Well, yes and no," replied the eagle. "The Dark One is wily so we must be sure that you did not steal it from the one who truly earned it."

Turning to Dark Wing she thought, "Can he be trusted?"

"The eagles have always been friends of Mahin although not always of the dragons, but I think you can trust him. Ask him his name as an act of faith first."

Turning back to the eagle, Aliyyah said, "Very well, however, I could say the same thing of you. Before I tell you what you wish to know, tell me your name first as I have told you mine."

"Did your dragon tell you to ask this?" staring at Aliyyah's surprised face. "We know that some dragons can talk telepathically with those they choose."

"Yes, he did advise me, but he is not my dragon, he is a companion who has risked his life to help me in this quest. He's a dear friend, as is the unicorn, and has suffered greatly protecting us from the Hodglings."

"They attacked you?"

"Yes, and Dark Wing was struck by dozens of their poisonous arrows whilst shielding us. It was only because I was given a Day Bloom by the Dryads that I was able to help him, but I had to use all the water I had and now I do not have even a drop to quench his thirst."

"You were given a Day Bloom? A precious gift indeed! Very well, my name is Night-breeze, cousin to Swift Wing. It was he who sent me to find out who you are. If you correctly answer my question and it is the correct answer, I will carry you up to his nest." Looking at Aliyyah he quickly added, before she could protest, "The dragon needs to rest and it would greatly upset the other eagles to see a dragon among their nests and their eggs. However, I will send some of our fastest eagles to fetch water and a plant that he can eat to regain his strength quickly. When you have finished I will bring you back here and then show you a way out of these lands that avoids the Hodglings."

"Thank you, Night-breeze, for your great kindness to us. The gifts I received in the city of Atlantis were two. One, a shell that contains all the knowledge there, and the second was a book containing all the protective spells of the elders. It could only be opened by the keys that I carry. Inside was a treasure that to me was even greater than the book, a letter from my father. Inside the sealed envelope was a key and this headband."

Nodding his regal head, Night-breeze told Aliyyah, "All that you have said is the truth and we welcome you, for it is a great honour to meet the successor of Ethos and daughter of King Dor, one of our most beloved friends." Then whistling in the strange tongue of the eagles he called several young eagles, who landed gracefully on the wide ledge. Night-breeze talked briefly with the eagles after which three of them remained on the ledge while the rest flew off.

"Princess Aliyyah, these are Day-wing, Storm and Zephyr. They will stay and look after your companions until we return. The others have gone to search for water and the plant I told you about. Now come, I have never allowed a human to ride me before." Then mischievously he said, "But I think I may just be able to permit a dragon friend and the wearer of the headband of Kumus to sit upon my back."

Smiling, Aliyyah thanked Night-breeze before gently climbing up upon his back. He was almost as big as Dark Wing and just as difficult to mount. As soon as she was seated the eagle cried, "Are you ready, Princess Aliyyah? Hold tight and please try not to pull any of my feathers out."

Sitting as comfortably as she could, Aliyyah held on as the eagle spread its powerful wings and soared upwards towards the top of the Cantun Mountains. Aliyyah felt a little giddy as the air became thinner the higher they flew. As she looked at the falling landscape, she realised why the eagles had chosen this place to nest. The sides were steep, almost vertical, and covered with razor sharp rocks that would rip the skin of anyone who tried to climb over them if that was possible. Nowhere was free of these cruel-looking boulders and rocks. Truly the only ones who could reach the top would be those who had wings.

Before long, the mountaintop came into sight. Here the rocks were softer and there were small ledges here and there crisscrossing the mountain face. Then, before Aliyyah's astonished eyes, a forest of stony pillars rose up before her. Each pillar had a flat top on which there was built the giant nest of an eagle. In the centre of this forest of stone there was one pillar that was taller and grander than all the rest. On top of this pillar was a magnificent nest in which a female eagle was patiently sitting while her mate, the proud, noble leader of all the eagles, stood by the side of the nest protectively.

The pillar that Swift Wing was standing on was wider than all the others, big enough for his nest and a great wooden chest that seemed to be somewhat out of place there. There was also enough room for several eagles to stand together to receive orders or report news to their leader.

As they flew nearer the nests a great commotion was heard as the females protested and the males rose up, ready to defend their homes.

However, as soon as they saw it was Night-breeze, they quietened down for a few minutes until they saw the young girl he was carrying was wearing the headband of Kumus. Straight away the terrible racket started up once more, this time, if it was possible, it was louder than before.

Just as Aliyyah thought her eardrums were going to burst she heard a loud, long screech and all the other eagles fell silent. Aliyyah looked at Swift Wing who was standing with his wings outstretched. She had not really realised until that moment how magnificent he was.

With one smooth movement, Night-breeze drifted down before his cousin and bowed gracefully before landing next to Swift Wing. Turning his dark eyes to stare at Aliyyah, Swift Wing remained silent for a while. Aliyyah was aware that all the other eagles were also watching her and their leader anxious to know what was going on.

Finally, Swift Wing spoke in the ancient tongue that bound all those who spoke it to tell the truth. "Welcome, Aliyyah, your father promised you would come one day and so you have."

"Thank you, Swift Wing I have come as promised and I thank you for your aid."

"We have not yet helped you," teased the eagle.

"But you have," protested Aliyyah. "By helping my companions and protecting them, I am in your debt."

"No more than I am in debt to your father. I am saddened that I was unable to repay him before his murder.'

"I do not understand," said Aliyyah. "One of my companions told me my father was an eagle friend. What does this mean?"

Asking Aliyyah to sit down and make herself as comfortable as she could, he ordered one of the eagles to fly and find some refreshment for their guest. After a while, the young eagle returned with some fruits and a coconut shell filled with clear water, which he held carefully with his beak.

"Aliyyah, please eat and drink, I am sorry that we can only give you such simple fare, however we do not usually have any visitors, especially one as special as you."

Embarrassed, Aliyyah took the food and drink gratefully before replying, "Swift Wing, thank you for your hospitality. For a weary traveller this is truly a banquet. However, I am not special, just someone who is trying to fulfil the task I have been entrusted with, and without the help of my companions I could not have come this far."

"Spoken like your father. He was also a great man."

"Please tell me about him as I never had the chance to know him.

He was murdered shortly after my birth."

"We know," replied the great eagle. "For your father had already seen what was going to happen to a degree before his death. Your father came here a few weeks before he died. He was brought by a dragon who I am sure you know very well."

"A dragon?"

"Yes, a great and wise dragon, a friend to all those who follow the light."

Smiling, Aliyyah asked, "It was not, by any chance, Greenthor was it?"

"Yes, indeed it was. He carried your father upon his back and the chest containing the book, he held in his claws."

"Didn't the Hodglings attack them?" asked Aliyyah.

"No," replied Swift Wing. "Who would dare attack the greatest of all dragons," then continuing, he said, "this was the second time he had come here, the first time was when he rescued my mate from the Hodglings. They had caught her and were preparing to kill and eat her when your father, who had been searching for something, bravely and somewhat foolishly attacked them and managed to kill their chieftain. The rest of the Hodglings fled, for they will not fight without their leader. My mate was seriously wounded and would have perished if your father had not hidden her in some thorny bushes. After which he risked his life yet again by climbing up the mountain, regardless of the danger. By the time he reached the ledge where your companions are he was exhausted and covered in blood where the rocks had scraped and cut his skin. Standing on that ledge your father shouted until some of the younger eagles went down to find out what was going on. My mate had given your father the headband of Kumus to show he was a friend, as she was, and is its guardian. When my people saw this, they called Night-breeze and myself down to the ledge. Your father quickly told us what had happened and where my mate was hidden, before collapsing.

"Leaving some of the eagles to look after and protect your father, we descended en mass, and rescued my mate. Four of us had to carry her up to the nests while others were sent to find the healing herbs we needed for both her and your father. Your father quickly recovered and after a few days with us he was ready to return to his home. For what he did for us we named him eagle friend, for not only did he save my mate, but also our priestess and protector of all our holy artefacts.

"Your father is only the second person to gain this honour and I am still indebted to him."

"I see, but what exactly is this headband and what powers does it have?"

"Before I answer that I must see if you truly have the key that unlocks the chest. If you do, you may open it and take the book. However, if you don't you will never leave here alive," stated Swift Wing not taking his eyes off her for even a second. Putting her hand inside her cloak she took out the letter and removed the golden key from it. Then with the great eagle's permission she carefully walked over to the chest and slowly placed the key into the lock. As she turned it she could hear the tumblers inside turning until, with a final loud click, the lid sprang open revealing the book covered in a dusty piece of heavy, yellow silk.

"Well done, Princess Aliyyah," came the eagle's dignified voice. "Please remove the book and place the headband inside."

As Aliyyah lifted the book out she saw several small boxes and artefacts all wrapped in yellow silk. Just underneath the book there was an empty piece of the same silk. Realising that this must be for the headband, she carefully put the book down before removing the headband and wrapping it in the silk before putting it back in the chest and locking it once more. Picking up the book, she put it in the bag she carried before giving the golden key to Swift Wind, who gave her a curious look before commenting, "Well done, Princess, you have what is rightly yours and we have what is rightfully ours. Now to answer your question." Motioning her to sit down once more, he continued. "The headband of Kumus is made from the first feather to fall form each hatchling that is destined to become one of our leaders. When the feather drops it is saved and when the old chieftain dies it is added to the headband, just before we crown him as our new king. Without the headband no eagle would be made our king and we would return to the old ways where every eagle fights for himself. The power and the magic of this headband is that it unites us and gives the ability of speech and knowledge that before we did not have. It is always worn by out priestess when she travels or when she officials at scared ceremonies. It shows to all who she is and gives protection to her from all other eagles."

"If that is the case, how did my father have it?"

"When your father brought the Book of Fazma here, he asked us to hide it form the Dark One. As we have no love of the Dark One and because of our debt to your father, we agreed. However, according to our laws, like the laws of the Merpeople, you cannot take something out of the treasury without putting something of the same value in. Your father knew our laws and he asked us to entrust him with the headband until his daughter reached the right age and came looking for the book. He wanted to be sure that none of our people would accidentally attack you. It was with a heavy heart that I agreed, especially when your father told me that he had

196

seen his own death in the Mirror of Dirtaq. He made me swear an oath never to give the book to anyone except the one who had the key and the headband. I swore the oath and have waited all these long years for your arrival."

"It seems like he cared deeply for me," said Aliyyah in a melancholy voice.

"Yes, he did. He also asked me to show you the way to the desert of the singing sands, which I will do, but first we must all go down to the ledge. There is a ceremony that must be performed before you leave."

Calling Night-breeze, he asked him to carry Aliyyah back down to the ledge.

Wondering what was going to happen now, Aliyyah once more climbed onto the back of Night-breeze. As they flew back down to the rock ledge, Aliyyah could see a long line of eagles, led by Swift Wing, following them. Aliyyah was overjoyed to see Dark Wing was fully recovered when she returned. Turning round she watched as one by one the eagles landed, until the ledge was so crowded that some of the eagles needed to hover nearby.

Clearing his voice, Swift Wing asked Aliyyah to stand in the middle of the circle of eagles, then in his deep voice he said, "Behold the one who has returned to us the headband of Kumus."

With one voice the eagles replied, "We behold."

Swift Wing continued, "Witness the one who has opened the chest and taken the book."

The eagles once more replied, "We witness."

"Remember her father saved our priestess, my mate."

"Yes, we remember."

"Now I ask all of you, my brothers and sisters, shall we honour her by our friendship? Shall we make her not just a dragon friend, but also an eagle friend and aid her whenever she calls upon us?"

With one loud voice they replied, "Hail to Aliyyah, dragon friend and eagle friend. May you live long and fulfil your quest! Hail Princess Aliyyah."

Overcome with emotion, Aliyyah felt the tears dripping down her cheeks as each eagle came before her and gave her either a feather or a small white crystal the size of a pea, but weighing almost nothing. Puzzled, Aliyyah asked Swift Wing what these gifts were

"Oh Aliyyah, if you ever need our help you only have to put the feathers together and recite, 'Elgot ne divn', three times and the feathers will fly back to their owners, who will come as swiftly as they can to aid you. The crystals you must keep in a bag and when you are unsure of the way you should go shake them onto the ground and they will point out the right way for you. They will work anywhere except for the desert of the singing sands, for there the only magic that can work is that of the Sand Wizard."

By this time the sun had begun to sink in the sky, so Swift Wing told Aliyyah that he would personally, with his cousin Night-breeze, show them the way to the desert of the singing sands the next day.

"But we, like the dragons, cannot enter it," he finished. He then ordered all the eagles to return to their homes, except for a few whom he ordered to collect some wood, twigs and small branches for a fire, to keep Aliyyah warm during the bitter night, and food and water for them to eat and drink and regain their strength. "I will keep you company during the night for we have much to discuss and many tales to tell."

Nodding her head, Aliyyah made herself as comfortable as possible and sat back to listen to all the giant eagle had to say. Throughout the long, cold night Aliyyah and Swift Wing sat by the warm fire, deep in conversation. So many of the questions that Aliyyah had long sought the answers to were answered that night. Swift Wing in his own way was almost, though not quite, as knowledgeable as Greenthor.

As the yellow threads of the coming dawn laced the sky, Aliyyah asked the great eagle, "You never found out what my father was seeking when he rescued your mate?"

"No, Princess. I asked him many times but he would never tell me. All I know is that it had something to do with the light." Then Swift Wing remained silent for a few moments in deep thought until finally he said, "I am not sure, but I believe your father may have been an elder like Mahin. His knowledge and understanding was much too great for any ordinary human. I do not know for sure. It is something you must ask the Sand Wizard. Your father told me to tell you that the answers to all your questions are with him."

Asking Aliyyah for her water flask he turned to Night-breeze. "Night-breeze, fill Princess Aliyyah's flask with water from the fountain of Calcus for she has a hard journey in front of her. Also bring water and food for our breakfast."

"Yes, my lord," Night-breeze replied, bowing before Swift Wing. Swift Wing then added quickly, before his cousin flew away, "Call some of the young and strong eagles to bring the sedan that Greenthor left here the last time he came"

Nodding his head, Night-breeze spread his wings and flew upwards towards the eagles' nests.

"The fountain of Calcus? What is that Swift Wing?"

"It is a fountain that is found right at the top of the highest mountain here. It is cool and clear and only one mouthful will quench your thirst. You will need it in the desert of the singing sands," answered the great eagle.

"Is the desert far from here?" asked Aliyyah.

"Not really, a two-day flight, no more."

"Not again," wailed Najputih. "Aliyyah, no, not again."

Dark Wing laughed at this and then explained when Swift Wing seemed puzzled. 'Great and mighty king of all the eagles, the unicorn is upset at the prospect of dangling in the air again. He has a great fear I may drop him or eat him," he added mischievously.

"No I do not," protested the angry unicorn.

Amused, Swift Wing told them, "Do not worry, little one. You will travel in style this time. I have ordered that the sedan be brought here. It is large enough for both Princess Aliyyah and the unicorn to rest in comfortably. Greenthor brought it just before he brought your father with the chest."

"I see," mused Aliyyah. "Once again it seems that everything has already been planned for me! At least I should be able to get some rest. I am very tired after talking all night."

Just then Night-breeze returned with another eagle, bringing her flask plus breakfast for them all. There was fresh water, fruits and fresh meat for the eagles and Dark Wing. Najputih shuddered at the sight of the meat, but said nothing. After all, as Aliyyah had already told him, all creatures have to eat to survive. No sooner had they finished their meal than they heard the eagles bringing down the sedan. It was being carried by eight young eagles, two each holding the poles that extended from the front to the back on both sides. It was completely covered by thick cloth, white and yellow in colour, that both concealed the occupant and protected them from the sun, wind and other elements. On the side were written many protective spells against black magic and evil creatures.

Landing on the ledge the eight young eagles bowed to Swift Wing then waited for further orders. Acknowledging his subjects, Swift Wing told them to prepare to carry Aliyyah and the unicorn to the desert of the singing sands.

"If you are you ready, please sit yourself in the sedan and we will carry you," he told Aliyyah and Najputih. "Don't worry, we will not drop you, and even if we did, your dragon, Dark Wing would save you."

"You know his name?" asked Aliyyah.

"Of course we do, we know all the dragons as they know us, and even though the younger ones are sometimes mischievous as all youngsters are, we have helped each other many times."

"Is this true?" Aliyyah asked Dark Wing.

"Yes, my Princess."

"Why did you not tell me?"

"Have you told me everything, Princess?" questioned the dragon.

"No," replied Aliyyah.

"Then why should I tell you everything?" Then he added slyly, "Besides, you did not ask me!" Laughing, Aliyyah got into the sedan followed by Najputih. Aliyyah was surprised by the luxury inside of the sedan. Two benches covered in soft cushions were at each end, the space between them being covered with thick, soft rugs. There was also a curtain tied at the side in the middle of the sedan that could be dropped to separate into two separate compartments.

"It is beautiful," commented Aliyyah. "Who does it belong to?"

Both Dark Wing and Swift Wing remained silent for a few moments before the dragon replied, "It belonged to your mother and you have ridden in this before, when you were just a baby."

Aliyyah was overcome with great sadness and sat down on one of the benches while silent tears slid down her cheeks. Najputih understanding her feelings, sat at her feet giving what comfort he could to the young girl.

As they sat there they felt the sedan being lifted up and the journey to the desert of the singing sands had begun.

All through the two-day journey, Swift Wing and Dark Wing flew on either side of the sedan and when Aliyyah was not resting they had long conversations. During this time she learned many things, especially the history of both dragons and eagles and how they had gone from being enemies to friends, both sworn to fight evil wherever it was found.

Aliyyah did not ask many questions being content for once just to listen.

Each night they would land and rest until the next morning and finally, in the middle of the afternoon on the third day, they reached the desert.

"Aliyyah, look out of the sedan, ahead is the desert of the singing sands." Opening the curtain that covered the door she saw ahead of her a shimmering white landscape.

"It still seems so far," said Aliyyah.

"I know, Princess, but soon we will have to leave you, for even now we are beginning to feel its magic and we dare not go much closer. Soon we will land, but we will wait with you until the night begins to fall and the temperature drops." With these words Aliyyah felt the eagles descending and in a few minutes the sedan was gently let down on the ground. Stepping out she felt the heat strike her so that she started sweating straight away.

"Princess, rest inside the sedan until the sun starts to sink, only then enter the desert," said Swift Wing.

"How far is the desert from here? It still seems quite far," commented Aliyyah.

"Not really, Princess, it is only about an hour's walk, but we can go no further," replied Dark Wing. "I wish we could, but I will be waiting for your call once you have left the desert, as will all my brothers, so be of good cheer. My advice to you is to avoid travelling in the afternoon sun until you reach the empty quarter. Travel at night only, if possible, and hide during the day. Now rest, the night will begin to fall in a couple of hours, rest."

Nodding her head she went back into the shade of the sedan, but instead of resting she checked her supplies, water and then began to read and reread the Book of Fazma until she heard Swift Wing calling her, "Aliyyah, it is time for you to go." Checking she had everything, she and the unicorn climbed out of the sedan ready to begin the final part of the hunt for the four treasures of the sacred Islands of Lamis. Putting her arm around Dark Wing's neck, she hugged him before saying a solemn farewell.

"Farewell, Princess, till we meet again, farewell," replied the dragon. "Take care, Najputih and look after Aliyyah," he added, as Najputih made an elegant bow before him.

Aliyyah then said goodbye to Swift Wing after thanking him for his help. "It was nothing, Aliyyah, I still have a debt to pay off and I will help you as much as I can." Then turning to Najputih he said, "You do not need to follow Princess Aliyyah into the desert, it is not a place for a unicorn. We can carry you to wherever you want, even the island of the unicorns."

Shaking his head, Najputih asked Aliyyah to tell the great eagle, "Thank you, but Aliyyah saved my life and I am honour bound to follow her until I have repaid my debt. Anyhow, I would never desert a person I have grown to love and respect as much as I love and respect Aliyyah."

Turning toward the desert, Aliyyah and the unicorn started their long trek, unaware of what lay ahead of them.

Chapter Twelve

The Old Man of the Desert

Waves of heat, one after another, relentlessly beat down upon the heads of Aliyyah and the beautiful white unicorn, who had been her constant companion since the beginning of quest. Slowly they made their way across the pure, white sands which had the fragrance of the most beautiful musk perfume you could ever imagine. Everywhere, haunting voices, mesmerising and hypnotic, rose up from the singing sands.

Once more breaking off pieces of the candle she carried with her, she had placed them in their ears before they started their journey across the sands two days ago. This was the second time she had used the wax to block her ears. She had already used the same defence in the Castle of Mirrors. The wax did not hinder communications between Aliyyah and the unicorn as they always spoke telepathically, without words.

They were searching for the Sand Wizard, the old man of the desert, who was said to live in the empty quarter of the singing sands, a place where the haunting voices ceased and not a sound, even of wind, could be heard.

It was the Sand Wizard alone who knew where the hiding place of the Sword of Ila was, for it was he who had hidden it from the Dark One long, long ago. This sword and this sword alone could destroy the Dark One and end his reign of oppression throughout the sacred Islands of Lamis.

It had been many, many years since anyone had seen the Sand Wizard and many believed that either he had died or he was just a myth, a legend, a fragment of an overactive imagination.

Mahin, however, had told her that he was very much alive and living in a deep cave that was hidden in the Emerald Mountains right in the middle of the empty quarter of the desert of the singing sands. His home was surrounded by treacherous quick sands that would swallow any intruders who tried to cross them.

There was, however, a path through the sands, but it could only be found by one who had in their keeping the Mirror of Dirtaq and the Book of Fazma. Mahin had told her that once the winds stopped blowing she would be on the edge of the empty quarter. She must continue until the sands turned from white to a golden brown and the smell changed from musk to an unknown fragrance. By this time she should be able to see the Emerald Mountains. As soon as she reached the golden sands she must use the Book of Fazma to show her the hidden path.

Aliyyah, her body aching from lack of sleep as well as the terrible heat, prayed that the winds would soon cease. Both she and the unicorn were finding this part of the quest to be the hardest and they both began to wonder if they would ever reach the empty quarter.

As they plodded on Aliyyah was so exhausted that she did not at first notice that the wind had ceased blowing and an unearthly quiet had descended. It was the unicorn who first noticed that there was no more wind and quickly asked Aliyyah, "There is no more wind. Is it safe to remove the wax now?"

Startled, Aliyyah stopped still for a moment and looked around her attentively. The sands were totally still, not a single ripple spread across their face. Her face and her skin no longer felt the sling of the biting wind and the air had become hotter and heavier. Surely, they must be near the golden sands by now? Straining her eyes in the falling gloom of the evening she could just make out a greenish glow. Aliyyah's heart leapt, surely that glow must come from the Emerald Mountains.

Turning back to the unicorn Aliyyah thought, "Yes, I think we can safely remove the wax. Wait, I will remove mine first and if it is safe I will remove yours. However, if I start behaving strangely, you know what to do."

Najputih nodded his beautiful white head and waited while Aliyyah removed a piece of candle from one ear. As she listened carefully she could hear no sound, nothing at all, not a whisper, no wind, nothing. Cautiously she removed the wax from the other ear to be greeted with absolute, perfect silence not a sound, not any creatures, no wind just silence.

Quickly she removed the wax from the unicorn's ears, who was overjoyed to be rid of the uncomfortable feeling of having pieces of candle blocking his ears.

Pointing to the green mountains, Aliyyah exclaimed, "Look, there, the Emerald Mountains, aren't they beautiful?" Then looking around her she continued, "We are so near now, but we had better not go any further tonight. It is much too dangerous to continue in the dark. We must wait until the morning before trying to find the path."

Nodding his beautiful head, Najputih settled down on the cooling sands to rest. Sitting down beside him, Aliyyah opened her bag and took out a small loaf of bread, which she shared with the hungry unicorn. They finished their meal with a few sips of their precious water. Still hungry, but no longer ravenous, they made themselves as comfortable as possible before resting for the night. Aliyyah, as the desert quickly cooled, covered both of them with her travelling cloak. Laying her head against the unicorn's soft body, she glanced at her ring and pendant to see if there was any danger, before falling into an exhausted sleep.

Before long both Aliyyah and the unicorn were in such a deep sleep that they did not noticed that a soft wind had suddenly sprung up from nowhere. As they slumbered on, the wind became stronger and in the distance a figure could be seen striding across the quick-sands.

Before long an oldish man wearing a long, blue cloak and a flowing blue turban approached the sleeping travellers. His face was fierce, a man who you could not play the fool with, yet at the same time it was kindly. His beard and hair were a surprising jet black with not a streak of white. Around his waist was strapped a long sword sheathed in its engraved scabbard, while in his right hand he carried a staff that was as tall as he was.

No sooner had he reached the sleeping travellers than his face broke into a wide smile. "Well, well, well," he said to himself. "At long last the seeker has come. I pray that she will be able to cross the sands tomorrow. She was wise not to try and cross them tonight."

Realising that both Aliyyah and the unicorn were exhausted, he called out, "Dukat, mila sikak." Before long a giant bird looking something like a condor, but big enough to carry a man, appeared and landed before the Sand Wizard. This bird was, in fact, the magical bird that used to live in the jewelled islands that dotted the eastern seas far away. It had many names, but most people knew it as the Samira or the Garuda bird. Dukat had been in the service of the Sand Wizard ever since he saved him from the evil magic of the shamans who served the Dark One.

"Dukat, guard them well until daybreak, make sure no evil comes to them. When you see that they are about to wake up, quickly return home. Make sure they do not see you!"

Nodding its head, Dukat moved a slight distance away from the sleeping girl and unicorn and settle down to guard them through the long night.

The Sand Wizard then left a bundle next to the sleeping Aliyyah. "I hope this will help you find your way tomorrow, as well as satisfying your hunger and thirst," he whispered, before returning the way he had come. As he left, the wind that had suddenly sprung up died down and perfect silence once more descended.

Hours later Aliyyah and the unicorn woke up as the dark of the night was pierced by the first rays of the coming dawn. As they stirred, Aliyyah thought that she heard the sound of flapping wings and quickly looked around expecting to see one of the dragons, even though they had told her that this place was forbidden to them. However, she saw nothing except a vague shadow, which could have been anything or just a trick of the light

"What is it, Aliyyah?" thought Najputih. "What is wrong?"

"Nothing, Najputih, I just thought I heard wings and I was hoping one of the dragons had come to aid us."

"You know this desert is forbidden to them. If they came here they know that the results would be disastrous. Their magic and the magic of this place can never be combined. You must have been dreaming."

Nodding her head she caught sight of the bag the Sand Wizard had left by her side. "If I was dreaming, Najputih, who left this bag here?"

Puzzled, the unicorn urged her to open the bag. Inside they found a flask, which when opened contain clean water. There were also three small loaves of bread as well as some dates and a small pot of dark, thick mountain honey. Also in the bag was a compass that only pointed towards the north east and a note which read:

To find the one you seek, first you must lose your way, for only those who have lost their way can be guided to the path that is true.

"Well," commented Aliyyah, "we definitely had a visitor last night and I have a feeling that it was none other than the Sand Wizard. However, what this note means I have no idea."

"Aliyyah," said the unicorn. "Let us have some food and drink first and then we will try to work out this riddle."

Smiling, Aliyyah took one of the loaves of bread, broke it in two and poured some of the thick, sticky honey on it. Giving one half to Najputih, she ate the other. As she took her first bite she felt strength flow back into her aching muscles and tired bones. Never in all her life had she tasted bread and honey as delicious as this, it seemed to melt in her mouth and she was tempted to share another loaf with Najputih. However, she resisted the temptation and shared a few dates with him instead.

"Aliyyah, could I have some water please, as I am very thirsty?"

"Of course, but only a little as we do not know how far we have to travel across this desert."

When they had finished their meal they both tried to work out what the note meant and where they were supposed to go now.

"Maybe we ought to open the book and see if it will show us which way we will have to take to find the Sand Wizard and the sword," suggested Najputih.

Agreeing that this was in fact a good idea, Aliyyah took the Book of Fazma from her bag. Although it was not very large, it was quite heavy and very, very old. It was bound with fine leather on which many a protective spell had been written upon it. The four thick, leather straps were held together with an intricate golden lock shaped like two dragons chasing each other's tails, the keyhole being where the two met. Taking the Keys of Hanaj, Aliyyah tried one after another in the lock until finally the second smallest key fitted. Slowly turning the key she heard the tumblers fall into place before the lock clicked and then opened. Removing first the lock and then the leather straps, Aliyyah carefully opened the book and stared at the yellowing pages before her.

At first she had difficulty reading the handwritten script as it was old and flowing in flowery writing, but after a while she began to understand the archaic words.

"What does it say?" enquired Najputih with great impatience. "What is written there?"

Shaking her head slightly Aliyyah replied, "The writing is very old and difficult to read, but it seems to contain spells and other forms of magical incantations. This is an amulet to protect against illnesses and this one against black magic, but I have not seen anything that can help us yet."

"Keep going," urged the unicorn. "There must be something in there that can help us. Keep searching."

Aliyyah struggled page after page until suddenly she exclaimed, "Here it is!" Then laughing, she added, "It says 'to find the one you seek, you must first lose your way, for only those who have lost their way can then be truly guided'." Then continuing she read, "'This spell can only can only be used by one who has in their possession the Mirror of Dirtaq and the Keys of Hanaj. Whosoever casts this will be able to open the doors to other world and dimensions and travel through them. To use the spell the weaver must first find the place where the compass always point to the north east, no matter what direction it is in. They must then place the Book of Fazma facing towards the north east with the Mirror of Dirtaq in front of it, reciting Tasik, tehra lasik dimn lasik risr' three limes. If said with sincerity, a door will appear before them with a golden lock. To open it the weaver must use the Keys of Hanaj. Do not forget to lake the book with you or you will not be able to return to where you once came from'."

When Najputih heard this he exclaimed, "What are we waiting for? Let us try this at once!"

Musing on this, Aliyyah finally said, "Wait, we must be very careful, Najputih. We dare not make a mistake or we may end up somewhere we don't want to go or become trapped in a place we cannot escape. A heart that is sincere? I suppose this doorway must be like the one on the Island of Mists that follows whatever is truly in your heart. Well, I truly want to meet the Sand Wizard and find the sacred Sword of Ila. Give me the compass, Najputih, please."

Picking up the compass with his teeth, the unicorn carefully passed it to Aliyyah.

The compass was quite small and hexagonal in shape. It was a dark blue, almost black, colour with golden runes inscribed around it. It had only one direction written on it and that was north east, although the needle at that particular moment was spinning around by itself. Placing the compass in her right hand she slowly started moving around until finally the compass needle stopped spinning and pointed to the north east. Cautiously she turned in a complete circle, all the lime staring at the compass needle. The first attempt was fruitless, so moving slightly she tried again. Again and again, she tried and it was only on the seventh attempt that she found the spot that no matter what direction she turned the needle remained pointing to the north east.

"This is it," she cried excitedly. "Come here and stand in front of me please, Najputih, I need your help."

Moving with grace, the unicorn walked in front of Aliyyah and stood perfectly still. Taking the Book of Fazma, Aliyyah laid it on the back of the unicorn and opened it at the page that contained the spell she needed. Then holding the Mirror of Dirtaq in front of her she recited 'Lasik tehra lasik dimn lasik risr' three times. At first nothing happened, but after a few minutes a beam of golden light started dancing in front of them. As they watched, spellbound, the beam continued to dance weaving a solid pattern as it went. Soon they realised it was weaving a door of light with an intricate golden lock. Faster and faster it span until finally it exploded in a brilliant burst of light, disappearing as mysteriously as it had appeared and leaving behind a shining, solid door shimmering before them.

Looking at the lock, Aliyyah realised that the second largest key on the ring should be able to open the lock. Placing the key into the strange lock she felt the door open even before she turned the key. Hurriedly picking up both the Book of Fazma and the strange compass, she and Najputih passed through the door together not forgetting to taking the Keys of Hanaj with them.

No sooner had they walked through the door than it disappeared, leaving them inside a large cave with a sand-covered floor. A gentle green light permeated through the rocks allowing them to see where they were.

"I think we must be inside the Emerald Mountains," said Aliyyah. "Maybe this is where the Sand Wizard lives."

"Yes and no," said a deep, rich male voice from behind her. 'Welcome, Aliyyah, daughter of King Dor and seeker of the four lost treasures. Welcome to my home."

Turning, she saw the Sand Wizard standing there, his face fierce, but his voice and deep eyes friendly. He was dressed as normal completely in blue with his long heavy sword in its sheath by his side and his stout staff in his right hand, while on his head was a dark blue turban.

"Are you the Sand Wizard?" asked Aliyyah politely.

"I am many things and I have many names," replied the old man. "Sand Wizard is just one of the names I have been given by those who have yet to learn who and what I am. Now come with me, we have much to discuss. Follow me to where we can be more comfortable."

Leading the way across the massive cavern they came to a smaller cavern that Aliyyah had not noticed. Entering, she saw that this chamber was a lot smaller than the main cavern. In one corner stood a carved wooden screen from behind which Aliyyah could just make out the shape of a sleeping couch. In front of it was a low table covered with scrolls and books covering every subject that you could possible imagine. There were also several wooden chests standing near the table that were also filled with scrolls, books and bits of parchment priceless beyond words. Arranged along the rock walls of the cavern were soft pillows and cushions, while exquisite rugs were strewn across the sandy floor.

However, the thing that most shocked Aliyyah was the great Garuda bird that was sitting in the corner of the cavern watching them with its mournful eyes.

"Welcome to my home," said the Sand Wizard. "Please be seated." Then looking at the stunned expression on Aliyyah's face, he chuckled, "Do not be afraid, Aliyyah, that is Dukat, my companion and my servant. I rescued him many years ago and now he refuses to leave me until he has repaid his debt to me."

"Just like Najputih," muttered Aliyyah.

"He was the one who guarded you throughout the night. You were wise not to go on any further. We were hoping you would have enough wisdom to use the book. If you had tried to cross any other way you both would have been pulled down to your deaths,

210

slowly and cruelly. We are the only ones who know the secret paths and ways of this place. No one not, even the Dark One, can cross those sands without the Book of Fazma and the Mirror of Dirtaq." Then crossing the cavern he went to small table and took a bottle of drink in an earthen flask, two cups and a bowl. Putting the cups, bowl and pitcher on another low table near Aliyyah, he then poured the drink, which was a rich, golden colour. After giving Aliyyah one cup he placed the bowl in front of Najputih so that it was easy for the unicorn to drink. Sitting down on the cushions opposite Aliyyah, he told them to drink.

Cautiously Aliyyah took a small sip, letting out a sigh of surprise as honey liquid slid down her throat, warming and refreshing her as it went. It was like nothing she had drunk before and filled her with a new energy as her weariness disappeared.

"What is this?" she exclaimed. "I have never tasted any drink quite like this."

Smiling, the Sand Wizard told her, "This drink is similar to the one you were given as a gift by the elder of the Council of Dragons. It is made from honey taken from bees that live only here in the Emerald Mountains, and dates augmented by certain spells and incantations. It will heal any injuries and restore vigour and energy to whosoever drinks it."

Waiting for Aliyyah and Najputih to finish, the Sand Wizard sat quietly before saying, "Aliyyah, so far you have done well, but you still have one more test to go. The Sword of Ila is kept in another cavern near here. You must go and take it. You will see and feel many things in that cavern, but if you are sincere and your heart is pure, what you see or feel will not harm you, but if not..." with this he let his voice trail off. "As soon as you have taken the sword, return here and I will tell what the next stage of your quest is. Are you ready, Princess?"

Putting her cup on the table, Aliyyah nodded her head and stood up ready to follow the Sand Wizard. However, he told her that first she must remove her travelling cloak.

"You must pass this test by yourself without any other help." Aliyyah, without question, did as she was asked and carefully placed the cloak and all its treasures on the pillow she had been sitting on. Najputih got up as well as he wanted to follow his beloved princess, but the Sand Wizard put his hand out to stop him. "You must stay here, you cannot follow." Then more gently he added, "Do not worry, she will not be long and Dukat will keep you company. Aliyyah, come, it is time."

Najputih looked uncertainly at the giant bird, not sure if he was safe with the Garuda or if he would be its next dinner.

Looking at the restless unicorn, the Sand Wizard laughed softly. "Do not worry, little one. He will not eat you and he tells excellent stories. Wait here, we will return soon."

Following the Sand Wizard, Aliyyah was led to an even smaller cavern.

"You must enter here, the sword is inside. Remember what I told you. Go and I will wait for you here."

Walking to the entrance of the cavern Aliyyah could smell a burning odour and could see the shadow of flames licking the walls. Walking through the opening her whole body began to tremble and she nearly fled in terror. She could see the sword lying on a golden table at the far end of the cavern, however, between her and the sword there was not only a raging fire that raced up and down throughout the cavern, but there were also cruel, sharp metal spikes protruding out of the floor, so close together that you could not step anywhere without one of them piercing your foot. How was she going to cross and survive?

Thinking rapidly she recalled what the Sand Wizard had said, 'All is not what it may seem'. If that was case, what was real and what was not? After a few minutes, Aliyyah decided she would have to try and cross the chamber, no matter the consequences.

'Remember, if your heart is pure you will not be harmed', the words echoed in her head. Saying a small prayer Aliyyah stepped into the chamber and at once she felt an excruciating pain shoot through her as she trod on the spikes. At the same time she could feel the flames licking her skin and smell her flesh and hair burning. "All is not what it seems," she kept repeating to herself as painfully she stumbled across the cavern, tears of agony flowing down her face. Inch by agonising inch she forced herself on, not daring to look at her feet or body for fear of what she would see, but keeping her eyes firmly fixed on the glimmering sword in front of her.

Finally, just when she believed she would fail this test, she somehow found a spurt of courage and pushing herself forward she grabbed the sword with her right hand while great sobs of relief and fear racked her body. No sooner had her hand touched the sword than the hungry, raging flames turned to brightly coloured butterflies while the ground beneath her feet became a carpet of beautiful and fragrant desert flowers. The smell of burning flesh and all the pain she had felt disappeared and when she looked at herself there was no sign of any injuries at all.

Picking up the sword in its jewelled sheath, she carried it out of the cavern to the waiting Sand Wizard.

"Well done," he said as he took the sword from her. "Come and I will tell you what you must do next."

Walking back to where the unicorn and Dukat were waiting, they sat down and Aliyyah gratefully accepted another cup of the strange drink. Before the Sand Wizard could say anything Aliyyah asked, "In that cavern, was the fire real or not? I felt the pain, but I am unharmed."

Grimly the Sand Wizard replied, "The fire and the spikes were real. If your heart was not pure and your intention not sincere you would have been destroyed. Now listen and listen carefully, the first part of your quest is completed and you must proceed to the second and more difficult part. I believe that someone has already told you that you cannot destroy the Dark One."

"Yes," replied Aliyyah. "On the Island of Mists I was told that I was only the Gatherer and that someone else who would be very close to me would be the one to destroy him. Do you know who this is?" "Yes I do, it is your son." said the Sand Wizard.

"What do you mean, my son? How? Who is my husband?" Laughing, the Sand Wizard replied, "One question at a time. It was written long ago that the son of the seeker who found the lost treasures of the sacred Islands of Lamis would be the only one who would be able to destroy the Dark One. The Dark One himself knew of this prophecy and made up his mind to kill you as soon as you were born. However, Mahin was too clever for him and hid you soon after your birth, so well that the Dark One could not find you, no matter how he tried. Frustrated, he used his dark arts to divine who you are destined to marry and then captured him. He did not kill him, as he feared you would marry someone else and still have the child that could destroy him. So he kidnapped him as an infant and trapped him inside a glass prison, under the black lake, in the land of eternal night. He hoped that one day you would try to free him and give him the chance to destroy both of you. You must, however, rescue him, as he alone can father your child.

You will have to cross many lands conquered by evil and fight many battles."

"How will I do that?" asked Aliyyah. "I am not a warrior."

"You must learn to be one, but you will not be without help, the dragons will look after you and you will find many surprising allies along the way," comforted the Sand Wizard. "However, Najputih cannot go with you this time."

"What?" cried both Aliyyah and Najputih at the same time. "Why not?"

Firmly the Sand Wizard replied, "I will take him back to his island where he can regain his magical powers, for you will need his help in the final battle. However without his powers he cannot aid you." Before either of them could protest the Sand wizard said in a firm voice, "Please do not argue with me."

Sulkily Najputih remained quiet as Aliyyah tried to comfort him.

"Don't be afraid or angry, my dearest Najputih. It is only for a while. We will soon be reunited and stronger so that we can defeat the Dark One. Take heart, with your powers regained nothing can stand in our way."

"But who will look after you until then? Who will keep you company and look out for you?"

Smiling, she replied, "Did not the Sand Wizard say I would find many allies along the way? I am sure there will be those who travel with me." Sensing the unicorn's emotions she quickly added, "But none of them will be as close to me as you are dear, dear Najputih!"

Finally, unhappily, the unicorn accepted that they would have to go different ways for the time being. "But," he thought, "as soon as I have recovered my powers I will search for you, no matter where you are I will find you."

Putting her arms around Najputih's neck she hugged him for a while, both sadden but both realising there was no other way.

When the unicorn had settled, Aliyyah straightened up and turning to the Sand Wizard she asked, "Who is this prince and how will I know him?"

"A wise question, Aliyyah. His name is Adam and he was born in the land of snow and ice. He is one year older than you, but born on the same day. You will know him by the small red birthmark he has on his right hand, shaped like a dragon. Once you have freed him you will have to fight many wars together against the Dark One and his allies until your son is old enough to fulfil his destiny," replied the Sand Wizard."

"But how will we protect him until that time?" interrupted Aliyyah with concern.

"Do not worry, we will look after him." In a tone that made Aliyyah both happy and fearful at the same time. "Now you must give me the sword once more and the Book of Fazma. They must remain here until you have succeeded. One more thing, you must remember to fulfil any promises you have made first or you will never be able to free Adam."

Nodding her head, Aliyyah gave the Sword of IIa back to the Sand Wizard before handing him the Book of Fazma. "Why did I have to find them if only to leave them here?" she asked.

"That you must work out for yourself," replied the Sand Wizard. "But there is a reason for everything, if you just look for it you will find it."

Taking the book and the sword, he went over to one of the chest, and opened the heavy wooden lid. Putting both the book and the sword in the chest, he removed a smaller and lighter sword from within it.

"This is for you, Aliyyah. It was made for Aliyyah the Pure and has seen many battles."

Taking the sword Aliyyah admired the intricate gilt work on the sheath and the jewelled handle of the sword. The handle had a blood- red ruby embedded in it surrounded by smaller rubies, set in a pattern that formed one of the strongest verses of protection known to mankind. It was a gift beyond price. Overcome, all Aliyyah could do was thank the Sand Wizard again and again.

"Use it well, Aliyyah," said the Sand Wizard. "Use it well!"

So ends the first book on the Chronicles of Lamis.

Appendices

Dragons

Dragons are one of the oldest and wisest beings of all living creatures. They have existed since the beginning of time and their life span lasts for many thousands of years. Although they are not eternal and will die eventually like all other creatures.

Most dragons are creatures of good, opposing the forces of dark, which are at all times trying either to destroy or control all other life forms. However, there are a few dragons that have been corrupted by evil and have caused great destruction whenever they have escaped their imprisonment by the other dragons.

Nearly all dragons belong to the Council of Dragons, which governs them and assigns to each dragon a specific task. The council, at any one time, consists of a minimum of ten members, but if a full meeting is called (once every five hundred years) there will be over one thousand five hundred members who attend. The council however is not led by a dragon, but by Mahin, the elder who stands between the light and the dark and whose lifespan is as long as the dragons'.

The dragons live on a great island of steep mountains and deep valleys hidden from sight by their powerful magic. Although this island is their home, the dragons spend very little time there being occupied elsewhere with their tasks. Most dragons return only to attend meetings, rest or mate.

Dragons mate once every five thousand years and from this mating there is only ever one egg. These eggs are incubated in a special nursery surrounded by light and goodness so that when they hatch they will become Dragons of Light, good and wise. If by some misfortune an egg is hatched in evil and darkness, the resulting hatchling will be evil as well.

Dragons' eggs normally hatch after five hundred years, but they can remain in their shells for an unlimited period of time (sometimes many thousands of years) unharmed, if the time for their hatching is not suitable.

The first dragons to live were Tisfir and his mate Trepa. From them all other dragons are descended. Greenthor is their great-great- great grandson.

The petrified remains of Tisfir and Trepa stand on either side of the pass that leads to the dragon's nursery, as though they are guarding it. A dragon's body, when they die, does not decay like other creations, but turns to stone, slowly eroding to become the hills and the mountains of the worlds.

The history of dragons and mankind have been interlinked since the beginning of time, although not always to the advantage of the dragons. At one time there was a very special relationship between certain humans and dragons. This bond was forged by magic, when an egg hatched and the young dragon and its human counterpart were joined spiritually and to a degree, physically. These humans, because they rode on the dragons, became known as riders and they would feel their dragon's physical pain as the dragon would experience theirs. They also shared a telepathic bond so that they knew and felt each other's thoughts and emotions. These dragons and their riders dedicated their lives to fighting evil.

However, after some time the dragons appealed to the council to abolish all such relationships, for the bond they shared was so powerful that if the rider died so too would the dragon. As a human's lifespan is only a fraction of a dragons', it was leading to a dangerous decline in the number of dragons as most would die before they reached breeding age. The council, in its wisdom, agreed that there should be no more dragon riders, on the condition that all the remaining dragons swore a binding oath to help all those who struggled on the path of light. All the dragons, except the wild dragons that lived in the highest mountains, swore the oath in the ancient tongue, thus binding them to aid and protect those who fought in the way of the light forever. The wild dragons, who had never permitted anyone to ride them, kept their independence and on the whole kept to themselves, but a few of them later on caused a great deal of trouble. One of these wild dragons was none other than Ne'alder, who later on became one of the most evil dragons ever to live.

There were also riders from among the unseen people, but as their lifetime is as long as the dragons there are still a few riders among them left. Now a human can only ride a dragon if that dragon agrees to carry them and not on a long-term relationship.

Each dragon has its own name, which they rarely reveal to anyone else. By the ancient magic, if a person knows a dragon's secret name they can them command the dragon and the dragon has to do as that person orders.

The only ones that know the hidden names of the dragons are those humans who have somehow managed to earn the trust of the wary dragons (a very difficult task). These people are known as dragon friends.

Dragons have great magical powers, stronger even than the unicorns. How great their powers are no one knows for sure, as they are generally very secretive and are rarely, if at all, seen by ordinary beings.

Every hundred years or so the dragons shed their scales so a new coat of shiny thick scales can grow back. At the same time they shed their old claws, teeth and where applicable their horns and grow new ones. This whole process takes about three weeks and the discarded scales, teeth, claws and horns are greatly sought after, to be used in the spells of greater magic.

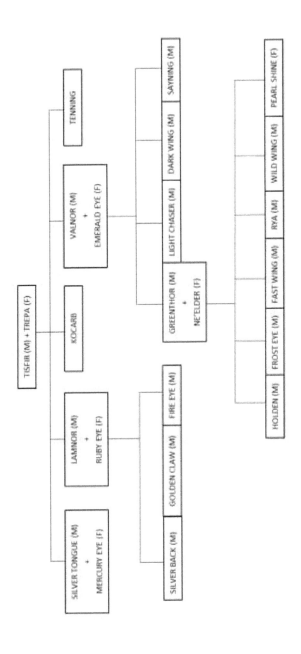

219

Unicorns

Unicorns are creatures of light resembling a horse with a long, pointed spiral horn on their foreheads. Normally they are white in colour although very rarely a grey or brown unicorn may be found.

The unicorns horn is said to be the source of their magically powers. Every seven years the unicorns shed their old horns and grow a new one in its place. The powder that is made from these shed horns is in great demand among witches and wizards for their spells.

However if a unicorn is killed for any part of its body the horn will straight away become useless as the magic within it will return to the Na'da, the source of the magic of all the unicorns.

The unicorns live on a secret island in the blue seas of Lanada. It is here that the Na'da, the source of the unicorns white magic resides protected in a castle of strong and powerful enchantments, day and night.

The Na'da came from the time before the worlds were as they are now. It is a living force of pure goodness powerful beyond anyone's imagination.

It was a gift to the inhabitants of the world to guard them and protect them from the wiles of the Dark forces .The unicorns were created by the Na'da as its guardians and they travel normally unseen among the lands doing the bidding of the Na'da.

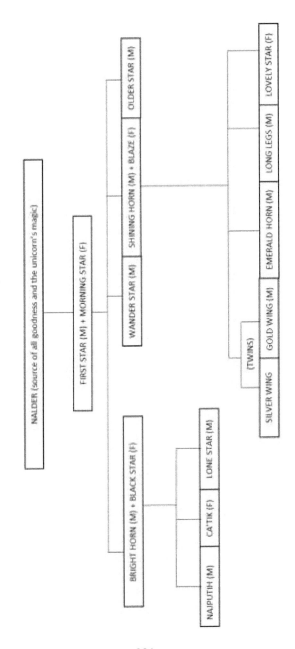

Fire-worms

Creatures of pure evil created from the pits of black and red fire in the land of Nastan. In appearance they resemble giant earthworms, however, as they travel flames and bolts of lightning shoot out of their sides of their bodies burning and blackening the trees and land around them.

Creatures of habit, they always follow the same paths that previous generations of fire-worms have used.

These creatures feed not on the physical body of their prey, but suck out the life force and the souls of any creation that is unfortunate enough or foolish enough to stray onto their paths, leaving their bodies to walk the earth like some unholy zombies. These zombies in turn will terrorise any and all living creatures, needing fresh meat and blood to prevent their bodies from decaying. They can only be destroyed by fire, which is strong enough to consume their whole body. Eventually though they will decay and turn to dust, although it will take many, many years.

If however if the fire-worm is killed before the body of its unfortunate victim starts to decay, the soul will return to its own body and the victim will be freed.

On the other hand, if the victim's body has already decayed then the soul will be forced to walk the face of the earth, a ghost until the end of time or until a seeker can release them from their torment.

Dryads

Dryads, or tree spirits as they are called, are the shepherds and gardeners of the wild woods and forests. Resembling trees in appearance they were created in the beginning to look after and guard the forests. Able to walk and leave the place they grew, they will nevertheless die if taken out of the woodlands and confined to a stone city. Drawing their nourishment from the soil and the fresh springs within the forests, they live for thousands of years.

In the time that the world was still young, the hidden folk taught them the language of mankind, although they have their own speech, which is much older than any other language. This language only the Dryads can understand and to the outsider it seems to be a series of creaks, groans, ruffling and whispers. It is a complicated and beautiful language and the Dryads are well known for their beautiful poetry among the hidden folk.

Generally unconcerned about what happens outside their forests, they nevertheless make terrible enemies if and when their tempers are aroused and their beloved forests are at risk.

Dryads rarely show themselves to humans, although they may be watching and following you when you travel through their domain.

These ancient creatures love all things good and hate evil in any form. They also, understandably, hate axes and fire.

Phoenix

A bird of great beauty and rarity said to have many magical powers. Originally from the green mountains behind the ancient lands of Egypt, they normally make their homes high up in inaccessible mountains. Protectors of the light, they aid those who fight evil in all its many forms.

The tears of the phoenix are said to cure all injuries and illnesses, even those caused by dark magic. Although able to speak all languages, they normally prefer to communicate telepathically.

Phoenixes tend to prefer solitude and rarely mix with others, even of their own species. Once thought to be immortal, because they burst into flames every thousand years to be reborn from the ashes of their own nest, the phoenix is, in fact, declining in numbers, so they are already considered very rare. However, because of their secretive nature, their true numbers are very difficult to ascertain.

The feathers, especially the tail feathers, are eagerly sought after by practitioners of both black and white magic, as they greatly strengthen all spells as well as being used in the preparations of wands and sorcerers' staffs.

Merpeople

Once human, they were given the choice of remaining human with a short lifespan or living hidden beneath the waves of the ocean, deep in its depths, to look after all the creatures and plants within it. In return they would be granted a lifespan that equals that of the dragons and the elders. Relagus, the forefather of all the Merpeople, chose the latter when he and all his followers left the land for the last time and entered the sea. No sooner had the waves lapped around their waists than they found their legs were changed into powerful tails and at the same time they were given the ability to breathe beneath the waves. Although they are still able to breathe above the waves as humans do, if taken out of the water for any period of time they will die.

Although not endowed with any magic powers, Poseidon, their king, does possess immense powers, which reside within his trident. This trident can only be used by the ruling king and will destroy anyone else who is foolish enough to try and use it.

The Merpeople are a gentle people who love beauty in all its many forms. However, if roused they make fierce warriors and even more deadly enemies. Poseidon is the great grandson of Relagus and like his great-grandfather is one of the protectors of the light. He is also a close friend of Mahin, being almost as old as he is.

The Screeching Owls

The Screeching Owls are descended from the great and wise owl known as Hootoon. It was he who rescued the princess of the song thrushes from the sprites of the black marshes. As a reward he was given a singing voice that surpassed the greatest singer of any other race of birds.

His descendants inherited this gift and later on became known as the singing owls of the beautiful islands of peace. However, after being cursed by the Dark One's evil black magic, they lost their beautiful voices so that all they could do was screech. Their islands were made desolate and the crystal clear seas surrounding them turned black and evil when the Dark One stole the pearl that guarded them from its cove. They remained in this condition until the seeker, known as Aliyyah, returned the stolen pearl to its shell in the cove of joy, thus breaking the Dark One's spell and returning both the islands and the owls to their original condition.

Suqaqusi

Guardians of the underwater gateways. Resembling giant blue squids, they have human faces and protect the portals to the hidden worlds under the sea. The leader is Diousni, the guardian of the gateway of Atlantis.

Kinasu

Is the queen of the Island of Gamic, also known as the Island of Sorceresses. She was the mother of the sea witch, Serena.

Serena

Daughter of Queen Kinasu, who after secretly studying the black arts, killed her own mother. She was turned into a sea witch and tried to destroy King Poseidon by turning herself into a giant whirlpool. Unsuccessful, she was trapped in this form until her destruction at the hands of Princess Aliyyah.

Alaneai

Alaneai is a living memory created by the elders of Atlantis just before their city was destroyed by a mighty earthquake. Realising, through the thoughtless acts and arrogance of their people, disaster would strike them, they nevertheless did not want all their knowledge destroyed. In order to prevent this they created Alaneai to preserve all the knowledge of the ancients and to act as one of the city's guardians. Proud and arrogant in bearing, she is in fact no more than a recording of the history, customs, sciences and all other knowledge of the ancient race and is incapable of any kind of feelings or emotions

It is said that when the city of Atlantis is finally destroyed she too will cease to exist. Before this happens, however, she will have to pass on her memories to a fitting keeper.

Ethos

Ethos, or the wise green turtle, is the oldest living creature of all creations. He was entrusted with the task of preserving all knowledge both good and bad. Since the beginning of time he has been one of the guardians of the light and has grown old and tired in its service. His true home was in Cepa in the depth of the Atlantic trench. However, he could not return there until he had passed his knowledge and responsibilities on to his successor.

Kara

The leader of the great white sharks, another protector of the many hidden worlds and enemy to the Dark One and all his servants. He and his followers patrol the watery ruins of Atlantis protecting it and its secrets. They aided Aliyyah in her quest when they realised that she was a true seeker. As soon as Aliyyah had left Ethos, Kara led his followers away from Atlantis before its total destruction, after which they were entrusted with the task of guarding another hidden gate to another hidden world.

King Err

A sea dragon who used to work with the guardians of the light against the Dark One. One of the few dragons that are able to live beneath the water in sea, river or lake.

Unfortunately, after becoming infatuated with a human princess and kidnapping her to be his bride, he broke dragon law and crossed over to the dark side. He has a daughter from this forced union called Errina who is half dragon and half human. With the daughter's help, Aliyyah managed to set the mother and her retinue free and force King Err to abandon his evil plans, thus making an eternal enemy of King Err.

Errina

The daughter of king Err, she is half human and half dragon. Disappointed and saddened by her father's behaviour, she helps Aliyyah to escape from his clutches.

In return, Aliyyah manages to force King Err to release Errina's mother and return her and her servants to their homeland. Errina later on becomes one of Aliyyah's greatest allies.

Ne'alder

Ne'alder is one of the wild dragons who refused to swear obedience to the dragon laws. At first, she worked for the light and was one of the members of the Dragon Council. She was also the mate of Greenthor before her pride and arrogance turned her to the dark side. After being imprisoned for her crimes she managed to escape with her last egg, after deceiving and then killing the young dragon who had been appointed as her jailor. However, Aliyyah managed to rescue the egg by defeating Ne'alder in the riddle game.

Ne'alder has sworn vengeance not only on Aliyyah, but all the other dragons as well, especially Greenthor. In her quest for power and revenge she has already killed three of Greenthor's sons, her own flesh and blood. She has no mercy or goodness left in her and is incredibly cunning and clever.

Hodglings

Hodglings are creatures of pure evil living in damp, dark places. In appearance, they resemble large rats. Highly intelligent, crafty and cunning they are the sworn enemies of the great eagles. They are also skilled archers.

The great eagles

An ancient race of birds, the largest ever to live. They aid the guardians of the light and oppose all things evil. Their king, Swift Wing, was a close friend of Aliyyah's father, King Dor, with whom he swore a pact of eternal friendship. After rescuing Swift Wing's mate from the Hodglings, the eagles made him an eagle friend, an honour that had only ever been given to one other person before, Aliyyah the Pure. They are the sworn enemies of the Hodglings.

Riddle game

The riddle game is an ancient game by which two opponents compete to see who can ask a riddle the other cannot answer. This game is bound by the ancient magic so that whoever loses must fulfil whatever they promised before the game. A favourite game of all dragons who seem unable to resist its challenge.

The four lost treasures of the sacred Islands of Lamis

The origins of these treasures are known to only a few individuals, but it is generally accepted that they were a gift from the Creator to mankind at the beginning of time and entrusted to the keeping of the rulers of the Islands of Lamis.

The Book of Fazma - this book contains the hidden knowledge of the past, present and future and can only be read by one who has a pure and clean heart. It also contains all the protective spells and amulets needed to defeat evil in all its forms.

The Mirror of Dirtaq - this mirror, when the correct incantations are recited by a true ruler of Lamis, can reveal what may happen in the future. Although it may be changed by the actions of the one who looks into it, generally speaking what is seen will happen.

The Keys of Hanaj - a set of nine keys that can open a multitude of different locks both secret and known. Each key can open more than one lock, including the doors that lead from one realm to another.

The Double-edged Sword of Ila - this sword was made from star-metal and augmented by countless protective spells and incantations. It was created to destroy evil in all forms and at all times and generally its keeper is the ruler of Lamis.

Vilena

The guardians of the secret gateways of the Island of Mists. Their leader is a young and beautiful woman called Quasa. Although the Vilena can appear in human form they, in fact, have no physical bodies being purely spiritual creatures of immense wisdom and power.

Dukat

A giant Garuda bird, one of the few remaining, who normally live in the jewelled islands of the eastern seas. He was captured by the evil shamans who enslaved him and tried to use him for their evil purposes. He was, however, rescued by the Sand Wizard, who freed him from the black magic and chains that were binding him. In order to repay his debt to the Sand Wizard he willingly became his servant. After some time a bond of mutual respect and affection grew up between the two and the Garuda became the Sand Wizard's constant companion.

Kathir

The oldest and most knowledgeable of all the healers, who live on the island of healers. Wise and kind, he is a close friend of Greenthor.

Mantrayrini

A giant stingray, king of all other rays, who carries Aliyyah and Najputih on its back over the great ocean.

Nogard

A dark mockery of a dragon made from the mists and shadows of damalion itself. A totally evil creature and one of the few creatures that could destroy a dragon.

Mimah

The keeper of the Book of Peace. She was trapped inside its pages by the evil dragon, Ne'alder. She was later released by the seeker, Aliyyah.

Maps

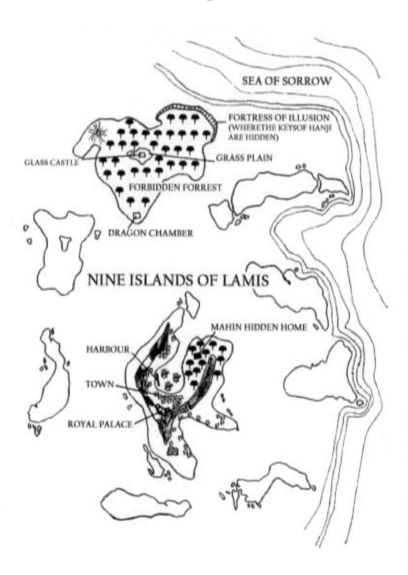

SEA OF SORROW

FORTRESS OF ILLUSION
(WHERE THE KEYS OF HANJI
ARE HIDDEN)

GLASS CASTLE

GRASS PLAIN

FORBIDDEN FORREST

DRAGON CHAMBER

NINE ISLANDS OF LAMIS

MAHIN HIDDEN HOME

HARBOUR

TOWN

ROYAL PALACE

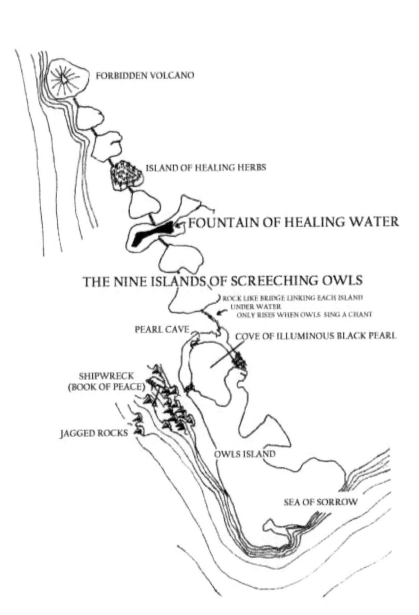

FORBIDDEN VOLCANO

ISLAND OF HEALING HERBS

FOUNTAIN OF HEALING WATER

THE NINE ISLANDS OF SCREECHING OWLS

ROCK LIKE BRIDGE LINKING EACH ISLAND
UNDER WATER
ONLY RISES WHEN OWLS SING A CHANT

PEARL CAVE

COVE OF ILLUMINOUS BLACK PEARL

SHIPWRECK
(BOOK OF PEACE)

JAGGED ROCKS

OWLS ISLAND

SEA OF SORROW

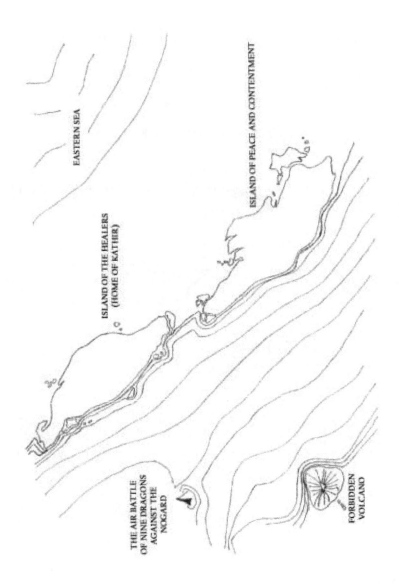

EASTERN SEA

ISLAND OF THE HEALERS
(HOME OF KATHIR)

ISLAND OF PEACE AND CONTENTMENT

THE AIR BATTLE
OF NINE DRAGONS
AGAINST THE
NOGARD

FORBIDDEN
VOLCANO

TO THE LAND OF
WHISTLING WIND

GATE UNDER
WATER

PALACE OF KING ERR

UNDER WATER PASSAGE
TO THE LOST CITY OF ATLANTIS
- HOME OF ETHOS

SEA WEEDS FORREST OF SARGOSS

EASTERN SEA OF ETERNITY

WHIRLPOOL

HIDDEN ISLAND OF GAMIC
(HOME OF WHITE SORCERESSES

KING POSEIDON PALACE
(UNDER WATER)

LINE OF MERMEN

OPEN SEA

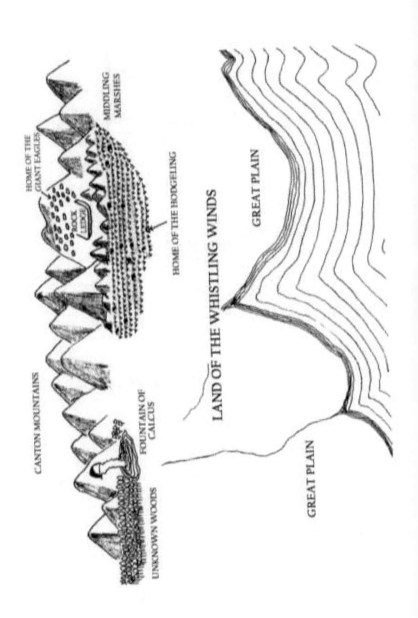

CANTON MOUNTAINS

HOME OF THE GIANT EAGLES

MIDDLING MARSHES

ROCK LEDGE

HOME OF THE HODGELING

FOUNTAIN OF CALCUS

UNKNOWN WOODS

LAND OF THE WHISTLING WINDS

GREAT PLAIN

GREAT PLAIN

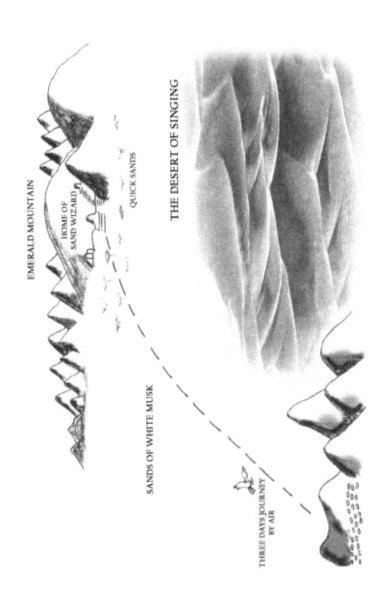

EMERALD MOUNTAIN

HOME OF
SAND WIZARD

QUICK SANDS

SANDS OF WHITE MUSK

THE DESERT OF SINGING

THREE DAYS JOURNEY
BY AIR

237